A Watergate Tape

Also by Roy Hoopes

Our Man in Washington

A Watergate Tape

Roy Hoopes

A TOM DOHERTY ASSOCIATES BOOK
NEW YORK

A WATERGATE TAPE

Copyright © 2002 by Roy Hoopes

A Forge Book
Published by Tom Doherty Associates, LLC
175 Fifth Avenue
New York, NY 10010

www.tor.com

Forge® is a registered trademark of Tom Doherty Associates, LLC.

Library of Congress Cataloging-in-Publication Data

Hoopes, Roy.
        A Watergate tape / Roy Hoopes.—1st ed.
        p. cm.
    "A Tom Doherty Associates book."
    ISBN 0-312-87899-0 (acid-free paper)
        1. Watergate Affair, 1972–1974—Fiction. 2. Washington
(D.C.)—Fiction. 3. Journalists—Fiction. I. Title.

PS3558.O6323 W38 2002
813'.54—dc21
                                                                2001058611

First Edition: May 2002

Printed in the United States of America

0   9   8   7   6   5   4   3   2   1

*Again, for the grandchildren, Lesley,
Sara, and Scott*

ACKNOWLEDGMENTS

I wish to express appreciation, from beginning to end, for the perceptive observations of my two editors, David Hartwell and Moshe Feder.

A Watergate Tape

PROLOGUE

It was almost, as Yogi is supposed to have said, déjà vu all over again when Sam Meyers, editor of *Washington* magazine, called me about doing a piece on the thirtieth anniversary of Watergate to be published in the summer of 2002. You remember Watergate? At first it was known as the "bugging incident." Then White House press secretary Ron Ziegler tried to discount it as a "third-rate burglary."

When the police arrived, they caught five men in the act of burglarizing the offices of the Democratic National Committee. Their names were James W. McCord, Bernard Barker, Frank Sturgis, Eugenio Martinez, and Vergilio Gonzales.

It was early on the morning of June 17, 1972, in the middle of a presidential campaign. And although thirty years later, McCord, Barker, Sturgis, Martinez, and Gonzales are virtually forgotten, the clumsy—and, as it would later prove, pointless—act would lead to the first incident in the nation's history to rival Teapot Dome for a place in the lexicon of government scandals.

At first, the Watergate burglars remained silent and their lawyers—who quickly appeared at police headquarters despite the fact that none of the burglars had called a lawyer—said their clients were not talking. But their connections were easily traced. Collectively, the men had several hundred-dollar bills on them, most numbered and in sequence, and several packets of numbered hundred-dollar bills were found in their hotel rooms (also in the Watergate) along with a telephone book that included the White House telephone number of E. Howard Hunt, who had had an office in the White House but was not attached to the Committee to Reelect the President (Richard Nixon). And it was easily established that one of the men—James McCord—worked for CREEP, as the committee was called. It was easy to trace the hundred-dollar bills back through Bernard Barker to a bank in Mexico to Kenneth Dahlberg, former treasurer of CREEP. It was also learned that Hunt and another CREEP employee—G. Gordon Liddy—had directed the break-in.

As the press, led by *The Washington Post* and its two young reporters, Bob Woodward and Carl Bernstein, began to uncover the true magnitude of what had happened, the Great Cover-up began. The cover-up was an obstruction of justice, which some very prominent Washington names, including former attorney general John Mitchell, White House aides John Ehrlichman, H. R. Haldeman, Charles Colson, John Dean, and eventually President Nixon, would come to appreciate was a crime.

Everyone who followed politics in Washington knew that "this Watergate caper thing," as we would later learn Haldeman was calling it in the confines of the White House Oval Office, must had had the sanction of Mitchell, director of CREEP at the time of the break-in. When Mitchell resigned from the campaign to return to his law practice, it gave credence to this assumption—especially after several cryptic calls from his wife suggested that she was a "political prisoner" and that Nixon was involved. Mitchell immediately called that "ridiculous," but considering how close Mitchell was to Nixon, many assumed that the president must have known something of what was going on.

As the full story began to emerge it became apparent that the Watergate break-in was just the most recent incredible incident in a deliberate plan of espionage and sabotage conducted by CREEP against the Democrats. And it is remarkable just how long the White House was able to effect its cover-up. Very little of the story surfaced during the presidential campaign of 1972 and Richard Nixon was reelected in a stunning landslide victory over Democratic candidate George McGovern.

On January 8, 1973, the trial of the Watergate Seven began in the court of John J. Sirica, chief judge of the U.S. District Court in Washington, D. C. The following month, the Senate empowered a special committee under the chairmanship of Senator Sam Ervin (D., N. C.) to investigate the Watergate affair. As the trial progressed, Judge Sirica repeatedly suggested that the defendants and others were not telling the truth about what had happened. But the Watergate cover-up did not begin to come undone until March 19, 1973 when James McCord wrote his now-famous and historic letter to Judge Sirica charging that he and other Watergate defendants were under "political pressure" to plead guilty and remain silent. Perjury, he said, had been committed at the trial and higher-ups were involved in the break-in.

By early May, White House legal counsel John Dean, suspecting that Ehrlichman and Haldeman were setting him up to take the fall, had decided to tell his story to the Senate Watergate Committee. But no one knew precisely what Dean was going to say or who he was going to implicate and at this date dozens of reporters and government investigators were still trying to uncover the truth.

Sam's call gave me that déja vù feeling, because it was almost thirty years ago in 1973— just after Dean had been fired by President Nixon—that Sam had asked me to do an article about the strange death of my friend, Tom Cranston. And as soon as Sam mentioned Watergate, I had this vision of Tom standing on the Delaware beach north of Fenwick Towers and shouting at the moon: "Hyyyyyaaaaaaa! They're all going to jail—Nixon, Haldeman, Ehrlichman, Dean, Mitchell! They're all going to jail!"

Well, Tom was right. They all went to jail—except Nixon who probably would have if President Gerald Ford had not pardoned him. And it was not long after this that syndicated columnist Joe Alsop said that he had begun "to think that the '70s are the very worst years since the history of life on earth."

Of course, there were a few other things that contributed to Alsop's gloom and doom—long lines to buy gasoline; the generational and sexual revolutions; women's liberation; drugs; personal computers; wage and price controls; the emergence of the snail darter as a force in environmental politics; Vietnam; the never-ending war in the Middle East; the massacre of the Israeli Olympic team at Munich in 1972; the cost of social security and medicare doubling every four years; the budget of 1972, over $200 billion; and the population explosion (summed up by Dr. Paul Ehrlich's prediction in his book *The Population Bomb*, that "in the 1970s, the world will undergo famine—hundreds of millions are going to starve to death in spite of any crash programs embarked upon now").

But Tom saw only the beginnings of some of these problems, and he never had the pleasure of seeing the presidency of the man he hated so much come crashing down. He was found on the beach one morning—May 3, 1973—dead. And that is where this story begins.

CHAPTER ONE

Wednesday afternoon, May 2, 1973

It was easy enough now to pinpoint the date. All I had to do was check my copy of *The End of the Presidency*, a chronological account of the events leading up to the eventual resignation of Richard Nixon by the editors of *The New York Times*. President Nixon had just announced the resignations of Attorney General Richard Kleindienst and White House aides John Ehrlichman and H. R. Haldeman and John Dean. In a televised statement the president took responsibility for the Watergate break-in but denied any personal involvement in the incident, However, there "has been an effort to conceal the facts," he said.

For those of you who don't remember or were too young to be concerned by your parents continually talking about the three White House aides and "what did the president know and when did he know it?", by then, all anybody in Washington, if not around the country, could talk about was what was going to happen next in Watergate. Every day the newspapers or the evening television news would report some new tidbit of information concerning the espionage tactics of the Nixon administration or the alleged wrongdoings of the president.

I had been resting my eyes when the telephone rang. It was just as well, because when I looked at the clock on the wall I noted it was almost 2:30 P.M. Time to be back to my typewriter.

"Hartley here," I said, picking up the phone.

"Raymer? This is Tom—Tom Cranston. I know it's been a long time, but I've got something important to tell you. You'd better take notes."

"All right, Tom. I'm ready. What the hell's going on?"

"I'm over here in Ocean City playing the White House game."

"The what?"

"Did you see Herblock yesterday?"

"Yeah. Oh. Watergate!"

"That's right." What Tom was referring to was yesterday's Herblock cartoon in *The Washington Post.* He had drawn a game board similar to Monopoly's and superimposed on it a White House game with a Watergate theme. It had such squares as "Go Directly to Jail and Shut Up!"; "Investigate Yourself and Go Free"; "Go Back 5 Spaces and Shred Paper." The stack of hundred-dollar bills sitting by the game had President Nixon on them, with the heavy growth of beard Herblock always gave him.

"Raymer, depending on what happens this evening, I may or may not be mailing you a little package."

My first name is Raymond, but ever since college, when a friend who thought that was too formal and didn't like Ray came up with Raymer, that is what most of my friends have called me. We had lost track of the Cranstons since their divorce and I had heard things were not going so well with him and that he was drinking a lot. But Tom sounded cold sober now and quite tense, as though he were in some kind of trouble. He said, "If the package arrives and you haven't heard anything from me in a day or so, I want you to deliver the package to Bob Woodward at *The Washington Post*. Got that? Bob Woodward!"

"Right."

Tom was working as staff director of the Senate Select Committee on Oil Reserves, which I was sure had nothing to do with Watergate. But Bob Woodward and *The Washington Post* did. Woodward and Bernstein had been leading the *Post*'s investigation. And Ron Ziegler had gone so far as to say that a *Post* story about White House aide Bob Haldeman having managed a "secret slush fund for political espionage" was "shoddy journalism."

But the *Post* and Woodward and Bernstein had been vindicated, and I said to Tom, "I heard this morning that Ziegler apologized to the *Post* for his criticism of the paper. Has this package you may be mailing me got to do with Watergate or your Senate committee?"

"Raymer, believe me, I can't take the time to go into it now. It's very complicated and personal, too. But if you don't hear from me, the person who can tell you all about it is named Beverly Turner. She's the wife of Arthur Turner. You may not remember, but you met them at Rehoboth Beach when you and Dory visited us there. They're neighbors. Got that? Beverly Turner."

"Okay," I said, "but I sure as hell would like to know what Ocean City has to do with Watergate. What are you doing over there?"

"Raymer, I can't tell you now. All I can say is that I've

learned what was really behind the Watergate break-in. There has been a bunch of guys working out of the White House; they're called the plumbers because some of them had offices in the basement. During the campaign of '72 they were wiretapping and breaking into offices trying to find out things that would help them during the campaign—who was responsible for leaks coming from the White House; especially who had leaked the Pentagon Papers about Vietnam to *The New York Times*. By the way, all this is strictly confidential."

"Right," I said.

"Could anybody be tapping your phone now," Tom asked, "for any reason?"

"I can't imagine why. I haven't worked on anything sensitive for years."

"Good. You might be in danger, as I am, if some of these people knew I had talked to you about this. Anyway," Tom continued, "these guys were in the DNC headquarters to improve some wiretaps they had already installed, which weren't giving them what they wanted."

"Jesus! They must have been out of their minds. So why were they in there to begin with?"

"Because they're stupid," Tom said. "They were trying to get information on Larry O'Brien, the DNC chairman, linking him to Howard Hughes."

"I can't believe they'd risk what they did just for that."

"But they did—and that's all I can go into now. But there's more. I think I know who was behind the whole thing and I know there's a cover-up going on, which is going to put some of them in jail. With any luck, I should be back in Washington in a couple of days. We'll have drinks and I'll tell you all about it. Promise." And he hung up.

Jeeeesus, I thought as I slowly put the phone back in the cradle. What the hell was that all about? I knew I was through working for the day, so I opened a beer, walked out on the deck, and sat in the warm May sun to try to decide what to do. We had known Tom Cranston for years. He and Elaine had come back to Washington in 1961 to take a job in the Kennedy administration, part of a large contingent of Californians who had worked for Governor Pat Brown and then come east to work for the Kennedy administration. They used to joke that the Californians in the Kennedy administration even outnumbered the Irish mafia from Massachusetts. Tom worked for a number of government agencies and finally ended up working for President Johnson in the White House in 1966.

It was unusual for a Kennedy man to work in the Johnson White House, but that's the way Tom was. He impressed everyone with his integrity and his increasing devotion to one overwhelming objective—keeping Richard Nixon out of the White House in 1968. Tom quickly justified the Johnson people's faith in him and he developed a number of projects important to the administration. As the 1968 campaign approached and Johnson announced that he intended to resign at the end of his term, Tom left the White House to work in the Humphrey campaign against Nixon. When Humphrey was defeated, Tom was out of work.

He was offered a job back in California as editorial page editor of *The Los Angeles Tribune*—a pretty good slot. But he elected to stay in Washington and take a job with the Senate Committee on Energy and Natural Resources. He also started to work on his book, *A Democrat Looks at the Future,* which was published in 1971. Tom not accepting the *Tribune* job surprised most people. He was one of the good guys who came to town because they believe in government and want to play some part in the events that shape their lives. Most people, I guess, are drawn to Washington by their natural instinct to be where the power is. But Cranston was one of those exceptions

who give this town its soul. He really believed in the democratic process and putting the government to work for the people. And he wanted to make a contribution to society. His
enthusiasm for what he was doing and his essential belief in the
system were infectious. But, I had to admit, something had
happened to him after the Humphrey defeat. And now he
seemed to be in the middle of something involving Watergate,
and in real trouble.

I tried to remember the Turners, vaguely recalling a quite
attractive woman with two young kids and a husband who was
in the construction business. It seemed to me that they lived in
Towson, a suburb of Baltimore.

Then there was the question of whether I should tell Doreen
about the call.

Not now, I decided. If I did, everyone in the neighborhood
would know about it by tomorrow, even if—especially if—I
told her it was confidential.

Before going out to dinner that night we watched the
evening news. That evening CBS had follow-up stories about
the resignations of Haldeman, Ehrlichman, Kleindienst, and
Dean, and already there was speculation about what these men
were going to do now—especially Dean. Were they going to
try to plea-bargain and get immunity or a lighter sentence for
telling everything they knew? Or were they going to fall on
their sword for Richard Nixon?

"Not likely," said Dory. "I bet they're scrambling all over
each other to see who can get a deal."

"But I'll be surprised if any of them get immunity," I said.
Dory agreed.

There was also the curious story of John Connally, the former Democratic governor of Texas who had been chairman of
Democrats for Nixon during the campaign and Nixon's first-
term secretary of the treasury. Believe it or not, with what

looked like some of the rats in the administration deserting or being pushed off the sinking ship, Connally was scrambling to get aboard. He had just announced that he was leaving the Democratic party and joining the Republicans!

Some analysts thought he was setting himself up for a run at the presidency on the Republican ticket in 1976, and nobody seemed surprised at his switch—considering his role in the 1972 campaign and his tour of duty in Nixon's cabinet. Governor William Hobby of Texas joked that George Bush (chairman of the Republican National Committee) and Bob Strauss (DNC chairman) had just made a deal: John Lindsay (the mayor of New York who had switched to the Democrats in 1971) for Connally, with the Democrats getting a first-round draft choice and a senator to be named later.

For dinner we went over to our favorite Chinese restaurant in Bethesda. The conversation, of course, centered on Watergate, but suddenly, out of the blue, Dory said, "I wonder what Tom Cranston is doing now? He must be jumping with joy, seeing the Nixon gang leaving the White House in disgrace, with Richard Nixon probably not far behind them. Didn't he take on a job with the Senate?"

"Yes, he did."

"I wonder if he's involved with the Ervin committee, which is getting ready to investigate the Watergate break-in. You know how much he hates Nixon. I bet he's pulling in every blue chip he has to get a job with that committee."

Doreen, with her usual intuition, had divined what was going on in my mind. And I didn't see how I could *not* tell her about Tom's phone call now. After what I felt was a very awkward pause, I said, "Doreen, there is something I guess I have to tell you. I got a very strange call from Tom Cranston this morning. At first I decided not to say anything about it to you—at least until after I knew what was going on. In fact,

Tom himself asked me to keep it confidential and even said it would be dangerous for me if some people knew Tom had involved me in what he is doing."

"He *is* working on something about Watergate, isn't he?" Dory said.

"He is—and understand this has to be strictly confidential."

"I understand."

"I don't think he's actually working for Senator Ervin. But he seems to have some information that he feels the committee could use, something that would be very damaging to a number of people."

"And you can't tell me what it is, can you?"

"No. In fact, I don't know everything Tom has turned up. He promised to fill me in when he gets back from Ocean City, where he is now."

"So what's he doing in Ocean City?"

"He's working on something."

"So are you involved?" Dory asked.

"Not yet. But I might be. He seemed to be convinced that he is in some danger. And if something happens to him, he says, I might be receiving a package from him that I should get to Bob Woodward at *The Washington Post* as soon as possible."

"Woodward, eh. That certainly means Watergate, doesn't it?"

"It does, but let's not speculate about it until we know more."

At home, I stayed up for the late news, to see if there was anything about Tom. If something had happened to him it would be on the local news.

"You're worried about Tom, aren't you?" she said.

"Yes. And let's hope he's not on TV tonight." He wasn't.

When the news was over I was still wide awake so I started to watch *The Tonight Show.* Johnny's guest was Burt Reynolds, who was pushing his new movie *Shamus.* But Dory persuaded me to watch *The Late Show,* which was featuring *The Left-Handed Gun,* starring Paul Newman as Billy the Kid.

"I can guess why you want to watch this old western," I said.

"Don't worry, if Paul gets me excited, you'll be the first to know."

"I hope you can wake me up."

I fell asleep before the first commercials came on.

CHAPTER TWO

Thursday morning, May 3, 1973

There was fortunately nothing in the *Post* about Tom so I decided to get some work done on my biography of James K. Polk. It was a few seconds before I realized that the noise intruding on the Mozart piano concerto was my telephone. I usually let it ring, hoping Doreen would answer it on the kitchen phone. But she must have been out shopping, so suddenly I had a Mozart telephone concerto going.

"Hartley here," I said, picking up the phone beside my typewriter.

"Raymer, this is Sam. Have you heard the news?"

I had known Sam Meyers forever. We had gone to Notre Dame Midshipman School together in 1943 under the navy's officer training program. After graduation, we both served in the South Pacific on landing ship tanks. Sam and I would occasionally run into each other at some officers' club on some godforsaken beach somewhere. Now he was the editor of *Washington,* a weekly magazine he and a bunch of Washington moneymen had started back in the early 1960s, right after the Kennedy election. It was still struggling along in 1973, trying to get out of the red and confirm its sponsors' dream inspired by numerous Press Club bar laments that "what this town needs is a *New Yorker!*" A call from Sam Meyers always meant an article assignment.

When he said news, I naturally assumed that it was something about Watergate, but then some sixth sense told me Sam might be calling about Tom Cranston.

"No," I said. "What news?"

"Thomas Cranston was found dead this morning on the beach in Delaware, near something called the Fenwick Towers. Nobody knows much about it—yet. I just heard about it from one of our people, who heard a sketchy news item on WTOP. But you knew Cranston, didn't you? Wasn't he a good friend of yours?"

Slowly and after a long pause, I said, "Yes, we knew Tom quite well."

Something prevented me from mentioning that I had just talked to Tom yesterday.

"He's a Democrat and I know he was working for the Senate. Is there any chance that Cranston's death had something to do with Watergate?"

"I have no idea. You knew Tom, didn't you Sam? Had you heard from Tom lately?"

"From time to time."

"Was he murdered?" I asked.

"Don't know. The news report said they're not sure whether it was murder or suicide. There was a gun found on the beach.

Small caliber. And he was shot in the temple. Maybe Elaine can give us a clue."

"Maybe so. She's gone back to California, living in Santa Monica now, I think. I was never sure what happened there. But I knew they were not getting along. She always felt—as Dory and I did—that Tom should've taken the job with *The Los Angeles Tribune,* which he turned down. You knew about that, didn't you?"

"Yeah," Sam replied. "Everyone did. I always thought it was strange, too, him going to work for the Senate instead of the *Tribune.* That was a pretty good job he turned down."

"I agree. But I didn't really know him then. Met him shortly after that. He told me he turned down the *Tribune* because it would be easier to write his book in the Senate job. Elaine wanted him to go back to California. That's where she was from. We hear from her occasionally. She was drinking pretty heavily before the separation and that may have been a factor. But then, Tom drinks—drank—quite a bit himself, I guess you knew that?"

"I heard he could put 'em down," said Sam. "But I don't think he was an alcoholic, do you?"

"Not when we knew him. We got to know him because of his book. When Humphrey was defeated by Nixon, Tom was offered a job with a subcommittee of the Senate Committee on Energy and Natural Resources and started to work on his book. He knew about my books, of course, especially the biography of George Creel, who always intrigued him. He called me for lunch one day and said he wanted some advice on how to write a book. One thing led to another and we began spending weekends at their place in Rehoboth. And then we eventually bought our own beach house in south Rehoboth— Dewey Beach."

"I remember," Sam interrupted, "and because I knew you and Dory have your place at the beach, and your friendship and all, I thought what happened to Tom over there would be of special interest, especially if his death was related to Watergate."

Funny that Sam should think there might be some connection with Watergate. And then I remembered something a lawyer friend had told us at dinner. He heard that next week John Dean and his wife, Maureen, were going to Bethany Beach to get away from the telephone and the media while he wrote his account of the Watergate mess. Bethany Beach is just north of the Fenwick Towers and it was unlikely that Sam knew about Dean's plan to go over to the shore, which was told to us then in strictest confidence.

"I would be interested in doing a piece on Tom's death," I said to Sam. "I've got the usual stuff going—mainly my biography of James K. Polk."

"Yeah. I remember Polk. Naturally he was a Democrat."

"Naturally."

By 1973, I was pushing fifty and had decided that without any doubt the most interesting and significant subject, next to history, was a human life span—and the more interesting and significant a life the better. For a fiction writer, this means a novel. But for a journalist, this means a biography, which someone said "is the mother of history." I knew my subject would be either a novelist, a journalist, or a politician. For my first biography, I chose George Creel, a crusading, muck-raking, turn-of-the-century journalist who impressed Woodrow Wilson in the campaign of 1916 and went on to become Wilson's propaganda chief in World War I. A fascinating my-kind-of-guy. *Creel* was published in the late 1960s, producing a fine collection of reviews and very little money over and above the publisher's advance.

So then I decided my next book would be not about a president's assistant, but a president.

Then there was my weekly newspaper column that I wrote for *The Berkshire Eagle* in western Massachusetts under the pseudonym Peter Potomac.

Ridiculous sounding pseudonyms have an honorable tradition. You may recall that around the time of the American revolution many journalists wrote under such names as "Peter Porcupine" (William Cobbett), "Publicola" (John Quincy Adams), and "Pubius" (used by Alexander Hamilton and James Madison for articles that were eventually included in The Federalist Papers).

The reason I chose to write an anonymous newspaper column dealing with politics and public affairs is that I worked for a number of publications and organizations that discouraged or prohibited such extracurricular writing. Eventually, I came to prefer anonymous writing. Sam, one of the few people in Washington, or anywhere, who knew that I wrote a weekly newspaper column, was noticeably impatient as I enumerated my commitments.

Never sound too eager to an editor. It might lower the price. So I hesitated long enough for Sam to feel he had to break the silence.

"How 'bout it? A thousand bucks and expenses?" Then he paused. "And another thousand if you are the first to determine that Tom was murdered. It will make a helluva story, crime or not."

"All right, Sam. I'd like to do this one. But look, don't count on me to solve this murder—if that's what it is, especially if it blows into something big, with government overtones. I'm a happily married man with a couple of kids, one just getting out of college and another nearly finished with law school. And I don't want to get into a position of withholding evidence until you can publish it."

"We'll worry about that when we come to it. Can you take off for the shore this afternoon? You know everybody will be over there working on this thing—maybe even Woodward and Bernstein if it's connected to Watergate. You'll have to move fast and stay on it."

I said yes, but then decided I had better get a commitment on one thing.

"Do the expenses include a trip to California?"

"Why?"

"To talk to Elaine Cranston."

"Can't you do it by phone?"

"Yeah, that'll be just the first move. But to find out what I need to know, I'll have to learn why Tom really didn't take the *Tribune* job and why they separated. And maybe she's not going to tell me over the phone. I'll have to get her at just the right moment, on maybe the second martini, but not the fourth."

"What makes you think Elaine Cranston's the key to it? My hunch is that it's government business."

"Maybe—maybe not. People don't usually kill or get killed over government business, even scandals." I still did not want to tell Sam about Tom's phone call.

"Alright, you think you've got to go to L.A., okay. But make it cheap and quick. I don't want to see any expense account for three days at the Beverly Hilton. What's your first move?"

"I'll go down to the shore this afternoon and find out what I can. Then, if I can locate Elaine, I'll fly out to L.A.—tomorrow, I hope."

"Well, good luck, Marlowe. Hope you break the case; but

mainly a good man is dead. Just bring me a good profile. Okay?"

"Okay." And we both hung up.

I looked at my notes on Polk. Suddenly the 1840s seemed long ago and faraway. Watergate was living history. Most people around Washington knew that the Nixon administration could not survive if the White House was involved in a cover-up. Nixon's only real hope of remaining in the presidency would be if Ehrlichman or Haldeman or John Mitchell stepped forward, said they were responsible for the operation and the cover-up, that the president knew nothing about it.

But more important than the potential Watergate aspects of Tom's death was the fact that because of Tom's call I felt personally involved in this article. Tom had been a close friend.

But what had happened to him? That old spark of his was gone. I remembered, in recent years, he would sometimes get that faraway look in his eyes when he was talking to you, as if he were intensely preoccupied with something.

But his death might well have had nothing to do with his personal situation, especially if he were working on the Watergate case. By then, everyone in Washington knew that the White House and the CIA were up to their necks in this thing. Recall that later in *All the President's Men*, Woodward and Bernstein said that "Deep Throat" (their name for their informer or informers) had told Woodward that the CIA had started electronic surveillance on the people who were investigating Watergate. "Everyone's life was in danger," Woodward said.

Dory and I did not really get to know the Cranstons well until after he started to work on his book, something we had in common.

I remember he came out to our house several nights for dinner and I gave Tom my standard lecture on how you approach a book, which, to the fledgling author, is overwhelming. Where do you begin? Well you begin, I told him, by first dividing the book into chapters and then approaching each chapter as a magazine article. Anyone can write a magazine article—and if you can't you should not be thinking about a book. So, you write one chapter and you see how easy that is, and you write another and then another and pretty soon you have written three or four chapters. And you are well into your book. From then it is just a matter of stamina, although a lot of writers—and especially journalists—can't stay the course.

Much to our surprise, Tom and Elaine eventually separated. We never really knew what happened, but we did know—because she told us—that Elaine did not like Washington and was very unhappy when Tom turned down the California job. That was one reason why we were all so surprised. Not only was it a good job, but his wife made no secret that she wanted him to take it. But he didn't. Elaine was drinking a lot at the time and Tom was too. Frankly, they became something of a problem couple before the separation. And maybe it was just as well. Neither of them was happy. We began to drift apart, although I would run into Tom around town from time to time and we would have lunch or drinks. He was becoming quite morose, but I cannot honestly say I ever really figured out what was getting him down. Maybe it was just living in Washington with Nixon in the White House. I remember when he went to work for the Senate committee. He was not much interested in the politics of oil; the job was just a way to make a living while he worked on his book, which did not bring a large advance.

But by the end of Nixon's first term, Tom was increasingly concerned and vocal about an energy crisis he said was approaching.

It was near lunch and quitting time, so I opened a beer and went out on the deck to sit in the sun. Did I really want to play detective? Hell, I decided, what is a biographer but a literary detective? However, nobody comes out of the archives and starts shooting at you. Who knew what I might run into writing Tom Cranston's biography. If he was murdered, at least one person had a stake in keeping anyone from finding out about it. Should I really be getting mixed up in this?

Suddenly, I thought of my Peter Potomac column. It was Thursday noon and I try to get it in the mail on Friday or, at the latest, Saturday morning. This gave us a little time in case there was a delay somewhere along the line. The *Eagle* was an afternoon paper then and the column appeared every Wednesday. There wasn't any problem picking the subject matter—Watergate! That's all anyone in the media thought about then. In the year before the president's resignation, thirty-one of Peter Potomac's fifty-three columns were about Watergate.

The break-in occurred in the middle of the campaign— June of 1972. But as late as August 29, the President was telling the press that "no one in the White House staff, no one in this administration, presently employed, was involved in this very bizarre incident. What really hurts is if you try to cover it up."

And he was getting away with it! So good was the White House cover-up that on November 7 Nixon was reelected in a landslide—60 percent of the popular vote, 97 percent of the electoral college vote. On November 1, a week before the election, Potomac wrote:

*There is the uncomfortable feeling that lurking beneath the
Watergate incident is the ugliest political scandal the
nation has ever known. The question is: If it turns out to
be as ugly as it appears, or even if it lies there unex-
plained, will the President be able to keep the support of
the people he needs to govern the nation?*

So Watergate would be the subject of next week's column.
But what would be the angle? Last week's column had been a
little sermon on how fortunate we were to live under a government of laws made by representatives of the people rather than
by men who made the laws as they went along. The Watergate
scandal was the direct result of men in power going too far,
first breaking the law, then obstructing justice by trying to
cover it up—men who had come to believe they were above
the law.

For this week, May 9, I decided to discuss the motives of the
men in the Nixon administration willing to risk all to obtain
information they felt would help them get reelected. Unlike the
scoundrels in the Grant and Harding administrations, Nixon's
men did not risk breaking the law for personal gain but to stay
in office another four years.

The door slammed and I knew it was Doreen coming
home from her shopping—thoughtfully in time for my lunch.
Marriage has its advantages. And I didn't have to tell her
about Tom.

"Tom Cranston's dead," said Dory, coming out on the
deck, assuming that I had not heard the news because I had
been working. "His body was found this morning on the
beach just south of Bethany. This is dreadful. Shouldn't we
call Elaine?"

"It's too early in California," I said, looking at my watch,
"I'll call her this afternoon."

"All right, but we simply have to find out what happened."

"I know," I said, "I just got off the phone with Sam Meyers. He agrees with you. He also said that, in addition to the article, someday I'll get a book out of it."

"You always do," said Dory.

CHAPTER THREE

Thursday afternoon, May 3, 1973

While Dory was fixing lunch, I went down to the gas station at Glen Echo to fill up the tank for a trip to the Eastern Shore. While waiting for my turn, I couldn't help but think about Tom and the fact that it was not the shortage of gas, per se, that worried him so much as the financial crisis it would ultimately produce.

When that little book *The Limits of Growth* predicted a shortage of petroleum it also predicted a shortage of a great many of the world's critical resources. But the most critical one was oil, most of which was owned by the Arab countries, and this would produce a balance of payments crisis, with the result that the Arab countries would amass a huge reserve of cash. And perhaps the fate of the free world's economy would depend on what they did with this cash.

I remember at the time that Tom had a theory, which we discussed many times and which he wrote about in a brilliant article. There was, he said, only one honorable solution to the balance-of-payments crisis, but it would inevitably speed up the day when the world's essential resources would be exhausted. The only recourse for the Arab countries was to pour all the cash they were amassing from the sale of their oil into developing the Third World, to reduce the poverty in the emerging nations and bring them into modern society. This would, of course, make them avid consumers of the world's resources, just as the nations that had benefited from the industrial revolution had been doing for a hundred years—which would obviously hasten the depletion of the world's resources.

This catch-22 depressed Tom, although I was never convinced that worrying about the fate of the world was what was causing Tom's depression in the early 1970s. As for the oil crisis then, he said all that was phony, although it sure depressed me. *The Limits of Growth* had predicted that if we continued to increase our petroleum consumption at an exponential rate, our oil reserves would be depleted by the year 1992. But even if we continued at our present rate, we would exhaust our oil supplies by the year 2005. I was in a funk for days, until I had lunch with Tom at the Press Club. He said lots of experts did not agree with those estimates, and, in fact, the Club of Rome backed away from them somewhat in its second book, *Mankind at the Turning Point*, published two years later. But Tom insisted that within the first two years of Nixon's second term there would be a phony oil and gas shortage produced not by OPEC but the U.S. oil companies in cahoots with the Nixon administration, which never made any secret of its friendship with big oil. "Mark my word," said Tom, "we're going to see a major scandal, if we can document the evidence we have at the committee."

Tom was not talking about Watergate. In fact, this was in the spring of '72, before the break-in. He was talking about a conspiracy to create an artificial shortage of natural gas and oil that would drive up the price of heating fuel and gasoline, which did happen. Ten years later, in his book *The Oil Follies of 1970–1980*, Robert Sherrill confirmed what Tom Cranston told me then and later.

I recalled how concerned he had been about the threatened gas and oil shortage. He was convinced there was a connection between the Nixon administration and the oil companies. He said the primary reason for the coming oil shortage was the continuation of something called the Mandatory Oil Import program. Early in 1973, Nixon appointed a committee, chaired by Secretary of Labor George Shultz (later to become President Reagan's secretary of state), to study the program and it voted 5–2 to scrap it.

But Nixon listened to the oil lobby instead. He permitted the mandatory quota program to continue until OPEC took over the price fixing of oil. If Nixon had followed his own committee's advice, the country would have had three years to avoid the oil shortages that Tom predicted—correctly—were coming. He said the oil companies had contributed huge amounts—some of it illegally—to the '68 and '72 Nixon campaigns.

At the time, I remember chalking it up to cocktail party talk, but last summer, when I ran into Tom at the Press Club bar, I came away with the distinct impresson that he was working on something big in this area. But he might have become involved with Senator Ervin and his special Watergate Committee.

Dory did the driving on this trip, while I sat in the front seat beside her writing my Peter Potomac column on a yellow legal pad. But I was having trouble concentrating. Although a world-class backseat driver, Doreen tended to speed.

"Slow down, will you! You're driving too fast." Then I mumbled, more to myself than Doreen, "Appointment in Delaware."

"What?" she said. "I thought you were writing your column on Watergate."

"I am, but I was just thinking about that Somerset Maugham story John O'Hara used as the template for *Appointment in Samara.*"

"I don't get it."

"You remember—the Baghdad merchant who lent his servant his horse to flee to Samara after the servant had met Death in the marketplace and she had motioned to him in such a way as to suggest he should leave town? Later, when the merchant himself met Death in the marketplace, he inquired as to why she had made a threatening gesture to his servant. 'That was not a threatening gesture,' Death replied, 'it was only a start of surprise. I was astonished to see him in Baghdad, for I had an appointment with him tonight in Samara.'"

"It is as if ever since his divorce, Tom has had his appointment in Delaware. There seemed to be some hidden force driving him toward destruction."

Dory was about to reply when station WTOP on the car radio came on with the latest report on Tom Cranston:

"Police in Delaware and Ocean City, Maryland, are still investigating the death of Thomas Cranston, a former White House aide under Lyndon Johnson and recently working for a Senate subcommittee. Cranston was found dead on a stretch of beach north of Ocean City, Maryland, in Delaware. Police said he was apparently shot with a thirty-two-caliber revolver, found near the body. Two shots had been fired from the gun, although only one bullet had entered Cranston's head. The police do not now have a motive or a suspect, and do not rule out the possibility of suicide. Ocean City police are also investigating a report that a man who appeared to answer the description of Cranston had been staying at the Admiral Hotel in Ocean City. Ocean City police have found Cranston's car, a little white MG, parked near the Admiral Hotel. What Cranston might have been doing in Ocean City is not known. Police are also investigating the possibility that Cranston was involved in a sensitive government assignment."

"Now, what the hell was Tom doing staying at a hotel in Ocean City," I said to Dory after turning down the radio, "when he has a house in Rehoboth?" Ocean City is only a thirty-minute drive south of Rehoboth.

"Maybe he had business in Ocean City and it was more convenient."

"You have any money?" I asked, holding out my hand. We were approaching the bridge that had brought urban tensions to the Eastern Shore. She gave me a dollar and a quarter for the toll and we breezed over the Chesapeake Bay Bridge without delay.

We were heading for Chestertown, Maryland, and by the time we reached that little college town on the Chester River I had finished my column. Dory had arranged to spend the afternoon visiting our friends, Roger and Thelma Clayton, and then have dinner with our daughter, Karen. Karen was about to graduate from Washington College and had to study for final exams. But she did agree to have dinner with her mother. It was a good thing, because Karen was very upset to hear about Tom's death. She had been close to the Cranstons during that period when we would go down on weekends to visit them at their Rehoboth house.

Washington College is located on a beautiful, rolling campus in Chestertown, probably the highest point on the Eastern Shore. Both the town and the college sort of got lost right after the revolutionary war and have only been recently rediscovered, after two hundred years of peacefully ignoring the rest of the country. Even the Bay Bridge, which was built across the Chesapeake in 1952, did not have much of an impact on Chestertown. When you crossed the bridge from Washington or Baltimore you had to head north to get to Chestertown. But most people just kept going due east to the ocean.

The Claytons lived a couple of miles out of Chestertown in a beautiful old house overlooking the Chester River. Roger used to be a journalist and had worked awhile for *The Washington Post*. But when his wife came into a substantial inheritance, they moved to Chestertown so he could write that novel he knew he had in him if he could ever get away from government and find some peace and quiet. Although there was virtually nothing but peace and quiet in Chestertown, the Claytons had lived there at least three years and he was still on the first chapter, I think. A fine couple, though. We visited them often; and they usually stayed with us when they were in Washington.

"I may be late tonight, but I'm sure the Claytons don't mind you staying here after dinner," I said to Dory as I pulled away from the Clayton driveway. We agreed that I would pick her up on the way back from the beach, we would drive home together that night, and I would fly to Los Angeles the next day, provided I could reach Elaine.

I took a back way from Chestertown, ending up on Route 1, the Ocean Highway, which took you to Rehobeth and then on down to Ocean City. My first stop was the Rehoboth

Police Department at the convention center in town. They told me the state police were handling the case and to see Detective Jenkins, who was working out of the local state police headquarters.

Detective Stanley Jenkins was a big, hulking man. It was immediately obvious that Jenkins was going to be one of those cooperative policemen, primarily concerned that you spell his name right. He had a photograph of himself in his briefcase, suitable for publication. He was even more cooperative with the Channel 4 Washington television reporter who was also asking questions. For an Eastern Shore country boy, Jenkins knew the score.

"This is an interesting case," Jenkins told several reporters from Baltimore, Wilmington, and Washington. "Cranston lives in Washington and owns a house at Rehoboth Beach but was staying at the Admiral Hotel in Ocean City registered under the name of Herman Sullivan. He's married but separated from his wife. Her name is Elaine and she lives in Malibu, California. We haven't been able to reach her yet. There's no answer at her house, just an answering machine. The L.A. police are trying to contact her now."

"Is that confirmed?" a reporter interrupted to ask. "Cranston was definitely registered at the Admiral?"

"Yep. We got a tip—from a woman—that Cranston drove a white MG with D.C. tags. So that's what we started looking for, up and down the shore. The Maryland police found it in Ocean City. They started making inquiries in the vicinity of where the MG was parked and they found he was registered at the Admiral under the name of Herman Sullivan. But there were papers in the room easily traced to Cranston."

"What were they?" another reporter asked.

"That's still under investigation. We're not at liberty to say at this stage. The FBI may be entering the case, if we find that Cranston was working on government business. Then you'll have to ask Washington. But that is not official yet."

"Anything else in the room that might be of interest?" the Channel 4 reporter asked.

"Yeah, one thing we can talk about. There were some ashes in one of the ashtrays. Looked like something might have been burned in it. We're having a lab in Wilmington analyze it. There'll be a report on that later today. There was also an empty cassette in the wastebasket and a tape recorder on the dresser. That's all for now. I'm taking the television crews up for some shots on the beach where the body was found and an interview. You know how they like it on TV, with the ocean and sand in the background. Any of you guys who want to can come along. We gotta get going soon, while we still got good light."

Jenkins was obviously a man of his times. Either that, or the Delaware State Police had begun sending their detectives to media school.

I started to Fenwick in my station wagon but before I reached there I decided to drive on down to Ocean City and sniff around the Admiral. I did not think there would be much to learn on the beach now and I wanted to talk with someone at the hotel before the media pack arrived.

The Admiral Hotel was one of those big relics from the 1920s and 1930s when Ocean City was a nice, quiet little place to bring the family, before the Chesapeake Bay Bridge brought the crowds and the high rises north of the original city, which gave it that Miami Beach look. The admiral was only four or five stories tall, but spread out over half a city block. At least half of its rooms had a nice view of the Atlantic. But its most attractive feature was a big, dark, oak-paneled bar and lounge where you could sit and drink and, from some of the tables, see the ocean. Very pleasant.

It was about 4:30 P.M. when I arrived. The cocktail hour was just getting started, but being midweek in early May there weren't many people around to distract Eddie the bartender— the man I wanted to see. He was handsome, sort of like an old comic-strip character. It was too early for the college boys to have arrived, and Eddie was obviously one of those resort drifters who spent his winters in Florida and the summers on the Eastern Shore in an endless search if not for the perfect wave then at least the perfect body. And I gathered he had already found one. She was sitting near the cash register where she could talk to him. She was across the bar from me and the counter hid half of her. But from the waist up, she was perfect.

After Eddie and I exchanged the usual preliminaries I told him I wanted to talk to him.

"You a cop?" he asked indifferently, but sensing immediately what I wanted to talk about.

"No. Working on a story about Thomas Cranston for *Washington* magazine. You know it?"

"Yeah, I see it around."

"Have the cops been in?"

"The Maryland police were in this afternoon."

"Well, you'll probably be hearing from the Delaware police soon. Detective Jenkins will be wanting to know what you know."

"All I know is what I told the Maryland cops. It ain't much."

"But it is something. Right?"

"Right. I saw this guy Cranston a coupla times recently. He's been staying here at the hotel for a few days and—"

"Ever seen him before that?" I interrupted.

"No, never. But he spent a lot of time in the bar while he was here. Not much else to do. At least he didn't seem to have much to do. Night before last, the night before he was killed, he got pretty blasted. Started drinking in the late afternoon. And he was acting real strange. Sorta like someone was after him or somethin'. At least that's what he told Jessica, here. But he didn't say too much about it, mostly his talk was just the usual: the weather, which restaurants are open now. Which was kinda strange, because until the last night—the night he was killed, or whatever—he never went out at night, always ate in for dinner. He seemed especially edgy after dark. He knew the shore. In fact, I understand he owns a place in Rehoboth."

"That's right. A town house on the north shore. Nice place. Did he say anything to suggest why he was staying here in Ocean City?"

"Nah. But I could tell somethin' was botherin' him."

"How?"

"I don't know. Just the way he acted. That last night, after he'd talked to a man at that table, back there"—and Eddie pointed with a glass he was wiping to a table far back in a dimly lit corner—"they left together as if they were going up to Cranston's room. Then when Cranston came back in here a little later, he was a different guy, cracking jokes, you know, and winking and pretending like he had a date with the hottest woman on the shore, things like that."

"Slow down a little, Eddie, you're getting ahead of me. Let's go back to the night before he died. Did anything happen that night?"

"Nah. Cranston just sat here drinking heavy until around eight, then he went to dinner in the little restaurant across the lobby there. He talked some to Jessica. He was in here the next night round six, and took that table back in the corner. A little while later a small, heavyset, well-dressed guy came in and they sat there for a while. I remember he wore very thick glasses. After a couple of drinks, they got up and left, heading toward the stairs up to the rooms."

"Did you talk to Cranston then?"

"No, he was too involved with this guy."

"So how come you decided he seemed so different?"

"That came later. After about an hour, he came back in alone, sat at the bar, and ordered a drink. That's when I noticed he was different. He started kiddin' with me and with Jessica— just not the same guy that was sitting in here broodin' and drinkin' the night before."

Tom had certainly convinced Eddie, I thought. Or maybe Eddie was putting on an act. But somehow Eddie convinced me too, and I decided, until shown otherwise, that whatever went on between Tom and that man in the corner must have been good news to Tom.

"What happened then?"

"Well," said Eddie, "he kept kidding around like maybe he had a date, you know, phony macho bar stuff. Nobody pays much attention to it. It was the changed mood that impressed me, and Jessica, too."

I looked over at Jessica who was, by now, listening to our conversation. She nodded and smiled.

"In fact," Eddie continued, "I'm not even sure he had a date, at least with a gal. After he had one drink, he said, 'See you tomorrow,' and went out. By this time, I was curious about him because of the way he was acting an' all. So I walked down to the end of the lounge there, where you can look out the window and see the street. I just wanted to see where he was going, and maybe if he met anyone. Well, he did meet someone on the street corner. A man, as tall as Cranston. It was dark by now and I couldn't see too well, but they were near the streetlight."

I cut in: "Any chance this was the same man Cranston had left the bar with earlier?"

"No way. This fellow was much taller and had on one of those Greek fisherman caps, dark, with a little bill, a tan jacket, looked like one of those corduroy jackets, the kind with brown patches on the sleeves. And dark slacks. No glasses. The man he was with earlier was much smaller and heavier, wore a suit and carried a top coat, thick glasses. Also, this new guy was just a little swishy—know what I mean? Not really queer acting, but he moved sorta precisely, like an actor or dancer. They talked a little on the corner, then walked across the street and up the next block, and got in a car. I could just barely see them. I couldn't tell much about the car, except I'm sure it was a station wagon. I could see that much when they drove off. Any chance Cranston was queer?"

Without really thinking, I replied, "Not a chance. I've known Tom Cranston for years. Know his wife and—well— he's separated now, but I know he likes girls the same way I do."

"You knew him?"

"Yeah. We were pretty good friends once. That's one reason the magazine assigned me to do a story on him. But I haven't seen him much lately."

"Well, maybe he changed. A lot of guys come down here to lead a double life, you know."

"Yeah."

"Happens all the time."

"Well, I don't figure Tom Cranston that way, but I'll think about it."

"May explain everything. May have been just a lover's quarrel up there on the beach."

"Yeah," I agree. "But who was the lover?"

Eddie shrugged, then suddenly looked at his watch: "Hey, I gotta get this place ready. People'll be coming in soon."

I nodded, and said, "Think I'll talk to Jessica."

Jessica had recently arrived from Florida and was about to start her summer job waitressing at the Phillips Crab House. She was very friendly and said she had talked to Cranston, thought he was a nice guy, but drinking too much. "He was obviously worried about something; the night before he was killed when he had too much to drink, he implied that his life was in danger, that someone was following him. In fact, he said that was why he was eating here in the hotel, not going out. If he did they'd get him."

Jessica said she usually did not pay much attention to anything she heard from guys in a bar. And she had heard plenty. But she also said that judging from the way he acted the night before last, when he invited her to his room for a drink, and then last night, when he left the bar, there might be something to it.

"When I went to his room, he was really down—drinking and obviously worried. He kept looking out the window, which was on the street side."

"Do you think he was homosexual?" I asked, and she shook her head quickly. "Hell, no. He was a hundred percent normal that night, at least as far as sex was concerned. But he was acting strange, as I said. He had this little box with a tape in it. And he said: 'If I send this to Washington—which I might—it's going to really make the headlines.'"

"Did he give you any idea what was on the tape, what it was about?"

"No. When I asked him what was was on the tape he said, "Never you mind. You'll be reading about it soon enough.""

"So he convinced you he was involved with someone or something, and it was pretty big?"

"That's right," Jessica replied, "And then the next night, the night he was killed—or shot himself—he was completely different. He acted like some great load was off his mind and he kinda made out like he had a real hot date, and he obviously didn't mind going out of the hotel now."

After staring at my drink a moment trying to absorb everything Jessica had told me, I said, "Can I buy you a drink?'

"You sure can," she replied as she moved her leg over to touch mine and put her hand lightly on my thigh, halfway up. "I'm not doing anything for dinner, either, if you're free."

"Oh, no, thanks. I gotta head back to Washington as soon as I make one more stop in Rehoboth."

"Sorry. If you get down to the Crab House, look me up."

I motioned to Eddie for a drink and the check. The local news was just coming on to the big TV screen behind the bar and Jessica, Eddie, and I focused on it, knowing that the Cranston case would probably be the first story. We were right. The local anchor gave the basic facts—nothing new. Then there was a live interview with Detective Jenkins on the beach. He was impressive and articulate. Seemed reassuring and on top of the case. But still nothing new.

Sports featured the Orioles game the night before and it was a dismal affair, unless you were a White Sox fan. The Sox beat the Orioles 4–0 behind the six-hit pitching of lefthanded knuckleballer Wilbur Wood. It was no fluke. Wood had pitched twenty-eight scoreless innings and last night's was his third straight shutout. Jim Palmer took the loss, although as usual he pitched good ball, giving up only five hits and a couple of runs before being lifted in the top of the seventh. The Birds had now dropped nine of their last twelve games and looked like they were starting to slide—after winning three straight pennants from 1969 to 1971.

When Eddie came with the check, I gave him an extra-large tip and thanked him for the information. "Very helpful, I'll mention you in the article. Watch for it."

Before leaving, I went over to the reception desk, told the girl minding the store that I was a reporter and asked whether she remembered Tom Cranston, the man whose body they found on the beach this morning.

"Yes, I do," she said. "I already told the police. Last night, right after I came on duty, he came down from upstairs and asked if I had any stamps for sale. I said yes, and he bought about two dollars' worth and put them all over this little package he had. He asked me where he could mail it and I pointed over there to the box. He said thanks, and that was all."

"Earlier, did you see him go upstairs with a small, heavyset man?" I asked.

"No."

"Did you see the man come down?"

"No."

"Was there anyone else around that might have seen Cranston with the other man?"

"No. The police asked the other girl, Mary, who is on before me. And I heard her tell them the same thing. She never saw another man."

"Could he and another man have gone upstairs without you seeing them?"

"Easy. I'm away from the desk sometimes, back to the kitchen, into that little office, the ladies' room. I could've missed them."

I thanked her, then walked over to the newsstand and paused, wondering what to do next.

I planned to drive back to the Delaware State Troopers' headquarters for one last talk with Jenkins, but I saw him coming into the lobby of the Admiral.

He must have driven straight down to Ocean City from his beach interview at Fenwick. "Hey, Jenkins," I said, trying to be friendly, "we just saw you on TV. Lookin' good. When you going on the Johnny Carson show?"

"Maybe soon," he replied, "if this case is hot, which I think it is."

Jenkins must have something new I thought. I motioned to the bar, and asked, "How 'bout a drink? It's on me; maybe you can get me on TV, too."

"Not now," said Jenkins. "I'm still on duty. Gotta talk to the bartender. The Maryland people say he has a story."

"Yeah, he just told me. Interesting. You must have something new—but you didn't say anything on TV."

"Didn't know then. When I got back to the car, before I drove down here, I phoned headquarters in Rehoboth and they had the lab reports from Wilmington. Most interesting thing is that Cranston wasn't killed by the bullet fired from the thirty-two-caliber pistol found at the scene. He was killed by another gun—a thirty-eight-caliber, which we have not found. The lab couldn't tell much about the burned stuff in the ashtray, except that it had been a photograph, some negatives, and the remains of an audiotape."

"That was quite a bit," I said. "What do you think it means?"

"Two things," replied Jenkins. "One: it means somebody was probably blackmailing somebody, and two: it means the FBI could be comin' in on the case. We think Cranston was working on something for the government, and if he was, just maybe somebody was blackmailing him. You don't know what he might have been forced to tell 'em."

"Well, don't start jumping to conclusions," I cautioned.

"You're going to be confused after you talk to Eddie, and watch out for Jessica. I can tell by the size of your waistline that you're a happily married man—and Jessica is bad news."

"I know a hundred Jessicas," Jenkins said with a wink and headed for the swinging bar doors.

"One more thing. Why don't you see if you can find the package Cranston mailed last night in that box out front? The girl at the desk can tell you all about it," I said, motioning toward the hotel desk.

Jenkins looked startled, then he moved fast toward the desk to talk to the young lady, while I looked at my watch. It was 6:30 P.M.—3:30 in California. A good time to call Elaine, before the martini hour.

There was a phone booth over in the corner, and after obtaining her number from information I dialed it.

The phone rang a few times before a man's voice answered.

"My name is Raymond Hartley. I'm a friend of Elaine Cranston, calling from Ocean City, Maryland. Do I have the right number?"

"Yes, this is her house, but she's not here."

"Well, it's really important that I get in touch with her. I don't know whether she's heard or not, but her husband was killed last night. Do you know how I can reach her?"

"I talked to Elaine about ten minutes ago. She just learned about it. She's been in an all-day seminar, but someone in the class heard about it on the radio and told her."

"Do you know where the seminar is, or where she's staying?"

"In Washington, D.C."

"Washington? That's where I live. We were Elaine and Tom's closest friends when they lived here. I would have thought she'd call us if she was coming to town."

"I don't know. Maybe she tried. The course is a three-day

orientation seminar put on by the Bristol Sound Corporation. She just went to work for them, but hadn't really made up her mind whether she wanted to stay with the company. I guess I talked her into it. So she decided to take the course. It was a last-minute thing. Maybe that's why she didn't call you."

"Maybe," I said.

"The seminar's at the Sheraton Park Hotel, and that's where she's staying. You know it?"

"I know it well. By the way, who am I speaking to?"

"Arnold Stein. I just happened to be here picking up my tennis gear when you called. Elaine and I are very good friends. We planned to get married as soon as she could get her divorce from Tom. In fact, that's one of the things she was going to do on this trip. Talk to him about the divorce."

"Did she ever reach him?" I asked.

"Not that I know of. I guess now . . ."

"That's right. The divorce is taken care of, but in an ugly way."

"Too bad. Very sorry to hear about it."

"Did you ever meet Tom?"

"Never did."

"Well, thanks for your help. I'm going to call Elaine right now. Good-bye."

"Good-bye."

"Damn," I muttered to myself as I hung up. If Elaine's still drinking, it would probably be too late to catch her sober.

I got the Sheraton Park phone number from the operator and called. They did have an Elaine Cranston registered, and the switchboard put me right through.

"Hello, Elaine? This is Ray Hartley. I'm just calling to tell you how sorry I am to hear about Tom and to see if there is anything we can do."

"That's sweet of you to call, Ray, but I'm all right."

"I called Malibu and your fiancé said you just heard about it."

"Yes."

She sounded fine; if she was still drinking martinis she was only on her first.

"It's terrible. But if you feel up to it, I'd like to see you—tomorrow, if that's possible."

"Well, I have a seminar beginning early, but we take a break for lunch. I'll have about an hour. Could you come to the hotel at noon?"

"That would be great. And Dory'll be with me."

"Marvelous. But you know, if it's inconvenient, you two don't need to hold my hand. I'm doing fine."

"That's good, Elaine, but Sam Meyers at *Washington*—you remember Sam—wants me to write a piece about Tom and I'm under a real tight deadline. He knows how much I liked you both and that we were pretty close at one time. I've done a lot of writing for Sam and he thought I'd be a good man for the job."

"He's right about that. I don't know how much help I can be, but I'll be glad to talk to you and happy to see you again."

"Same here. I'm in Ocean City right now, but will be leaving for Washington soon. I'm picking Dory up at Chestertown, where she's visiting Karen."

"What are you doing in Ocean City?"

"Just asking about Tom. You probably heard he was staying down here when he was killed."

"Yes, I did hear that," said Elaine, "and it struck me as strange. He still owned the house at Rehoboth—you remember it. That was always his house. He bought it with money inherited from his father. I wonder what he was doing staying at a hotel in Ocean City."

"A lot of people would like to know that. And I suspect when we find out we'll know a lot more about what happened. But we can talk about that tomorrow. Sure there isn't something I can do for you?"

There was a pause, then she said hesitantly, "Well, there is one thing, as long as you're down on the shore. Tom had a secret hiding place at our beach house, where he kept his papers and other valuables. He said they were a lot safer there than in our Washington apartment. It's behind a phony panel in the second-floor bathroom. He built it himself and nobody knows about it but me. Would you look in there and see if there are any papers—probably in a brown leather folder tied with a heavy string. I think his will is in there and I need to see it. I haven't told the police about it. Maybe it's not the right thing to do and if you'd rather not get involved, I'll understand."

For a moment I considered the legality of what Elaine asked me to do, and then I said, "No, Elaine, I'll do it. Give me the details."

She told me precisely how to find the hidden panel, how to open it, and where the key to the house was under the back steps. I told her I would bring her whatever was in the hiding place tomorrow.

Now I wanted to avoid seeing Jenkins, so I left the Admiral immediately and had a quick sandwich at a little grille up the street. Next door was a large drugstore, where I bought a small hammer, flashlight, and a couple of screwdrivers. They might come in handy.

When I reached the row of town houses in the north shore of Rehoboth, they were dark and seemed to be deserted, except for one about three houses from Tom's on the south side. I remembered meeting the people who lived there once at a party they gave when we were visiting Tom for a weekend, but I could not remember their names. I decided it would be best to check in there first, to keep them from calling the police when they saw me go into Tom's. Also, they might know something.

I took the station wagon into the driveway and parked behind a brown Cadillac and a green BMW, both with D.C. tags. When I rang the bell, a very attractive woman in her mid-forties answered the door. It would be hard not to remember her, but I'm not sure she recognized me.

"Evening. My name is Raymond Hartley, a friend of Tom Cranston's. I think I was here once a couple of years ago, when we were visiting Tom, at one of your parties. I'm a writer. Maybe you remember?"

"Of course, of course, I'm Arlene Bradshaw, come on in." She took me up to the living room dominated by a bar, on the other side of which was the kitchen. The curtains were open at the ocean end of the room. There was a spectacular view of the Atlantic. As we entered the room, another attractive woman in her mid-to-late thirties stood up from her seat at the bar and smiled at me. She was holding a half-empty old-fashioned glass in her hand. "This is Brenda Hollingsworth. Brenda and I are enjoying a week by ourselves. Our husbands are coming down Friday after work. Bill, my husband, and I were down last weekend and I decided to stay the week and asked Brenda down and we're both getting an early start on our tans."

Arlene's husband, I recalled, did something in the bureaucracy or maybe Republican party politics. Brenda I recognized from *The Washington Post* Style section as being the wife of Republican congressman Herb Hollingsworth. A very stylish couple. I accepted a scotch and water, then told them what I was doing and asked if they had, by chance, seen Tom around lately. They were pleased and a bit excited to be asked about their possibly murdered neighbor. Arlene said no. "Brenda and I weren't around much on Wednesday. She came early and we went down to the bay to see our boat and then had lunch in Fenwick. We went back to the boat and spent the afternoon just sunning on the deck. We got back here around cocktail time, had a couple of drinks, went out to eat, then came back here. We didn't see anything at Tom's house. No sign of him. And we didn't see him before that night. That's about all."

Then she paused for a moment before saying, "No, there was one more thing which seemed a little strange."

"What was that?"

"Well, last night, I don't remember what time but it was well after dark, there was a light on in the Turner house, next to the Cranstons', you know. There was no car in the driveway when we got back from the boat. But after we returned from dinner, the lights were on and I think it was the Turners' blue Cadillac parked in their driveway. But I can't be sure it was their car."

"The Turners?" My interest picked up considerably, as I remembered Tom mentioning Bevery Turner.

"You must remember them. They live near the Cranstons. The Turner house is the one just to the north. They were good friends. We're also friends with the Turners. I'm sure you remember them."

"Yes, I do. And you say there were lights on there that night but you didn't see anything?"

"That's right. They were on for maybe an hour or two after we got back from dinner. Then I heard a car door close and the car drive away. A little bit later I noticed the lights were out, and they never came back on that evening. I thought it a little strange at the time, the pattern, that is. Usually when someone arrives in the evening it means they're going to be here at least overnight and into the next day. But just to come to the beach one evening, stay for a couple of hours and then leave and not come back that night is definitely not normal. Know what I mean?"

I understood. So I asked, "Are you sure the car there was a Cadillac and not a station wagon?"

"Absolutely. The Turners have a station wagon but it was definitely a Cadillac. I can't be certain of the color or whether it was theirs. Or for that matter, even if the driver was one of the Turners. It could have been someone else."

We speculated for a while as to who it might have been and what Tom Cranston was doing in Ocean City and what could have happened to him. Then I realized it was getting late and I still had to drive back to Chestertown and then Washington, so I said I had to be going. I mentioned, as casually as I could, not to be alarmed at lights going on in the Cranston house tonight because I had talked to Elaine Cranston this afternoon and she asked me to bring her something—a little personal thing she wanted to remember Tom by—tomorrow in Washington. I told them I knew where the key was usually kept and if it was there, I would only be a few minutes in the house. They seemed to think that was fine—a nice thing for me to do. And we said our good-byes.

The key was just where Elaine said it was and so was the secret panel. Working as fast as I could with the tools I had concealed in my briefcase, I hoped to get out of there before the police arrived. I removed a wooden container about twice the size of a cigar box from the hidden chamber, replaced the panel, and left in a hurry, holding the box to my side away from the Bradshaw house, just in case the ladies were trying to see what Elaine Cranston wanted me to take to her.

*   *   *

As I was nearing the end of the stretch of road that runs parallel to the ocean, I could see a Delaware police car approaching. Seeing that it was Jenkins, probably headed for Tom's house, I motioned for him to stop. I pulled up beside him and we talked through our windows: "What the hell are you doing here?" Jenkins said, but not really showing displeasure.

"I thought I'd talk to some of Cranston's neighbors. I met them before. They're in the house next to his—with all the lights on."

"Learn anything?"

"Not much. The Turners live on the other side of the Cranstons and one of their cars was here for a while the night Tom was killed. Ask the neighbor, Mrs. Bradshaw. She'll tell you about it."

"I will."

"Here's something else. Elaine Cranston is in Washington—at the Sheraton Park Hotel. She's attending a seminar. Give her a call. Maybe you can arrange to see her before she goes back to the coast."

Jenkins took out a pad and made some notes. "Thanks. 'Preciate it. Let me know if I can help you any."

"Don't worry, I will." I waved good-bye and took off.

When I was back on the highway heading toward Five Corners, I could not help pulling over to the side of the road and stopping for a quick look in the box. The leather pack was there all right, but on top of the packet was a black-and-white photograph of a very attractive woman wrapped in a towel, sitting on the edge of a bed. Next to her was a man dressed only in his Jockey briefs. They both looked distressed, as if someone had caught them alone together; their features were clearly distinguishable. The man in the Jockey shorts looked vaguely familiar and I was sure I had met the woman somewhere. There was also something familiar about her. I would bet that the woman was Beverly Turner, whom he had mentioned on the phone yesterday.

Tom Cranston was involved in blackmail. But he was not being blackmailed; he was doing the blackmailing.

CHAPTER FOUR

Friday morning, May 4, 1973

I was up early to read *The Washington Post* in my exercise room, also watching the little TV I had hooked up in front of my treadmill. I was hoping there would be something on the Cranston case, but there was nothing. Dory was still asleep, so after the workout I climbed back into bed and started gently shaking her shoulder, reminding her that we had a luncheon date with Elaine. "And I have a deal you can't pass up," I whispered in her hear. "If you'll type my column and get it in the mail, I'll make love to you." This brought a sharp elbow in the ribs—but she did do the column and mailed it.

After breakfast, I spent the morning the way most detectives, reporters, and housewives do—on the telephone. The first person I called was Jenkins, to ask him about the package Tom mailed that afternoon.

"I'm not very optimistic," he said. "It was not registered or certified. The post office people put a tracer on it but they don't hold out much hope. I'll let you know if they find it. You got any idea who he might have sent that little package to?"

This was the moment I was dreading. Not to tell Jenkins about Tom's call to me, and about the people in the photograph, amounted to withholding evidence. "Damn it," I muttered to myself, but said, "No, I don't have a clue. But if I run into anything, don't worry, I'll let you know. But I did learn one thing from Mrs. Cranston; maybe she told you, too? The Cranstons, at one time, were very close to their neighbors on the North Shore, where Tom still owns a town house. Their names are Arthur and Beverly Turner. You should check them out," I said, hoping that my giving the detective a little helpful information would somehow compensate for withholding real evidence.

"Yeah, I've already talked to Mrs. Turner. She's coming to Rehoboth early next week and we have an appointment. But you know, Mr., er, uh . . ."

"Hartley," I said. "Raymond Hartley."

"Yeah, right. Well, there's something really strange about this case, if you know what I mean. First place, we talked to a couple who have a condo in Fenwick Towers, which is only a couple of hundred yards from where Cranston was shot. They were sure they heard what sounded like a gunshot that night. But they only heard one, not two. They got kind of nervous when they heard it, so they tried to look up the beach but couldn't see nothing.

"And here's a curious thing. They said they also looked out a window that looked down on part of their parking lot. They were sort of checking their car, which was a Pontiac Le Mans. And when they looked—this was just a moment after the shot—they could see a station wagon gunning out of the lot and heading north. But considering where Cranston's body was found, if that was the shot that killed him, whoever was driving that station wagon couldn't have fired it."

"Did they recognize the wagon?" I asked.

"No, it didn't look familiar. But they couldn't be sure. Lots of people who live there, they said, have station wagons."

"Did you check the other people?"

"Yeah, and as best as we could find out there was only one other couple staying there that night. They own a station wagon but did not drive to the beach that trip. They also own another car, a Buick Skylark, and that was the car they were driving then. They don't remember seeing another car that night, except their neighbor's blue Le Mans. But the couple who heard the shot think they remember seeing another car in the lot that night—a light-colored one. But they aren't sure.

"Then there was Cranston himself. He was really acting weird at the Admiral Hotel, according to all those people who worked there. First he seemed afraid, and then later he wasn't. He was depressed and morose, and then he got happy. He was seen talking in the bar with one guy and then went off with another—all the time staying in a hotel in Ocean City when he owned his own house only thirty miles north of Rehoboth. That's definitely not a normal pattern."

"No, you don't have to go to detective school to figure that out," I replied. "What's your explanation?"

"Damned if I know—yet. But it's beginning to look less and less like suicide. One thing they did teach us in detective school was that nine out of ten murders have something to do with the victim's personal relations. The wife or husband, a neighbor or a jealous lover. Somethin' like that. Of course, this one could be government business. And that would bring in the FBI."

"I hope it doesn't come to that," I said hastily, I don't know why.

I was anxious to hang up so I could call Beverly Turner. The Turners were probably in town this weekend if they were not going to the beach until next week. "Look, Jenkins, I gotta run now. I'll be talking to you next week, okay?"

I looked up the Turners in the phone book, called the number, and when Mrs. Turner answered, I explained that I was a friend of Tom's, that I thought we had met a few years ago when we used to visit the Cranstons at the beach and that I would like to talk to her in connection with the *Washington* magazine profile of Tom that I was writing. I was prepared to hint about the photograph and Tom's mentioning her if she was at all hesitant to see me, but she said she would pleased to see me and talk about Tom. We made an appointment for tomorrow afternoon for cocktails. That's nice, I thought as I hung up. The Turner address was in the suburb of Kenwood, Maryland, and I could just smell big money coming out of the phone. That meant some good Black Label or Chivas Regal, which at $18.99 a halfgallon was out of my league.

Then I retired to my office and darkroom for the afternoon to block out the Cranston article and to make additional prints of the photograph Tom had hidden away in his beach house. I put Tom's photo on my light board, shot new pictures and made some prints, enlarging a few so that I would have better images of both faces.

I still had plenty of people to interview, of course, and I had to sketch two tags for my outlines—one if he was murdered and one if it was suicide, which might still be a possibility. And what about Watergate? Was that part of the story?

And the tape, if that's what was in the package Tom mailed.

And who did he mail it to? I kept listening for the mailman, and when he came, I rushed out to the box, though there was no package, just the usual junk mail.

Tom originally wanted to achieve something for his country in accordance with his beliefs, and of course be part of history. I fully understood that. But what happened? After two unsuccessful campaigns that would no doubt have meant a White House job for him had they won, did he lose that idealism? Did he become discouraged, bored? And what part—if any—did whiskey and women play in his downfall?

And what about money? If Tom really was blackmailing the woman in that photograph, or the man, what was he asking? Had he suddenly developed a need or urge for money?

Dory and I left the house for lunch about eleven-thirty, and as we approached the Sheraton Park the car radio said, "John Dean has announced that he removed Watergate-related documents from the White House to protect them from what he called 'illegitimate destruction.' Dean said he was now asking the U.S. district attorney to take charge of them."

"Well, now, who in the White House, do you suppose, would illegitimately destroy such papers?" said Dory, in that sardonic tone for which she is famous at area bridge tables.

"Can't imagine," I replied. "The people who stand to lose the most if the facts about Watergate come out are the president of the United States and his two chief counselors. Certainly *they* wouldn't do such a thing."

"Damn it," said Dory, staring out of the car window, "do you think Tom was really mixed up in this ugly mess?"

"I don't know," I said. "The photograph suggests it might have been something personal, although I'm sure the man in the photograph was someone I've seen around town, or in the media."

When I had shown Dory the photograph I found in Tom's secret compartment in his beach house, she too thought the woman looked familiar. She agreed it could have been Beverly Turner, whom we had met at the Cranstons' when we used to visit them at Rehoboth Beach. "Tom's photograph collecting seems to have taken a kinky twist," she said. "But it does, as you say, seem to suggest that he was blackmailing people."

Elaine Cranston was a tall fading blonde who had been quite attractive when she married Cranston. But years and overindulgence had taken their toll. And it had not helped her to have Tom remain so handsome and debonair, as he did. Tom did not seem like a womanizer when we knew the Cranstons, but there were rumors that after the McGovern campaign he not only began to drink too much but became involved with other women, or at least one woman.

In many ways Washington is like Hollywood, with a lot of very attractive, ambitious young ladies running around using every means at their disposal to advance their careers. Often this means going after that very attractive man in a powerful job, who more often than not has a wife in the boondocks whom he married back when he was just starting up the political ladder. This highly charged and often sexual atmosphere had been too much for Elaine.

When she walked toward us in the Sheraton Park restaurant where we were waiting, she looked much better than I had expected. She was stunning in a tan corduroy jacket and gray flannel slacks. Dory's first reaction was: "Oh, it's obvious Elaine has a new boyfriend!"

When she arrived at the table we hugged all around, and Dory said, "Elaine, you look so good. What have you been doing to yourself?"

"Well, first, I've stopped drinking! Just a little wine now and then. And I've started getting regular exercise. Arnold is responsible for that. He's also responsible for my new job. The company—Bristol—makes professional sound equipment for the studios and theaters. Arnold's a producer of documentaries and he got me the job. Anyway, you're right. I'm a new person these days."

"You look it," I said.

"Anything new at the beach?" Elaine asked, launching a brief conversation about the old days.

"Not much, except of course for Tom's death. That seems to dominate the party talk."

"What about your neighbors—The Carters? Isn't that their name? Are they still there?"

"Oh yeah," Dory replied, "They're still there. And Donnie hasn't changed a bit; same old Donnie."

Elaine was referring to Donnie and Mary Carter and their three kids. Elaine and Tom had met the Carters a couple of times at our house. They never were particularly close. We had several other friends in our area, some of whom the Cranstons knew.

After exhausting the neighborhood gossip, we finally got around to the number two topic of party talk—beach house prices. Elaine thought there was a possibility that she might have inherited their town house at the North Shore.

This gave me the opportunity to take out the packet of documents I had taken from Tom's house, commenting, "Maybe this will provide an answer."

She opened them immediately and was looking through them while we were studying the menu, when suddenly she exclaimed, "Well, this is a surprise! I'm still the beneficiary of Tom's insurance policy and the house. I thought surely he would have changed it by now—in which case there would be a rider, wouldn't there?"

"Yes. How much is it for?" I asked.

She paused a moment while she double-checked the amount. "The same as it was: two hundred and fifty thousand dollars."

"A quarter of a million dollars," Dory exclaimed. "Why, Elaine, you're a rich woman!"

"I don't know," said Elaine. "I guess I am. But I feel sort of guilty about it, if you know what I mean. After all, we are separated, and he did die in a terrible way."

"But you're still his legal wife, aren't you?"

"Yes, I am, but I've been trying to get a divorce. That's one of the reasons I decided to come east—to talk to Tom about that."

"Did you manage to talk to him before he was killed?" asked Dory.

"No, I called him at the apartment and left a message and tried to reach him at the beach house. But I never did."

I wanted to know from Elaine why Tom had turned down the job with *The Los Angeles Tribune*.

"Ray, I don't know how much of this you can use in your article, but Tom was having an affair with another woman—a married woman. That, pure and simple, was why he would not leave Washington; I only learned about that later, but the woman refused to break up her marriage. She had children, a comfortable life, and thought everything was just fine as it was. But she didn't get along too well with her husband. Then the affair broke up and Tom seemed to start going downhill. Naturally, as the wife, I don't know all the details."

The waitress took our orders, and when she left I knew we did not have much time remaining, and I needed to know about that photograph. So I took it out and showed it to Elaine.

"Well, I'll be damned," she exclaimed. "I don't know the man but I sure know the woman. That's Beverly Turner, our lovely neighbor at Rehoboth. No mistake. God! I wonder what Tom was doing with this."

"I found it in that box at the beach house."

I tried delicately to question Elaine about the love affair, asking whether it might have been with Arlene Bradshaw, who lived a couple of houses away from them at Rehoboth. I told her about my meeting Mrs. Bradshaw and her friend last night and commented that she was certainly attractive enough— although perhaps too Republican for Tom.

"No, no, it wasn't Arlene," said Elaine, laughing for the first time. "Tom didn't have enough money—or power—for her. No, this one was someone more intellectual, the kind of woman that always appealed to Tom."

"Well, I know it wasn't Arlene's friend, Brenda Hollings-worth," Dory said. "Her husband is a Republican and she is definitely not Tom's type. What about Beverly Turner? You said Tom was attracted to her?"

She shook her head and said, "I don't really know."

"How about another drink?" I asked, looking around for the waitress.

"No, this is my quota," she said. "Gee, it's good to see both of you again. I wish you could come out to Malibu and spend a week or two with me. Dory, you've never seen California, have you?"

"Yes, once upon a time when the kids were little. But maybe we'll take you up on that."

I leaned back and looked directly at Elaine. "Elaine, Tom never really discussed his affair with me, but he hinted about it once, enough to give me some idea who it was. Would you tell me, if I guessed right?"

"I don't know, Ray. Maybe."

"I think it was Beverly Turner."

Elaine looked at Dory, then slowly started to sip at a glass of water. Then suddenly, deciding that perhaps I knew already, or maybe just what the hell, it doesn't make any difference now, Elaine said, "Yes, it was Beverly. But of course you can't use that in print anywhere. And I hope you will keep this strictly confidential."

"I'll do my best," I replied quickly. "But it would help if I could let Mrs. Turner know that I knew about her and Tom as lovers when I interview her."

"Well, use your own judgment. But be tactful. Frankly, I'm not sure Arthur knows anything about it yet. I know I've never told anyone and I don't think Tom did either, although he may have confided in you."

"No, never specifically," I said. "But I will tread carefully with this. I assume you didn't mention Beverly to Detective Jenkins when you talked to him on the phone?"

"I did not, and I don't intend to," Elaine replied emphatically. "But I don't mind telling you and Dory now." There were tears in her eyes, and I was frankly a little uncomfortable.

But damn it, I decided, despite the profile, I was not insensitive. And while I was a journalist, for better or worse I was also a detective, though an amateur one. And I really felt it was important that we know how he died and why.

Dory had been silent and a little embarrassed for Elaine. Now she said, "Elaine, I'm sure Ray will understand if you would rather not talk about it—especially now, so soon—"

"No, Dory, it's all right. I trust Ray to handle it discreetly." She took another sip of water. "It all started in 1968 just before the campaign. You never know where your husband is during a campaign and apparently Tom was spending quite a lot of time with Beverly. The Turners had moved over from Baltimore, where they used to live. Tom, you recall, as a longtime Humphrey man—even before Kennedy—had a prominent role in the campaign. The affair continued on into 1969, as Tom and I drifted further and further apart. I didn't really know much about Beverly until later, when one night he broke down and told me. He was ready for a divorce but Beverly would not hear of it. And I think she was losing interest, although he was still intensely involved. I finally went back to California."

"You said the affair eventually ended. You know when?"

"No. I really don't, and frankly, I didn't care. Beverly worked in the Nixon campaign, which was supposed to get her a job in the White House."

"Oh," I said, somewhat surprised. "Do you know who she worked for or what she did there?"

"I have no idea. But I'm almost certain she and Tom had broken up by the time she got involved in the '72 campaign. Tom, you probably know, took leave from his Senate job to work for McGovern."

I nodded. "Elaine," I said uncomfortably, "can you account for your time Wednesday night—the night Tom died?"

"Why?" she asked, obviously surprised at the question.

"Well, I hate to say this, but I'm afraid you're going to have to explain to Detective Jenkins of the Delaware police what you were doing that night."

"I know I have to talk to him. He called me last night and wants to see me this afternoon. He's even coming up to Washington for the interview."

"I just hope you have someone who can prove where you were that night," I said. "That insurance policy and you being a jilted wife means the police have no choice but to consider you a suspect. And it won't help when he sees you wearing that tan corduroy jacket and slacks. The bartender at the Admiral Hotel says Tom met a tall man wearing a tan corduroy jacket and a Greek fisherman's hat that night when he left the hotel."

"Well, I'm pretty tall, but I'm not a man," she replied.

"Under a streetlight and from a distance, it might be hard to tell the difference. I assume you don't wear a Greek fisherman's hat."

"No, I never have."

"Another thing," I said. "They are going to think it odd that you showed up in Washington after all these years just on the day he was killed. And you have the motive, not only the insurance but wanting a divorce, which maybe he wouldn't give you."

"But he would," said Elaine.

"But he hasn't said anything about it lately."

"No," she responded. Then she asked, "What about suicide? Isn't that what they think?"

"It's still a possibility. But the police have not ruled out murder."

Elaine shook her head and started to think.

"Surely," Dory said, "you must have been with someone from your company, someone who can testify that you were in Washington that night?"

Elaine was staring at her coffee cup and still thinking. "Gosh, this is terrible. That was the first night of an all-day seminar. I was exhausted. I just went right to my room, called Arnold, and collapsed. I ordered dinner and drinks in my room, so there would be a record of that. And the waiter would probably remember. Frankly, I had a little more wine than I usually do—a whole bottle, in fact. I started watching an early movie and fell asleep before I even finished dinner. I woke up in the middle of the night with the tray still in bed with me. It was a mess. But I didn't talk to anyone in the seminar from late that afternoon until the next morning."

"And you had no idea," I said, "where Tom was. You had tried to reach him on the telephone and never did?"

"That's right. How could I have known where he was?"

"That'll be in your favor," I said, "but I think the police will still want a corroboration."

"Nonsense," said Dory. "How could they expect her to come in exhausted from the seminar, find out where Tom was, rent a car, drive to Ocean City, find him on the shore, shoot him, drive back and then be able to go to her seminar the next morning? Impossible!"

"Unlikely," I said, "but not impossible. They are going to have to investigate you, Elaine, and satisfy themselves that you couldn't have done it."

"Oh, this is dreadful," said Elaine, looking at her watch and standing up. "I've got to run."

We both gave her a hug, and as she ran off to her seminar, I yelled after her, "We'll be in touch. And don't forget to wear something else when you see Jenkins."

CHAPTER FIVE

Saturday, May 5, 1973

Saturday morning, like every morning during those Watergate days, was devoted to reading *The Washington Post* and *The New York Times*. There was only one small story about Tom's death and it was buried in the Metro section of the *Post*. Apparently the press had not yet made a connection between Tom Cranston and Watergate.

The editors were still viewing it as either suicide or, if murder, for personal reasons.

The *Post* carried a front-page story by Woodward and Bernstein, which said that President Nixon's speech last Monday had failed to "shift either public or White House attention to other matters as the president had hoped," and quoted one White House source as saying; "There's a crisis mood continuing. We can't run away from it—the issue is still presidential credibility." Then the story went on to tabulate all the president's problems—John Dean and the Senate Committee investigation; the renewed grand jury investigation under the Justice Department and its new attorney general, Elliot Richardson, who faced mounting pressure to name a special prosecutor; the uncertain fate of Haldeman and Ehrlichman; a New York grand jury investigation of a $200,000 cash contribution to the Nixon campaign by financier Robert Vesco; and the investigation into the 1971 break-in to the office of Daniel Ellsberg's psychiatrist. Ellsberg, as you may recall, had leaked what came to be known as the "Pentagon Papers." There was another front page story on Egil Krogh, the Nixon White House aide who said he took full responsibility for the break-in, although sources maintained that Krogh was at too low a level to authorize such a potentially damaging act.

Inside the *Post* were stories on Howard Hunt and a file he kept on Daniel Ellsberg that Hunt had loaned to the Justice Department, and Nixon's appointment of General Alexander Haig to take over H. R. Haldeman's duties in the White House.

The *Times* lead Watergate story was on the Ellsberg break-in and a possible CIA connection. There was also a front page story on Lawrence Walsh, a New York lawyer rumored soon to be appointed special prosecutor in the Watergate affair. The News of the Week in Review section had a long roundup of the latest Watergate developments, and the *Times* magazine contained a profile on Haldeman.

The Turners lived in the Maryland suburb of Kenwood, just beyond the District line. The house was adequate for a small family, but the parking area looked like a high-tone used car lot. I could not identify them all, but I could not miss the big blue Cadillac. I felt a little shabby with my standard Ford station wagon. Next to the Cadillac was a mint-condition tan

Oldsmobile station wagon. A dark-haired woman in a tennis outfit came out to meet me, introducing herself immediately. "I'm Beverly Turner, and of course I remember you from Rehoboth."

We shook hands and I said I remembered her too. She was the towel-clad woman in the photograph. We walked onto the patio and toward a cluster of chairs where there were several people. There were also eight or ten children of all ages splashing about in what could have been a heated pool, running over to the chairs every now and then.

"I invited some other people over who also knew the Cranstons. I thought they might help you on your article," Mrs. Turner said. I tried to imagine Tom and Beverly together and wondered what the attraction might be. She was obviously a nice-looking woman, but nothing exceptional at first glance. But she had a way about her, a sense of confidence, of being in control, of knowing what she wanted and how to get it, which made it easy to see why a man would like her—if she wanted him to.

But if Tom were going to be attracted to anyone in this group, I would have thought it would be the first woman Beverly introduced me to. "Ray—that is what they call you, isn't it?"

"That'll do," I mumbled.

"Ray, this is Bernadette Harrigan. You may have met her at the beach at one of our parties. The Harrigans have a house on the shore at Easton, but they come over to visit us at Rehoboth. Tom knew them. Bernadette and I went to college together."

I shook hands with Bernadette and her hand lingered in mine just long enough that I could feel its sensuality. It was hard to let go. Now, here was a beautiful woman. She was wearing tight white tennis shorts and a loose-fitting T-shirt which, loose as it was, could not hide large, well-rounded breasts. She was tall and had auburn hair, which she wore pulled back on her head in a little bun.

"Bernadette and I were playing tennis this afternoon," Beverly said, "and she agreed to come over. She knew Tom fairly well and is deeply upset, as we all are, about his death. And naturally we all want to know what you have learned about what happened."

Interrupting herself, she continued the introductions. "Ray, this is my husband, Arthur, and this is Robert and Christine Eckersley. They have a house at Rehoboth, too, and knew the Cranstons. They stayed in Washington this afternoon especially to talk to you. I tried to get the Bradshaws and the Hollingworths too, but they're all at the beach."

Arthur Turner invited me over to the bar, offering me a wide selection.

Turner was of slightly less-than-average height, but very well built and muscular. He wore a brown track suit and moved quickly, suggesting that he was in excellent condition. Elaine had said he was a builder and he obviously spent a lot of time outdoors on construction sites.

Bernadette was anxious to know everything I knew about Tom and what might have happened. But I did not feel any compassion there. Underneath her incredible beauty was a hardness that began to make me a little uncomfortable. Beverly Turner was also anxious to know what I knew. Only the Eckersleys acted the way you would expect two people to act who had once known Tom Cranston as a beach neighbor. Despite all the professed willingness to cooperate, it was obvious that I would have to see the two Turners and Bernadette Harrigan (her husband was out of town) separately if I were going to learn anything. But I did manage to glean some basic information.

The Turners were both from the Baltimore area and had lived

in Towson, Maryland. In the late 1960s, about the time he had bought their Rehoboth town house, Arthur Turner also started construction of a large shopping mall halfway between Baltimore and Washington, which made it just as convenient to live in a suburb of Washington as a suburb of Baltimore. Jack Harrigan, Beverly said, persuaded Arthur to move over from Towson to Washington. They had become very good friends with their next-door neighbors at the beach, the Cranstons, although they did not see as much of them after the Cranstons had separated.

Dusk and the mosquitoes were arriving and I looked at my watch. It was almost six-thirty. I stood up prepared to leave, and as I said my good-byes, a curious thing occurred. Arthur Turner came out of the house saying to his wife that his Greek fisherman's cap was missing. He insisted that he had left it on the hall table the other night, but it was gone. Beverly said, no, it must be where he usually kept it—and she went quickly into the house. A moment later, she returned with the hat in her hand.

"Here it is," she said in a manner suggesting that she often corrected her husband in such things, "exactly where I thought—in the hall closet."

It was a little dark blue Greek fishing hat, like the one Eddie at the Admiral Hotel had said the man he saw on the street corner with Tom Cranston that night was wearing.

My first thought was that I ought to tell Jenkins about this. But then I decided the hat was probably a coincidence. Arthur was not nearly as tall as the man the bartender said Tom met. And Arthur was definitely not swishy.

As I walked toward my car, the gorgeous Bernadette appeared at my side. She had disappeared in the search for Arthur Turner's hat, but now she was carrying her tennis bag, apparently headed home.

"Just thought I'd walk you to your car, Mr. Hartley," she said, with just a suggestion of flirtation.

I was probably fifteen years her senior and she knew I was married and had children. But this was the fast lane, and there were, I knew, women who were attracted to older men, even preferred them. In fact, someone back on the patio had made a remark suggesting that Bernadette's husband himself was an older man, older than I, perhaps. I replied, "Well, that's very nice of you, although you'd better get in your car. You aren't wearing much and I know if I were a mosquito, I'd certainly want to bite you." I knew I could explain this seductive remark to Doreen. All in the line of duty, you know.

"Then I'd just have to squash you and rub you into my thigh, or wherever you chose to bite me, wouldn't I, Mr. Hartley?"

Did she really want to play? Or maybe Bernadette Harrigan was conducting her own investigation. As I got into my station wagon, I said, "Well, Mrs. Harrigan, thanks for walking me to my car. I understand your husband is out of town. Would you like to have lunch tomorrow? At the Angler's Inn? You know where that is? At the end of Falls Road, where it runs into MacArthur Boulevard."

"I would love that, Mr. Hartley. But why don't you come by my place in Georgetown for lunch? We could be much more comfortable there, and, of course, less chance of being over-heard. I know some of the things we're going to be talking about are confidential."

"That makes sense," I replied. "Where's your place?"

"It's in the book, on O Street. You won't have any trouble finding it. See you around twelve-thirty."

Bernadette Harrigan's suggestive invitation to a private lunch at her house produced a twinge of excitement some-where deep inside me. And as I pulled out of the driveway I noticed in the rearview mirror that she was opening the door of what I presumed to be her car—the big yellow Mercedes sedan.

Now, just what was she up to? And I wondered whether I should tell Doreen who I was having lunch with tomorrow. I couldn't help but think that Bernadette would make a good name for a hurricane.

CHAPTER SIX

Sunday, May 6, 1973

Sunday, as usual, began with the papers. It took most of the morning to get through both the *Post* and the *Times*. Dory and I usually read them together, exchanging sections, making comments and muttering expletives with each new revelation. But that Sunday the *Post* did not have a single front-page story devoted to Watergate, which was rare for those days. The war in Cambodia; the treatment of POWs; Mexico releases thirty political prisoners in exchange for the U.S. counsel general in Guadalajara (who had been taken hostage by rebels); and the day-old cease-fire in Lebanon seemed to be working. These were the top stories, which I had a hard time concentrating on.

When I finished the *Post,* Dory was still engrossed in the *Times*, so before I took my shower, I glanced through the *Post*'s Book World pausing to check the best-seller lists, a move calculated to put me in bad frame of mind. The top fiction sellers were *Once is Not Enough* by Jacqueline Susann, *The Odessa File* by John Forsyth, *Jonathan Livingston Seagull* by Richard Bach and *The Taking of Pelham One, Two, Three* by John Godey.

The non-fiction annoyed me even more: *Dr. Atkins Diet Revolution* by Dr. Atkins himself, *I'm O.K., You're O.K* by Thomas Harris, that perennial best-seller that must have sold more than the Bible by now, *The Joy Of Sex* by Alex Comfort, and near the bottom of the list, a real book, in fact a superb one: *The Best and the Brightest* by David Halberstam. Naturally, what annoyed me about all these books, except for Halberstam's, was that my biography of George Creel, good as any of these best-sellers, had never come close to any best-seller list and, no doubt, neither would the book about Tom's death that even then was beginning to take shape in my mind.

After finishing the papers, as I rose from the table, heading for the shower, Doreen said, "Shall we pack a lunch and take it down to the canal for a walk? It's a beautiful day."

We often took weekend walks on the C and O Canal and sometimes packed a lunch. But there was that date with Bernadette Harrigan and I had to keep it. "I forgot to tell you, I'm having lunch with one of the women I met at the Turners' yesterday. She seemed anxious to talk to me, I don't know why. But as I said, if I'm going to get anything out of these people, I have to talk to them separately and alone. So I'm starting today."

"Which one?"

"Bernadette Harrigan."

"Where?"

"Her house in Georgetown. She suggested it. I would have preferred Angler's but her place has its advantages. I want to use my tape recorder and that would attract a lot of attention in a restaurant."

"Is her husband going to be there?"

"Er, uh, no. I'm not sure. He was out of town yesterday. He may be back today, maybe not."

"What's she look like?"

"Oh, tall, well built. A tennisy, Georgetown type, you know. They're quite a bit younger than we are." I was trying to sound as disinterested as I could, but I wasn't very convincing. When I was getting ready to take my shower, Doreen appeared at the bathroom door with an old copy of a Washington society magazine—the kind full of beautiful people whose names are always in boldface type. Doreen was holding the magazine open to a full-page color photograph of two beautiful people— the John Harrigans—standing beside what looked like a poolside bar at what the caption said was their home in Easton, Maryland. Both were holding cocktails as naturally as if the glasses were part of their hands and, she was wearing a tight-fitting sweater and even tighter slacks. He was wearing white ducks, a tan corduroy jacket and a blue yachting cap, with tufts of white hair protruding from the sides. Harrigan was obviously elderly, but appeared to be in excellent physical condition. They were both tall, about the same height, and deeply tanned. "Is this the tennisy type you're having lunch with today and her young husband?" Doreen asked.

"I didn't say her husband was young," I countered, taking the magazine from her, hoping the story would tell me something about them. Jack Harrigan was a very prominent Republican elder statesman. He had come down from New York to work for the old Federal Power Commission (now the Federal Energy Regulatory Commission) before setting up a law practice. Most of his clients were involved in the oil and gas business.

Bernadette was his second wife, a former model and actress. And, as Doreen was quick to point out, it was strongly hinted that their marriage was one of convenience, that they both led their own lives, separated often weeks at a time, while he traveled to Texas, the Middle East, and Europe on affairs of oil.

"I know this mannequin is not Tom's type," Doreen said acidly. "He liked women with some substance. But you! I know how you'll react if she puts her hand on your knee today. I can see you getting hard now, just looking at her picture."

"That's right, I like beautiful, well-built women. That's why I married one. And if you want to make sure I'll be out of harm's way when I go to lunch today you know how to do it." She was still wearing her bathrobe, which I took hold of and tried to pull her into the shower with me. She resisted and escaped. Recalling that old joke about the British lord, I yelled as she was going down the hall, "Okay, Dory, lay out my baggy tweeds. I'll just have to smuggle this one into Georgetown."

When I was out of the shower and went into the bedroom, Doreen had a tweed suit laid out for me but she was also lying in bed without the bathrobe.

Bernadette's house was on O Street on the White House side of Wisconsin Avenue. It was one of those huge, old Georgetown mansions that had been completely renovated within the last five years and was something of a showplace. I was sure it had appeared in as many architectural magazines as the Harrigans appeared in society magazines.

Bernadette came to the door in a trim luncheon suit with a short skirt, not in the lounge pajamas I half expected—or maybe hoped for. But it was quickly apparent that this was not a seduction, and not just because of her choice of clothes. There was something cold in her manner, all business. She had no objection to my using a tape recorder, which I plugged into an outlet near the fireplace and set on a coffee table in front of a couch where I assumed she planned to sit. Looking at the tape recorder, she said: "Well, I can see this might drag on awhile, so would you excuse me for a moment while I go to the ladies' room."

As she left she pointed toward the bar and invited me to fix a drink, saying she would have a glass of white wine. Her cooler had a nice collection of imports, including a six-pack of Heinekens, one of which I opened. And while she was gone I indulged in my favorite form of intellectual snooping—I examined the books in their library. You can usually learn a lot about people from their books. And I don't mean just the titles. Anyone can buy nice shiny new editions through the book clubs or in the stores of books that have become modern classics. What I look for are old, original editions that might have been bought when the book first appeared or from a used-book store. Books that have been collected one at a time have become comfortable in their place on the shelf and look at least as though they have been savored.

The Harrigans' collection was in a little study off the living room. There were a lot of fancy leather-bound editions—not old, but book club volumes. And many Book-of-the-Month Club selections. There were also the usual current books about Washington and, of course, books on the oil industry and energy, including the little Club of Rome book. And he had one volume which I thoroughly approved of: *George Creel: A Biography,* by Raymond Hartley. Every author loves to see one of his books pop up in someone's library. Harrigan's *Creel* was included in an excellent collection of books about World War I. He also had another fine collection on World War II. During war the world does its best to burn up as much petroleum as it can in as short a time as possible, hence it is not surprising that Harrigan had a special interest in war.

But there was one curious section in their library I thought must be hers—several titles that I was sure were primarily about lesbians and lesbianism, including the classic *Well of Loneliness* by Radclyffe Hall. There was also *Portrait of a Marriage,* about the marriage of convenience between British diplomat-historian Harold Nicolson and his wife, the poet and novelist Vita Sackville-West, who was also in love with another woman.

When Bernadette returned, I was still standing in the library. I pulled *Creel* off the shelf and, trying to be cute, remarked that I admired her husband's taste in biography. "Oh, how nice," she said, "I apologize for not knowing Jack had your book. I don't read much in his library. I read mostly novels."

As I readied my tape recorder, I recalled Norman Mailer's remark when he went off to Plains in 1976 to interview presidential candidate Jimmy Carter for a *New York Times Magazine* article: "By God, Mailer would even bring along a tape recorder. This, for him, would be a long fall from grace."

But not for me. By 1973, along with most of Washington's press corps, I was using a tape recorder. It had become indispensable for getting it right and having it on record. Who knows what our history would read like if they had had tape recorders from the beginning. Studs Terkel said, "What if there was a tape recorder that day at Calvary when Christ was crucified?"

The interview was a strange one. She seemed eager to talk and yet as I tried to draw her out about Tom Cranston she was not responsive. She wanted to know what I knew as much as I wanted to know what she did.

So I decided on a more direct approach: "As you may have guessed, I'm not only writing a piece about Tom, I'm trying to find out if I can what happened to him. And frankly, I've offered to give Detective Jenkins, who's handling the case for the Delaware State Police, all the help I can. Could I ask you where you were last Wednesday night—the night of Tom's death?"

She seemed a little startled at the question, suggesting as it did that she might be considered a suspect. But she replied quickly enough: "I was right here in this house with my children, Beverly's children, and our housekeeper."

"Why Mrs. Turner's children?"

"We often take care of each other's children when we go out of town. Or sometimes when they just want to play together."

"Was Mrs. Turner out of town that night?"

"No. She had just had a bad day and wanted to take a sleeping pill and go to bed."

"Look," I said, "I know from my inquiries so far that Tom Cranston and Beverly Turner had an affair at one time. Could she have been going to Rehoboth that night to see Tom? What do you know about the affair and do you know if her husband knew about it?"

Bernadette paused for a moment and sipped her wine. I was still wondering why she wanted to meet me here if not to talk. Maybe she did intend to seduce me. "Beverly and Arthur have been estranged for some time. So Beverly and I, going way back to our student days at Goucher College, have become rather close. I knew all about Tom, and for a while, she was really in love with him. But then she got bored with the whole thing. Washington affairs generally tend to break up when the man is out of power, don't they? But I know something happened to him. He seemed to lose his confidence. Maybe it was built on achievement and power, rather than a personal sense of worth. I don't know. But he definitely began to change. He became ugly sometimes, seemed to be obsessed with her. And he wanted her to leave Arthur, but she wouldn't do it because of the children."

"And the money, the comfortable life?" I suggested.

"That too, I guess. It's unlikely that Tom could ever have supported Beverly and her kids the way she preferred, unless Arthur took the kids. At least that's the way Beverly figured it. And she didn't want to be separated from them, even part of the time."

"Did Arthur know about the affair?"

"Yes," Bernadette said quickly.

"How?"

"I'm not sure why she decided to tell Arthur," Bernadette said, and I was sure she was lying.

"How did Turner take the news that his wife was having an affair with Tom?"

"He was furious."

"How do you know?"

"Well, I went over to their house the night Beverly told him. She called me. Arthur had stalked out of the house and, in fact, didn't come back that night." Bernadette paused and looked at the ceiling. "It was just the other night, Thursday."

"The night Tom Cranston was killed?"

"That's right," she said, "it was."

"Was that his tan Oldsmobile station wagon I saw in the Turner driveway yesterday?"

"Yes. In fact he must have been driving it that night, because I remember the Cadillac was still in the driveway. They only have two cars."

"What was he wearing?"

"I don't know. I wasn't there when he left."

"Maybe Beverly will know," I said. "Does she know where Arthur went?"

"She knows where he said he went. He told Beverly he spent the night with an old girlfriend over in Baltimore. Said they went to the Orioles game and he stayed all night with her. Maybe you should check that out."

"I'm sure the police will do that. Is Beverly seeing anyone else now?"

"I doubt it, She had a brief fling with an American University professor. But that was it—except, of course, for Dick Herson in the White House."

"How's that?"

"Well, I'm not sure I should talk about that. Maybe you should ask Beverly."

I took the photograph out of my briefcase and showed it to her. "Do you recognize this man? Would it by any chance be Herson?"

Bernadette was visibly surprised, After looking at the photograph a minute, she said, "It looks like him without his glasses. Where did you get it?"

"From some papers Elaine asked me to bring to Washington for her. They were in Tom's beach house. It looks like blackmail, of course."

"It would appear so."

"But who was he blackmailing and what did he want? How did Beverly get mixed up with Herson, anyway?"

"She worked for him in the '72 campaign. He promised her a job in the White House if they beat McGovern. But after the election, when Herson went to the White House, he reneged on his promise. He said her job had to wait, that they were involved in a huge reorganization of the government and she had to be patient until the dust settled."

I knew all about that. Right after the 1972 election, Nixon surprised everyone in town by asking for the resignation of all his Schedule C political appointees. Then he slowly rebuilt the government, rehiring only those men and women whom he knew to be completely loyal during the first term. And there were many dissidents, especially after the Watergate break-in, which most everyone in politics knew must have had White House connections.

"So how did Beverly take that?" I asked.

"She was furious, at least at first. I'm not sure how she feels now. I don't know anyone who wants to work in the White House today. Tom knew about her working in the campaign, of course, and he was mad. But there wasn't much he could do about it."

We were abruptly interrupted by the telephone, which was sitting on a little table beside the couch. She picked it up, listened for a moment, then said, "Well, guess who's sitting here in my living room and we're about to have lunch?" There was a pause. "Raymond Hartley, a good friend of Tom Cranston's. He's doing a story on Tom for *Washington* magazine."

Another, longer pause, then she said, "I know. He showed it to me," and putting her hand over the mouthpiece she said to me, "Jack says to tell you that he has your book on George Creel and he admired it very much."

I nodded appreciation and stood up to find the bathroom, giving her a few moments to talk in private. When I returned she was hanging up the telephone. "Jack's just leaving the Commodore in New York. He's taking the shuttle and wants me to pick him up at National at four."

I looked at my watch as we both decided we had better get on with the conversation. She said, "Where were we?"

"We were talking about Beverly and the committee."

"Oh, yes. Well, Beverly never was a Nixon loyalist. In fact, I'm not sure exactly what she is politically. I think she got involved with Republicans simply out of of boredom. All their friends are Republicans. She probably felt more com-

fortable with them. In 1972, Nixon was our man. We were
stuck with him."

"I assume you and your husband support Nixon?"

"Of course. It's no secret that my husband is a Republican. I
don't pay much attention to politics myself."

"Did your husband raise money for either of his campaigns?"

"Some. I don't know how much. I know we gave one fund-
raiser in 1972."

"Who came? Mostly oil people?"

"Not all. I can't remember. In fact, the only person I really
remember was Arthur Turner."

"Beverly's husband?"

"That's right. He's really apolitical, but Jack talked him into
giving quite a bit of money. He convinced Arthur it was 'good
business.' But I guess someone else, who impressed him like
Jack did, could have persuaded him to give money to the
Democratic party."

"Did you know that Tom might have been working on
something to do with an oil conspiracy—or maybe Watergate—when he was killed?"

"Or shot himself," Bernadette said. She seemed genuinely
surprised at my question, but I could not be sure. She was a
perfectly controlled woman. There was something cold and
forbidding about her, despite her physical attractions. I had to
find out more about Jack Harrigan and his connections to big
oil and the Nixon White House.

"Do you think their political differences contributed to Beverly's and Tom's break-up?" I asked.

"No, I'm sure it didn't. That happened before Beverly ever
heard of Herson, or had shown any political stripes one way or
another. It was strictly personal. A passionate affair that ran its
course."

Then she looked at the clock and said, "Maid's day off. But I've fixed some chicken salad. Shall we see how it is? I never know how anything I do in the kitchen is going to come out."

We went into an informal, well-lighted little room just off the kitchen. It had a small glass-topped table and two very expensive decorator chairs, modeled on the old ice cream parlor seats. I plugged in my tape recorder again and pulled out a chair.

We mostly talked about the Turners and the Harrigans and how Tom's affair came about.

The story began in 1967, as Bernadette described the disillusion and boredom that gradually overtook Beverly's marriage and her life in Towson, Maryland.

Beverly and Arthur were born and grew up in the Baltimore area. Arthur went to the University of Maryland and she attended Goucher College.

Her roommate and best friend was Bernadette Conroy, who married a young actor she met in New York when she was pursuing her modeling and acting career. That quickly proved a mistake and they were divorced. She abandoned her modeling career after subsequently marrying an older man, a Wall Street corporate lawyer named John Harrigan. He had two children by an earlier marriage and the Harrigans had one boy soon after they were married. They moved to Washington in 1969 where Harrigan worked briefly in the upper echelons of the Federal Power Commission before he took the revolving door out into private law practice, working primarily for the industry he had been regulating, an old Washington story.

Arthur Turner, Bernadette continued, was the son of a Maryland builder. He went to work in his father's small construction business after he graduated from college in 1955 and then took over the business in 1960 after his father died suddenly of a heart attack. They were married right out of college and when they matured they were different people, especially

Arthur. He developed into the Eastern Shore prototype of the male chauvinist pig. There had been some physical attraction and compatibility in their courtship and early marriage, but according to Bernadette, Beverly was not an ardent participant in the lovemaking and did it because she thought that's what you have to do if you are married. This encouraged Turner to drift into the after-work, let's-have-a-couple-of-drinks-with-the-boys crowd, where all the talk was about the Baltimore Colts, the Orioles and women, especially the ones who hung around the bars with them. The result was a casual affair between Arthur and a woman in his office, producing a confrontation from which Beverly never really recovered. Arthur thought a third child would help, but the idea repulsed Beverly. Neither of them wanted to go through a divorce.

Beverly tried to immerse herself in the problems of child-rearing, but that was not enough. She also tried volunteering for one thing and another, including the gubernatorial campaign of Spiro Agnew in 1966, although she was not serious about Republican politics.

There was one bright spot in her suburban prison: summer at the beach. Every year they rented a cottage at Rehoboth Beach, Delaware, and down there she felt better. She had more freedom, often spending a week or more at the beach without Arthur. And they met interesting people from all over the East—Wilmington, Philadelphia, Washington, even New York. But Beverly found the Washington people the most interesting and exciting. They were always on top of things, so vitally interested in what was going on in the world, in contrast to her circle of friends back in Towson who talked mostly about sports, their businesses, and taxes. One day driving home from the beach at the end of their vacation, Arthur said: "God-damn it, Beverly, it's about time we bought a place at Rehoboth. It's too good a tax deal to pass up, and you and the kids always have so much fun down there. What do you think?" She agreed.

The Turners' new three-bedroom town house at Rehoboth was one of a row of eight on a strip of ocean about a mile north of the Henlopen Hotel and maybe two miles south of Cape Henlopen. It was modern in design, with a beautiful view of the ocean.

There were many interesting people in the complex. One couple they knew casually from Baltimore. There was also a family from Wilmington and one couple from New York. Very attractive, but you never saw much of them; they were primarily in it for the investment. Most of the couples were from Washington and one in particular—Tom and Elaine Cranston—seemed very compatible.

The Cranstons were from California. Tom had been a political reporter with *The Los Angeles Tribune,* and among other things had covered Richard Nixon from his first campaign against a congressman named Gerald Voorhis. Beverly had never met anyone who hated Richard Nixon as much as Tom Cranston did.

Elaine Cranston was aware that women were attracted to her husband and that he responded to them. One of her antidotes for this situation was alcohol. It was not apparent at first, or to casual acquaintances, but Beverly got to know the Cranstons better and the situation became more and more obvious.

Beverly was also scared. She had read enough to know that extramarital affairs inevitably led to trouble, and sometimes tragedy. She decided to talk it over with Bernadette, who had just moved to the capital from New York.

Bernadette said she sensed immediately what had happened: her friend from college, who married a hick from the Eastern Shore and was dying from boredom and neglect in a Baltimore suburb, had finally met a really interesting, exciting man and fallen head over heels in love. Bernadette said she tried to warn Beverly of the hazards of an affair in Washington. The men are usually wedded to their work and when there is a conflict between the job and the love affair, the job usually comes first. Then she told Beverly about an affair she had had with a senator, which ended in heartbreak and bitterness, and her decision to stay away from men. All in all, said Bernadette, her counsel was negative.

She did not tell Beverly the senator's name.

After lunch, however, Beverly wandered around town staring into store windows but seeing nothing, her mind preoccupied with Tom. Then she went to a phone booth and called the White House.

Beverly fell in love not only with Tom but with Washington, and when Bernadette launched a campaign to persuade the Turners to move to Washington—or at least a Maryland suburb—Beverly was ready. Arthur was now well into his huge building development between Baltimore and Washington, which was actually a little closer to Washington. And Tom convinced Arthur that the new three-stage raises government employees had begun to receive would eventually make Washington the most attractive housing market in the country.

"Mark my word," said Tom, "in four or five years, all those bureaucrats are going to have big incomes—bigger than anyplace in the country including Westchester County. They'll all be wanting bigger houses and be able to afford them." Arthur suddenly became interested in Washington.

Then came the second Tuesday in November 1968, and Tom's world was shattered. Hubert Humphrey was defeated. Not only was Tom out of a job but the one man he hated most in the world was elected—Richard Nixon!

Beverly was delighted because she thought now she would have Tom all to herself. And to make her even happier, Arthur agreed to move to a Maryland suburb of Washington, and with Bernadette's help, Beverly started to look for a house.

The affair progressed beautifully in 1969. At first, Tom tried to keep it casual, more in the Washington tradition, and not become too involved. Tom's big dilemma was that he did not know what to do after being suddenly thrown out of his political job—a not-uncommon problem in Washington. However, it was compounded by his being in the throes of an increasingly passionate love affair—also not uncommon in politics. Then Tom had his job offer in Los Angeles, but it meant leaving town. And by now he did not want to leave Beverly.

This was a major crisis. Elaine Cranston wanted very much to return to California. She had come to hate Washington.

Beverly said Tom could not leave her after she had moved to Washington to be with him. So he stayed in Washington, to write his book and then take a Senate job he had also been offered.

Then in the spring of 1971, the love affair began to run its course. Tom's lack of interest in his wife had led to an increase in Elaine's drinking to the point where it got out of hand. And in 1970 she returned to California without a divorce or a legal separation, telling Tom he could stay in Washington.

Elaine's health was seriously deteriorating and there had been one strange little incident where she had to be rushed to the hospital one night. Tom, somewhat cruelly, I thought, felt she was headed for an institution anyway, so he did not see much sense in uprooting his life to return to California.

By 1971 Beverly was finding the affair untenable. And Tom's personal and economic situation was deteriorating. His book, *The Democrats Look at the Future,* came out and was a financial flop. His Senate position, at least then, was not very interesting. Ultimately jealousy, professional reverses, and a boring job began to take their toll. Tom simply was no longer as exciting and attractive as he was when Beverly first met him. It was a familiar Washington pattern; the disintegration of a man dedicated to politics and public affairs but no longer in an exciting or demanding job because of a defeat at the polls.

Inevitably there came the day when Beverly woke up to reality—and she decided she had had enough.

It was a long story Bernadette told me, and not over yet. After lunch we went back into the living room for coffee and brandy, which I declined, though she had a small glass.

"Nice library," I said as I sat down on the couch. "You have an interesting collection about lesbianism. No significance, I hope."

She seemed, for a moment, startled by my rather direct question.

But she recovered quickly. "None whatsoever. I'm a happily married woman, and as you could see yesterday at the Turners, our friends are normal, with kids and typical marriages. But I must admit the subject—homosexuality—intrigues me, especially living here in Washington, where we know couples who are that way but maintain a front of complete normality."

Then as she sat on a chair directly in front of me, her short skirt permitting me just a glimpse of the inside of her thighs, she added, "And I am not especially shocked by it."

"Do you think Tom Cranston was gay? The bartender at the hotel where he was staying in Ocean City thought he might be—especially after Tom went off with a man that night after acting like he had a hot date."

"As I said, you never know, which is one of the reasons the subject intrigues me so." Then she crossed her legs slowly, my eyes going in the direction they were invited to go.

She paused for a moment and fixed me with an odd stare. Suddenly, she began unbuttoning her jacket, which pulled open, revealing that she was not wearing a bra or a slip. Then, after a moment and noting my eyes were riveted on her bare skin, she said, "Tom's reaction to me was much like yours."

"I'm convinced," I said. "But there is such a thing as bisexuality."

"That's true, Mr. Hartley. And I tried that, too, in college. I think we all did. But this is what I prefer. And assuming you are still a happily married man—as you were when we first met at the beach—I will button up."

"But I assume you are not?" I replied.

"Not what?"

"A happily married woman."

"But I am. Jack and I have the most mature and intelligent relationship imaginable—giving us both complete freedom."

She slowly buttoned her jacket. Then she leaned back in her chair and crossed her legs in a very ladylike manner, and laughed.

It was obvious the interview, lunch, and flirtation were over. She had finished most of her brandy, so I stood up slowly, saying, "I don't know how much of it I should use in the magazine article, but all this might help me find out what happened to Tom out there on the beach that night. Maybe it *was* suicide. Tom sure seems to have been self-destructive."

"I hope you find out," Bernadette said as she cleared the table. "Suicide wouldn't surprise me.

"Did you ever hear of Tom being involved in any aspect of the Watergate investigation? He's always been something of a Nixon authority—and hater—you know."

"True," said Bernadette. "But I never heard anything. I guess from that photo that somehow Tom was involved with Dick Herson. Maybe he can tell you."

When I reached home, there was a note from Doreen on the hall table: "Certainly a long lunch. I hope it was satisfying. I have gone for walk on the canal."

I spent the next hour or so phoning friends, trying to find out as much as I could about E. Richard Herson, and whether anyone I knew might have known if Tom Cranston was involved in the Watergate investigation. No one could shed any light on that, but I did learn that Herson was a hard-line right-winger dedicated to keeping liberals out of the government. He had once worked for the CIA and was now making his way up in the Republican party, having enhanced his position by marrying Carlotta Bessie, the heiress to a midwestern industrial fortune and a big contributor to the Republican party. E. Richard Herson was expected to eventually play a big role in Nixon's second term.

Then I had an idea about Arthur Turner. I called Ed Murchison, who used to write pieces for *Washington* magazine. Ed was now doing editorials for *The Baltimore Sun* and was a big Orioles fan. We had gone out to many games. I knew there was a better than even chance that he had been out to the ball game the night Tom was killed. A dull Wednesday, a beautiful May evening, perfect for a few beers with the guys after you had closed the page and then gone out to the stadium. When I reached him on the phone, Ed confirmed that that was just the way it happened.

"Look, Ed, I can't take time to explain it now, but I'm trying to check the story of a guy that says he was at the ball game last Wednesday night. You remember? Wilbur Wood beat Palmer with a six-hit shutout?"

"Yeah, I remember. Dull game. The O's look lousy."

"You tellin' me," I said. "They're dead. Only Rettenmund and Baylor look like they're playing ball. But what I want to know is, did anything unusual happen? Anything complicated? Something my man couldn't learn about from reading the *Sun* the next morning?"

"No, Raymer, there really wasn't. About as dull a game as

you can imagine, unless you like good pitching, which I do, of course. But no big hits, except maybe Pat Kelly's first inning triple, which later produced the Sox first run—enough to win it."

"Okay," I said, with another idea. "Let's think of something that didn't happen! You know that big blonde—what's her name, the one with the huge breasts who every now and then in some city pops out of the stadium, runs on the field and kisses the nearest player? You know who I mean?"

"Yeah. I've read about her. But I don't remember her name. And I've never seen her, except on TV."

"That's right. She usually makes the highlights. I assume she didn't show up that night—or she'd have been on the TV I saw the next night."

"That's right. I can swear she didn't show up that night. I only left my seat once, and that was while the Sox were at bat around the fifth or sixth. She only comes on between innings, never while the game's going on."

"Great, Ed. That's all I need." I hung up and settled down to transcribing the tape of my conversation with Bernadette Harrigan. I was still on my first scotch but very relaxed when Dory came home and entered my study just as she heard Bernadette saying on the tape: "Maid's day off. But I've fixed some chicken salad. Shall we see how it is? I never know how anything I do in the kitchen is going to come out."

"How convenient," Dory said. "The maid's day off. Did her husband join you for lunch?"

"He's in New York. Or was. Should be back by now."

"Surprise. The perfect day for her to have you to lunch. Didn't you ask her if her husband was going to be home?"

"Are you kidding? They are a very sophisticated couple. He travels a lot and I'm sure she lunches there alone with men all the time. This is the 1970s—ten years after the 1960s. And yes, she is sexually liberated. In fact you aren't going to believe what she did at one point."

"Took your arm and dragged you screaming and kicking into the bedroom."

"Even better. She flirted outrageously, exposing her breasts."

"You resisted, of course."

"Of course." I cupped my hands and gently and slowly pushed her away. You would have been proud of me."

"What a fantasy."

"You see, you were pretty smart to make sure I didn't wear my baggy tweed pants."

"So it was your inability that prevented your responding. Aren't you the faithful one. What prompted her to stage this little show, anyway?"

"Well, I asked her if there was any significance to the fact that she had a pretty good collection of books on lesbianism in her library. She said absolutely not, but that the subject did interest her. And I asked her if Tom was gay.

"But then she suddenly said, in effect, 'Better yet, I'll show you what my reaction is to being alone with an attractive man.' And whammo! She did. I think she was just teasing."

Dory paused for a moment or two, looking truly perplexed. Then she said, "What a fantasy. Maybe someday you'll tell me what really happened."

"You wouldn't believe me if I told you," I said as she left the room.

CHAPTER SEVEN

I was up early Monday morning and read the *Post* in the exercise room. There was no story on Cranston. President Nixon was swimming, sailing and walking on the beach at Key Biscayne where his friend, Bebe Rebozo, had a house. However, Martha Mitchell, wife of the Attorney General John Mitchell, made the front page with one of her nocturnal phone calls to UPI reporter Helen Thomas. In this one, she told Ms. Thomas that President Nixon should resign because of Watergate—he should "say good-bye" in order to restore credibility to the Republican Party and the country. And with Jim Palmer pitching a shutout, the Orioles were beginning to look like their old selves with a 5–0 victory over the California Angels.

When I finished working out, Dory was still in bed, so I joined her, hoping she might be in the mood. She definitely was not. And as she started getting out of bed, I said, "Dory, you know we're missing the sexual revolution that's going on in this country."

"We're not missing anything because it's not happening in our generation. It's Karen and Junior who are involved—their generation, in case you haven't noticed. Besides, we just did it yesterday morning and I doubt if you're ready yet."

"Try me."

She ignored that and went into the bathroom, so I yelled, "In case *you* haven't noticed, it's our generation—specifically the women of our generation."

"You wish," she yelled through the bathroom door.

"You should read that book, *The Sensual Woman*. The author says that's what we men want and she's talking about our generation. And she says it's about time that American women learn about oral sex."

"You mean talking about it?" Dory replied.

"No I don't mean talking about it, I mean doing it. There's a new book out that says a husband's unsated sexual appetites are a threat to hearth and home."

"And our whole neighborhood," Dory shouted.

"The author says that the woman who just submits is a hausfrau, but a mistress seduces. That's what you ought to be doing."

"Does she have any specific suggestions?" Dory said, coming out of the bathroom and heading for the kitchen. She was just wearing her robe.

"Boy, does she."

That got her attention and she stopped a moment at the bedroom door.

"Such as?"

"Well, she says you could greet your man at the door when he comes home at night, wearing something sexy, like a cheerleader's outfit, with high heels or maybe an apron and nothing more."

"That's some book you've been reading. How 'bout just wrapping herself in Saran Wrap?" Dory said.

"You got the idea. And an outstretched hand holding a scotch on the rocks. The author got downright ecstatic describing how she put her children to bed early one night, met her husband at the door in something exotic."

Dory just stared at me with that incredulous look she has.

Later, I started working the phone. My lawyer friend told me he heard that John Dean and his wife were still planning to use the cottage at Bethany Beach as a retreat for writing his Watergate testimony. I thought this was significant. By now Tom Cranston's death had been widely reported in the media, although there had only been one hint on a local TV station that it might be connected with the Watergate investigation. However, if there was a connection, Dean would most likely know something about it, and by now would probably have found someplace else to write his story. There is nothing a reporter would like better than to discover John Dean hiding out in a cottage just a few miles north of the spot where they had found the body of Thomas Cranston, whose death was now thought to have something to do with the Watergate investigation. The fact that Dean was still going to Bethany suggested to me that he, at least, did not think Cranston's death had Watergate overtones.

I also called Detective Jenkins. I was anxious to let him feel I was cooperating, and I had a tip for him. "You're investigating the whereabouts last Wednesday night of all the people who were involved with Cranston, right?"

"You bet."

"All right, here's one for you. John and Bernadette Harrigan are good friends of the Turners and knew Cranston. Although they're on opposite sides of the fence politically, Mrs. Harrigan, I'm pretty sure, was in her Washington home that night. They also own a home in Easton. But her husband was in New York staying at the Commodore Hotel. Maybe you ought to check that out."

"Why?" asked Jenkins. "Where's the connection?"

"I don't know yet. But she's even more beautiful than Mrs. Turner, and who knows, Cranston might have been involved with her."

"All right. I'll check him out."

"Good. Anything new down there?"

"I talked to Cranston's wife. I'd have to say she had the motive, and it does seem suspicious that all of a sudden she shows up in Washington just before her husband's death,"

"Yeah, but she had a plausible explanation," I replied, "and I don't think she had the opportunity."

"She has no alibi for that night. She could have gone to the shore."

"So check out the rental car agencies."

"I'll do that," Jenkins said, "And here's something else. The post office still can't trace that package. They think it's already been delivered or lost. You got any idea who that package might have been sent to?"

"It wasn't me, obviously," I said.

I hung up on Jenkins, but could not help thinking about the tape that had apparently been burned in the hotel. Was that the one he was going to send me for Bob Woodward? Maybe Tom decided to send the one he mentioned to me to Woodward directly. Shouldn't I call Woodward and ask him?

But I decided against that. Maybe Tom had given the tape to one of the two men he met that night. Or maybe, after he felt a threat to his life had been removed, as Eddie and Jessica suggested, there was no need to send a tape to anyone. Or maybe after the threat he decided it was safe to bring whatever information he had back to Washington himself. I decided there was no use wasting any more time in speculation until I had more information.

I made an appointment with Senator Trowbridge for 11:00 A.M. and then called Herson. Although the White House was stonewalling almost everything now, I had a hunch that when I told Herson's secretary that I was calling about Tom Cranston, he would be on the phone in a hurry.

"Dick Herson here. What can I do for you, Mr. Hartley?"

I told him that I was writing a profile of Tom Cranston for *Washington* magazine and that I was aware he'd had some contact with him recently. I knew I had his attention.

"Yes, I've had some business with Cranston. Why don't we have lunch and talk about it. Today?"

"That would be fine," I said. "How 'bout one o'clock? I have an appointment on the Hill this morning."

"Good," Herson said, sounding maybe a little too cheerful. "Okay, I'll meet you at the corner of Nineteenth and G."

Then I called the Turner house. The maid said nobody was home but the kids. Mr. Turner was at work and Mrs. Turner had gone to Rehoboth Beach. Mrs. Turner left the children with her because they were still in school. I made a note that this would be an excellent time to talk to the maid and decided to go straight out to Kenwood after my meeting with Herson.

And just as I was leaving for my interviews on the Hill, Sam Meyers called. "How's it coming, Marlowe? You hot on the case?"

"I'm just going to interview Senator Trowbridge—Tom's boss."

"Good. You onto anything I haven't read about or seen on TV?"

"Plenty. But I'm not ready to talk about it. I don't have a direct lead to Watergate yet, but there is a helluva complex personal story developing. I'll call you in the next couple of days."

"Okay. I know you're hoping to get a Peter Potomac column or two out of this, but I don't want you breaking any story you dig up for me in your *Eagle* column. Agreed?"

"Agreed. Don't worry, I get plenty of column ideas about Watergate just reading the newspapers and watching TV."

"So tell me Raymer, why do you continue doing that column under a pseudonym? You don't have a job now that would keep you from using your own name."

"Well, I might get another one someday. But it's more than that now. This may sound crazy, but frankly Peter Potomac is a better writer than I am."

There was a moment of silence before Sam spoke. "What the hell are you talking about?"

"I don't blame you for wondering. Let me try to explain— and I'm speaking now as Peter Potomac, not his alter ego, Ray Hartley."

"You'll always be Ray Hartley to me," Sam replied, sounding like he thought I was a little nuts.

"Here's the thing. My alter ego, Hartley, is very much locked into the establishment. When he writes under his own name—like in an article for your magazine—he has all kinds of hang-ups. He's afraid to say what he really thinks in the way he wants to say it because he's worried about how people who know him will react. It's only when he sits at his typewriter pretending he is someone else that he can achieve the spontaneity and looseness that produces his best writing."

"Bullshit," Sam said.

"It has to do with E. M. Forster's comments about the two personalities of the human mind, one on the surface, one deep down. The Upper personality has a name, says Forster—like

Raymond Hartley. It is conscious and alert, does things like dining out and answering letters. But the Lower personality is a very strange person and cannot be labeled with a name. It has something in common with all other deep personalities. And unless a writer can tap that deeper source, he cannot produce good writing. Hartley is aware of this and it makes him mad— and jealous."

"You gotta be kidding!"

"No, Sam. Ray would rather have been Peter. But it's the old story. He knew he couldn't make a living just writing whatever he wanted in the manner he wanted. So he gradually developed this split personality, which gave him the best of both worlds."

"Christ, I'm beginning to think you *are* a split personality."

"Dory's convinced of it."

"Okay, Pete, tell Ray to call me when he gets a chance. And one more thing: how 'bout you writing the Cranston article for me? Now that you mention it, based on the few columns Ray has shown me, I think you *are* a better writer than he is."

"Thanks. I'll tell him." And I hung up.

Senator Porter Trowbridge had that perennially tanned and well-tailored look of the wealthy. He was also one of the new TV-age politicians—trim, handsome, graying around the temples, and very articulate. As he escorted me into his paneled office I noted that there was a young lady waiting there. "I've asked Alice Burton to join us," the senator said. "I have to leave for a committee meeting in twenty minutes, and Alice knew Tom better than anyone on the staff—professionally and socially. She'll probably be more help to you than I am."

"Do either of you mind if I use a tape recorder?" I asked, opening my briefcase.

"Not at all," said the senator, indicating that he was speaking for both of them. "Everybody uses them these days." Then seating himself behind a huge desk and in front of flag-draped windows, he said, "What can we do for you, Mr. Hartley? Have the police turned up anything on the Cranston case?"

"Not anything we haven't seen on TV or in the papers," I replied. "And what they're still trying to determine, as I am, is whether Tom's death could have had anything to do with his work or whether it was a personal matter. I'm hoping you can shed some light on that."

"Well, of course I'm not as free to discuss Tom's work with you as I was with the FBI agents—and I have been talking with them over the weekend. But, in a general way, I can tell you what Tom was working on. I suppose you know about the mandatory oil import quotas and the threatened shortage of gas and oil?"

I nodded. "I have discussed them from time to time with Tom, and I know a little about them."

"Tom was convinced there was a direct correlation," the senator continued, "between the oil import quotas and Nixon's huge campaign war chests in both 1968 and 1972. He also was convinced that the oil shortages we are expecting are contrived. In 1970 Nixon overrode a recommendation by the commission he had appointed to study them that the oil import quotas be scrapped. And in the spring last year Canada virtually begged us to take more Canadian oil, but the Nixon administration declined." The senator paused and I looked at Ms. Burton. She was stone-faced.

"We were all waiting for the president's energy speech last month," the senator went on, "but it was a big disappointment. Then at the same time we had this curious article in *Foreign Affairs* by a man, I forget his name, who had worked in the White House—hence the article had some weight to it. It was titled 'The Energy Crisis: This Time the Wolf Is Here.' The article said, in effect, that there were only two things we could do about it: one, give in to the OPEC nations, or two, go to war. Tom was convinced this was intended to encourage the OPEC nations to raise the price of oil. And naturally, all the big oil companies will benefit from this raise that we're all convinced is coming."

"So what was Tom doing—or trying to do about all this?"

"First, he was trying to convince the key people of this select committee and the various subcommittees that his interpretation of events was correct. Second, he was trying to prove the link between campaign contributions—and maybe even some money that went to pay for the Watergate cover-up—and the oil shortages."

"Was Tom working for the Ervin committee? I know they won't begin public hearings until May seventeenth, but they are gathering information now and interviewing sources."

"I don't think so," the senator replied. "In fact, I would almost say for certain that he was not. I'm sure he would have told me—or Alice." Ms. Burton nodded.

"Senator," I said, "is there any reason for you to believe that Tom's death was in some way related to his investigation of the oil money–White House connection? I mean, people do get killed in such cases, don't they? In fact, from talking to people down on the shore, for a while at least Tom appeared to be hiding out in that hotel and felt someone was after him. Do you have any ideas about this?"

The senator spun his chair around and stared out of his window for a moment. Framed by the flags, he looked every inch the public statesman, the servant of the people—and also I suspected the servant of the oil industry. Most senators of both parties on the energy committees and subcommittees have accepted campaign money from the oil companies.

Turning around at last, the senator said, "I've thought about that quite a bit over the weekend, and frankly, I don't know. My first instinct is to say 'Absurd—these things don't happen outside of the Washington spy novels.' But then we can't be positive. There've been stories, as you know, that the crash of the plane carrying Mrs. Howard Hunt—who had ten thousand dollars in one hundred dollar bills on her when her body was found—was not accidental. There are billions of dollars at stake in the oil business, and the most powerful office in the free world seems to have been bought off. People have been killed for far less." Then, after another pause, "So I just don't know. I'd naturally prefer to think it was something personal— or a suicide. Tom had been acting very depressed. But then Alice can tell you more about that." And looking at the clock on his desk, he said, "I have to run over to the hearing room now. But we can talk again—anytime. Just give my secretary a call and she'll set up an appointment."

I thanked the senator for his time and said he might be hearing from me. When he was gone, I turned to Alice Burton. She was a trim, obviously intelligent woman of around thirty-five. She wore a pinstripe suit befitting her role as legal counsel for the committee. Although she did not try to display it on the job, it was apparent that she had a nice figure. I guessed Tom had dated her.

"Yes," she said, "I knew Tom well. We've been out to dinner. I've been to his place, he's been to mine. In fact, I was half expecting a call from him from the shore that night or the next day. He had told me if he could settle some business he was working on that he'd be free and he wanted me to join him at his place in Rehoboth for the weekend."

"And you never heard from him?"

"No."

"I knew about Tom's place at Rehoboth," I said, "and it puzzles me why he was staying at the Admiral in Ocean City when he had a house only thirty miles north of there. You have any ideas about that?"

"No," she replied. "I figured it must have had something to do with the business he mentioned to me when he left."

"And you had no idea what that was?"

"No, although I've been speculating about it. I have a hunch it had something to do with the White House."

"Why's that?" I asked quickly.

"Well, just recently he mentioned talking to someone in the White House, someone I'd never heard of, so I don't think he had a very significant job. His name is E. Richard Herson. I've since looked him up and he's a second-level legal counsel who works on special assignments."

"Have you told the FBI this?"

"Yes," she said, and I felt somewhat relieved. At least I could not be accused of withholding evidence if I knew the FBI knew about it.

"Did he tell you what his involvement with Herson was?"

"No, he didn't. But if I had to guess, it was something to do with Watergate. Before he left he hinted that he was onto something big. In fact, I thought he was being a little overdramatic."

"Why not big oil? Wouldn't that be more likely in Tom's case?"

"Yes. But I am sure Herson's not involved in oil. I know all the energy people in the White House. Herson's not directly involved in the Watergate business, either. I've done some checking on that. In fact, as near as I can make out he's working on some sort of reorganization of the government."

"Well, that doesn't sound like the sort of thing people kill for."

"True," she replied. "That's why I think it must be Watergate. Tom could have stumbled onto something. He knows most of the people on the Ervin committee staff, although I agree with the senator, I don't think he's doing anything official for them."

"What about Tom's personal life and the suicide theory?"

She thought a minute, then said, "Tom was very depressed for a long time. And I know it concerned another woman. We've worked together very closely, often late into the evening. Tom had made a few casual passes, but I stood him off—before he separated from Elaine. If there's one rule I follow religiously in my career, it's not to get involved with married colleagues."

"But when Elaine left Tom, that made a difference, right?"

"Right. But it didn't change things significantly. He told me early on that he was involved with another woman, and because he never dated anyone openly, I assumed it was a married woman. He admitted that, and for a while, as far as we were concerned, it was almost as if he was married. Then things began to change. And not long ago he told me he had broken up with his married lover, although he still seemed involved in some way. It was about then that his drinking seemed to become a serious problem, although he always drank a lot. But it was under control. As the senator said, he was increasingly depressed, sometimes even morose."

"Then you think the suicide is a possibility?"

"Yes," she replied. "But there could also be a love triangle of some sort. I do know that whatever he was involved in lately was pretty messy. He said as much a couple of times."

"Did you two become lovers?"

"Not as much as I had hoped. But I do think if he had resolved whatever he was involved in that we were moving in that direction."

"Do you think Tom was queer?"

"Oh, God," she exclaimed, "not a chance. Why do you ask?"

"A bartender in Ocean City says that the man Tom went off with seemed swishy."

"Well," she said emphatically, "I doubt Tom was involved in anything like that."

Of course, I thought. The bartender had told me that Tom said he had a hot date and acted like it. It could have been a woman dressed as a man and wearing a cap to hide her hair.

I asked her a few more questions about Tom's personal life, but she didn't have much more to tell me. I had a long walk back to my car and did not want to be late for Herson, so I packed up my tape recorder and she walked me to the door. I gave her my telephone number and she promised to call me if she remembered anything that might be significant. She said she had no objection to me talking about her affair with Tom in the piece I was working on; she had told the FBI. She had nothing to hide, she said, and I believed her.

Which was more than I could say for the senator, although that may have been unfair. The problem with politicians is that for any issue or subject on which they expect to be asked questions, they work up a safe or noncommittal answer, with little regard for facts or the truth. By the time they get to be senator, giving a reporter their "prepared statement," which usually ignores the facts, is a routine thing.

As I walked to my car, I recalled several conversations I had had with Tom about the politics of oil and his concern that Nixon supported the big oil companies' desire to maintain the mandatory oil import quotas, with the result that the American oil companies were able to maintain a twelve-dollar price for a barrel of American oil while continuing to exhaust American oil reserves. I remember him quoting one geologist as saying,

"A child born in the 1930s, if he lives to a normal life expect-
ancy, will see the United States consume most of its oil during
its lifetime."

Tom saw it happening and it depressed him. Maybe it even
got him killed.

CHAPTER EIGHT

Monday afternoon, May 7, 1973

I arrived at the corner of Nineteenth and G at 12:13, pulled over to the curb just north of G Street, and waited. Suddenly, there was a rap on the window and a man opened the door. He was wearing dark glasses, a trench coat with the collar turned up, and a crumpled, tweedy hat with the short brim turned down in front and back. He looked like the Spy Who Came Out of Robert Hall's. It was E. Richard Herson and he said we were having lunch at a restaurant in Southwest.

The restaurant, called The Place Where Louis Dwells, was, indeed, the darkest public room I have ever been in. It was down near the Arena Stage and the Environmental Protection Agency, and has long since gone out of business. But in 1973, it would have been a perfect place for a married White House aide to have lunch with another man's wife.

Herson was about average height, heavy, and had blond crew-cut hair. His face was roundish and he had a forced, toothy smile. Without his glasses, he looked like an aging prep school athlete. I could not be sure that he was the man in the photograph, although I was sure I had seen his picture in the paper.

When the waitress arrived, I held the menu close to the little red candle on the table, ran down the beers and picked a Heineken. Herson had a margarita. Then we got down to business, with Herson taking the initiative. "Now, Mr. Hartley, just what kind of business do you think I had with Thomas Cranston?"

"Well, it's not exactly government business. But I understand both you and Tom Cranston had a very good mutual friend—Beverly Turner."

Herson quickly took off his thick glasses and started cleaning them with his handkerchief—not that he could see anything with them in this light anyway.

When he put them on I knew he had his prepared response. "Yes, I know Beverly Turner. She worked for me during the campaign. And I believe I do remember her mentioning knowing Tom Cranston, although I had forgotten it. When I heard about his death the other day, I remembered. But I still can't remember in what context she mentioned his name. I think they were friends or neighbors at the beach—something like that. Have you talked to her about it?"

"Yes, but your name didn't come up. Of course, we were in a group on her patio and the conversation didn't get very personal."

"Then how'd you figure I had any connection with Cranston?"

It was obvious Herson was going to stonewall it, so I decided there was no use wasting any more time. Taking out the photograph, I said, "Mr. Herson, the reason I thought you might have more than a passing acquaintance with Tom Cranston is this, which I found in his beach house. Perhaps you could explain what it's all about?"

I had to admit that Herson looked different without his powerful glasses, and I thought, *If he stonewalls it now, what will I do?* He stared at the photograph a few moments, turning it over a couple of times to see if there was anything on the back. Finally he said, "So? An interesting photo, but I can't imagine what you think I know about it."

"One person, who I'm sure you know, says it looked, and I quote, 'like Dick Herson without his glasses.' I'd have to say I agree with her."

"Was it Beverly Turner who said that?"

"No. I can't tell you."

"Well, she doesn't know me all that well. I don't see the resemblance. And, as you say, this man's not wearing glasses."

"Most men take their glasses off when they make love," I said. "I use reading glasses myself, but I've never worn them to bed, except to read. But I'm sure Beverly Turner will identify the man. She's the woman, of course. And if she refuses to cooperate maybe Mrs. Herson will help police identify the man. She would know."

At the mention of his wife, a slight note of hysteria was injected into Herson's already high-pitched voice. "You haven't shown the police this, have you, Hartley?"

"No, I have not. But that someone, who thought it was you, says you were having an affair with Beverly Turner, and furthermore, that Tom Cranston was using this photograph to blackmail you and Beverly Turner."

I paused for a moment, giving Herson as much time as he wanted to absorb what I had just said. He was in deep trouble and he knew it. And when he finally answered, it was obvious he knew that I knew it. "All right, I admit that's me—and Beverly. Who else has seen the photo—except Beverly and the person who said it was me?"

"Just me and Elaine Cranston. She did not recognize you. And if I can find out what happened to Tom without going public, I won't. But it's my ace in the hole. Tom was my friend. If I can't find out what happened to him, I assure you I'll tell the police all I know."

"Well, if you can guarantee you'll keep it confidential, I'll tell you what I know—if you give me that photograph to make sure my wife never sees it."

"I'm holding it for now. We'll see."

I asked Herson if he knew both the Harrigans. He said yes, and I said, "Bernadette Harrigan is a beautiful, fascinating woman, but I can't quite figure out their marriage."

"Carlotta, my wife, says there're rumors around that she's a lesbian and they're not sure about Jack either. He's a very successful lawyer and, like Turner, a big contributor to the party, but he may be a homo. Some people think their marriage is just a front; you couldn't go public with homosexuality and get around in Washington socially. But all that's just talk, I don't really know."

"I've found a lot of things to suggest that whatever happened to Tom might have had something to do with his work—on the energy subcommittee or maybe even Watergate. The people I talked to on the Hill don't think he was working officially on Watergate, but that he might have stumbled onto something. And one of them thinks what he stumbled on most likely came from you. What do you say?"

The hysteria was gone from his voice. He was now cool and contained, which meant that Herson had composed his prepared statement on Tom Cranston. "Here's what happened,

Hartley. It's a weird story and you may not believe it. But these are weird times."

We were interrupted by the waitress and we both ordered Greek salad. Then Herson started talking. I casually put my tape recorder on the table, hoping he would not notice it in the darkened room. But he did, and protested. So I reminded him that I had the photograph and that I was setting the ground rules. He started talking, interrupting himself only to let the waitress set us up with our salads—and another Heineken.

He had had an affair with Beverly Turner during the campaign and it continued for a while after the election. One day Cranston followed Herson to the hotel where he was meeting Mrs. Turner. He surprised them by bursting into the room after they had ordered lunch. They thought he was the waiter. He was brandishing a gun and acting very convincingly like the jealous ex-boyfriend. He forced them to sit on the bed, together, then brought out a camera, took some pictures, and left. They were stunned and did not know what Cranston was up to.

A few days later Cranston contacted Herson and threatened to show the photo to both Beverly's husband and Herson's wife, unless Herson told him everything he knew about the Watergate break-in. Herson told him he did not know that much about Watergate and said Cranston was bluffing, and that if he did what he threatened it would only make him look like a fool.

Cranston persisted. He also threatened to send a tape of what he already knew to a reporter on *The Washington Post*. Herson said he had foolishly told Beverly as much as he knew about the White House problems before he realized that Beverly could not be trusted with confidential information, especially about Watergate. She had decided she did not like Nixon and did not really care what happened to him. And Beverly had told Tom enough to incriminate Herson if Tom linked Herson's name to it. This concerned Herson, he said, because he had managed to keep out of the Watergate affair—that he had been busy executing Nixon's plan to take over the government.

Cranston later continued his threats, and to convince Herson that he was not bluffing, he sent an incriminating little note to Arthur Turner, implying that Beverly was having, or had had, an affair with someone in the White House. Arthur suspected that the man she was having an affair with was Herson because he knew Beverly had worked for him during the campaign.

Arthur had seen Cranston at the beach sometime earlier, when he was on a stag fishing weekend. He mentioned to Cranston that Beverly was working with Herson during the campaign and that Herson suggested this might lead to a job in the White House. Cranston, who was drinking a lot that weekend, made some insinuating remarks, suggesting Herson and Beverly were sleeping together.

Arthur was furious and threatened to have Jack Harrigan complain to the White House about Herson playing around with his wife. So Beverly had decided to tell Arthur about the *old* affair with Cranston, figuring it would be easier to handle a dead affair than an ongoing one with Herson. In fact, she told Arthur this the day Cranston was killed. Beverly told Herson that Arthur did not come home that night and was not heard from until the next day. That might bear investigating, Herson said.

By this time, according to Herson, Beverly was screaming at him to comply with Cranston's blackmail demands.

A few days before his death Cranston had called Herson at the White House and said that if he had not heard anything by Friday, May 4, he was going to the Ervin committee with what he had and to Herson's wife and Arthur Turner with the photographs. "He also demanded that I produce a list of people who had contributed to the Watergate cover-up fund—the money used by the White House to finance the defense and living expenses of the men who had broken into the DNC."

Herson said he could not get that list, but Cranston said that was not true, that Herson knew his way around the White House well enough to find the list. It was either provide the list or the photograph went to Herson's wife. Herson said he was afraid Cranston would carry out his threat, so, at great risk, he had gone through the files of the man who probably had the list, and found it.

Cranston called later and said he was in Ocean City, waiting for Herson to comply. Herson agreed to meet him there, tell him everything he knew, and give him the list—if Cranston would give him the photograph and the tape he said Cranston had made telling what he knew about Watergate.

He met Cranston in the bar at the Admiral Hotel in Ocean City. Then they went up to his room, where he told Cranston, in detail, everything he knew about Watergate, stressing the fact that he was not really involved at all. Then Cranston burned the photograph, all the negatives, and the tape. Herson said that Cranston walked him to his car, and they said good-bye. Cranston mentioned that he planned to see Senator Ervin the next day.

Herson had been so intense in his monologue that he hadn't finished his salad, but he seemed to have come to the end, so I decided it was a good time to speak. "Tell me this, both the bartender and a girl who met Cranston in the hotel said Tom was obviously greatly relieved about something after he talked to you, that he implied someone was stalking him, maybe even trying to kill him. How do you explain that?"

Herson thought for a few minutes while gulping down the rest of his salad and shaking his head. Then he said, "I can't help you on that one. He obviously would have been happy about getting the information I gave him. That might have made him seem relieved. But I can't imagine who'd be trying to kill him. In fact, the police have not eliminated suicide."

"You're telling me that after all Tom had been through with you and Beverly over this blackmailing business, that when he finally had the information he wanted and was going to the Ervin committee the next day, that he'd shoot himself the night before? Come on."

"It must have had something to do with his love life—a personal thing."

"Or maybe somebody in the White House decided to get rid of him."

"Jeeesus, Hartley, you can't believe that! We've made some mistakes, but shit! Not murder!"

"What about Mrs. Hunt?"

"What about her?"

"A lot of people think that plane crash was no accident."

"Yeah, and a lot of people still think some pro-Johnson group killed President Kennedy. Those rumors always go around after someone gets killed. Look, if we were going to kill anyone don't you think it would be John Dean, not someone like Tom Cranston?"

"Well, I don't know. Depends on how much Tom knew. I have a print of the photograph which I found, so why don't you tell me what you told Tom?"

"Hey! You said you were going to give it back to me if I told you what I knew about Cranston."

"Wrong! I told you I would *not* show it to your wife, and I won't."

"Look, Hartley," Herson said, becoming agitated again. "I made a deal with Tom Cranston. He promised to burn all the photographs and the negatives if I told him what I did. And when I told him, he burned them and the tape about me. He apparently kept one print of the photograph hidden away, which he didn't tell me about. But I lived up to my deal, and you ought to honor his!"

Herson paused a minute, and then continued. "Anyway, John Dean is the loose cannon now, and I doubt if there's much on that tape I told Cranston that won't come out soon."

It was getting late and I wanted to drive out to Kenwood and talk to the Turner maid. I assumed Doreen and I would be driving to Rehoboth that night to interview the Turners. So I said, "Okay, I'll honor Cranston's deal to the extent that I won't show it to anyone, especially your wife. But if I have to, I'll use this photo and anything else I can find to break this case. I didn't tell you, but Tom said he was mailing me a tape to go to *The Washington Post* if anything happened to him. Something did happen to him, but the tape has not arrived. You say he burned yours. But another tape might still arrive. So we'll see. *Meantime,* I keep the photograph!"

Herson frowned, but there was nothing he could say.

I reached for the check, and while I was paying it I asked Herson if he thought Bernadette and Beverly were having an affair.

"I don't know. But I do know she was never interested in me; just playing me for a job in the administration. It was a good thing—for a while."

I drove Herson back to the White House, then found a parking place on Pennsylvania Avenue and went into a drugstore to call Beverly Turner at Rehoboth. I told her that I was coming down to the beach that night and would like to talk to her first thing Tuesday morning and her husband, too, if he were going to be there. I said we had a lot to discuss, that I had talked with Bernadette and E. Richard Herson, and that I knew

Tom was blackmailing her and Herson with a photograph. I assumed she had already talked with Bernadette and knew I had the photographs.

She was obviously upset. She had talked to Detective Jenkins yesterday and he seemed to think she and Arthur were the main suspects because Elaine Cranston had told Jenkins about Beverly's affair with Tom Cranston and because Arlene Bradshaw had told him about seeing a light on for a while, early in the evening at the Turner town house. She said Arthur was coming down that night and they were both being interviewed by Jenkins tomorrow. She was sure Arthur would talk to me, too.

I asked her if she had told Jenkins about Cranston blackmailing her and Herson, and that Herson was the man Cranston talked to in the bar.

She said no.

Good, I thought, I'm not sure why. But I was already thinking about a use for the photo if it didn't go public.

As soon as I hung up on that call I dialed home and asked Doreen if the mail had come and if there was any package for me.

"No," she said.

"By the way, you can start packing for the beach. I'll be home in about an hour or so and then we're going to Rehoboth tonight. I have to talk to Beverly Turner tomorrow morning."

"Does she look as good in her bikini as Mrs. Harrigan does in hers?"

"How would I know?"

"I thought you saw her at her poolside Saturday."

"She was wearing a tennis outfit."

"Couldn't you tell from that? I could."

"I guess she's not my type. I'm going out to interview the maid now, and she's not bad either. We'll probably take a swim while we talk. Want to join us?"

Ignoring that one, Doreen said, "I'll be ready for the beach when you get home—and I hope you're going to tell me what's going on. We've hardly had a moment to talk since you took this assignment."

"You're right, but I'll tell you all about it on the way to Rehoboth. And don't forget, pack your bikini. The water's still chilly, but I'll keep you warm."

Driving out to Kenwood, I drifted into a mental dialogue, trying to unravel the mystery of the missing tape, when suddenly the Turner driveway loomed on my right. Neither Turner car was in the driveway but off to one side was a vintage Pinto, which I presumed belonged to the maid.

The Turner maid was a middle-aged black woman. She was a substantial person, one whom you would feel comfortable leaving your children with when you went out of town. She was reluctant to talk at first, but something about her suggested she would be amenable to persuasion, which I tried in the form of a fifty-dollar bill. When I showed it in my hand and promised complete confidentiality, she began to loosen up: The Turner children were going to visit friends after school and would not be home until dinnertime. Mr. Turner had already said he would be late, so it was agreed that if we talked fast, I could be out of their driveway before anyone would know I'd been there.

On the morning Tom's body was found, as near as the maid could remember, Mrs. Turner had a long call from her husband. "I didn't know what in the world they were talking about, but this much I do know: Mr. Turner was mad! And I could just tell from the way Mrs. Turner was talking, she was so upset she hardly knew what to do.

"After she hung up she went out and was gone most of the day. She came home around five-thirty. The children were here, but Mr. Turner didn't come home. I don't know where he was."

"What was the car situation?" I asked. "I mean, which one was driving which car? Do you remember?"

"Oh, yeah. Mr. Turner usually takes the station wagon and he had it that day. Mrs. Turner was driving the blue car."

She said Mrs. Turner told her she could go home around six o'clock that evening and she did. The next morning when she arrived there was a note for her on the hall table telling her that the children were spending the night with the Harrigans, as they had often done, and that the Harrigans would take them to school. Mr. Turner was not home when she arrived, which was around 7:00 A.M. "And I guessed he had not been home that night because he would have left me the breakfast dishes if he had eaten and gone to work or somewhere early."

There was also a note from Mrs. Turner for Mr. Turner on the hall table, but either he had not seen it or had not been home that night because the maid said he would not have left it on the table if he had seen it.

I asked her if she knew how Mr. Turner might have been dressed that night—was he wearing his Greek fisherman's cap? She said he was not wearing the hat. It was sitting on the hall table next to the note. She did not notice whether it was still there the next morning.

I had gleaned about everything I could, and I did not waste any time getting away. And driving back into town, I recalled Arlene Bradshaw's remark that the night before they found Tom's body, a large sedan, probably a Cadillac, had arrived at the Turner house for a while, then it left and did not come back again that night, and the house lights did not go on again. This was very curious. Beverly Turner had not spent the night at her beach house the night her ex-lover, who was blackmailing her, was killed. Where did she spend it?

Another thought hit me: if the package Tom mailed was not sent to me but to someone else—and if it contained the tape outlining all the information Herson had given Tom about Watergate—then the most logical person Tom would be sending it to would be someone on the Ervin committee. I could check that out.

I was also increasingly worried about all the evidence I was accumulating—and withholding from Detective Jenkins. If I didn't wrap this thing up soon or go to the police with everything I knew, maybe, like a lot of people around town, I would be heading for what we hoped would be a minimum security prison.

When I arrived home, Doreen was ready to go and I threw a few things in a valise. We had plenty of gas and I rushed, hoping to beat the rush-hour traffic around the Beltway. But first I made a phone call to Alice Burton. "I wonder if you could help me on one point?"

"Sure," she replied.

"You remember we were speculating about whether Tom was doing anything for the Ervin committee? Well, it could help if you follow up on that a little. Could you ask around among the people on the committee if Tom was doing anything for them? And this is important: try to find out if they received any kind of package from Tom. It probably would have come in the mail this morning. I really need to know about that package."

"What do you think's in it?"

"It is probably a tape cassette with information relating to Watergate. But don't say you know anything like that. Just try to find out if anyone received a package from Tom, and if so, what was in it, although they probably won't talk about it if it was a tape."

"Okay, Ray, I'll see what I can find out. Are you going to call me, or should I call you?"

"No, I'll be moving around a lot. I'll call you in the next couple of days."

My plan was to be at Fisherman's Inn across the Bay Bridge in plenty of time for cocktails and an early dinner. It was agreed that on this trip Doreen would just have one martini and I could have a few scotches; this time she would drive us on to the beach. Sometimes it was the other way around.

However, I drove to Fisherman's Inn, and as soon as we were around the Beltway and onto Route 50, heading for the bridge, I began telling Doreen everything I had learned so far. I was still talking when we were seated at Fisherman's and the drinks arrived.

"So what's your guess, based on what you know now?" she said.

"Well, Dory, one thing I'm certain of: Tom was killed! I don't know why or by whom—yet. But I can't imagine someone getting himself in a lot of trouble blackmailing people for information about Watergate, getting that information, then suddenly driving to a secluded place on the beach in someone else's car and shooting himself. I'm sure he could hardly wait to get to the Ervin committee with that information. But the fact is, he *did* meet someone at the hotel, probably a woman— and there were several women he knew who might have been at the shore that night. And don't forget, Tom was acting at the hotel like a man who thought he was being stalked by a killer. And he *was* involved in a dangerous game of blackmail."

I paused a moment while we both thought about that, then said, "But I think we're at the heart of it with the tape business. Tom said he might or might not send me a tape to be delivered to Bob Woodward at *The Washington Post* if something happened to him. Something *did* happen to him but the tape has not arrived, although it should have been here today if it was mailed Thursday evening from Ocean City. The girl at the desk of the Commodore said Tom bought stamps from her for a small package, which she saw him mail.

"The tape Herson said Tom burned must have been the one he was going to send to me, which suggests that his deal with Herson took the pressure off, justifying Tom in destroying the tape intended for the *Post*. One would assume that at that point, Tom had decided his life was no longer in danger—which meant Herson must have had something to do with the threat to Tom's life."

"Maybe that explains it," said Doreen.

"What?"

"Maybe Tom sent the tape to the Ervin committee in that package because he still didn't trust Herson. If Herson had been threatening Tom in some way and had promised to call off the threat if Tom burned the photographs and *The Washington Post* tape, maybe he told Tom that evening that the threat was off—but Tom didn't believe him! After all, Tom still had copies of the photograph hidden at his beach house and now he had an even better tape, containing more information. Maybe he thought Herson might double-cross him or maybe even try to kill him—or have him killed—to silence him. So Tom decided the smart thing would be to send a tape containing new information to the Ervin committee that night in case something happened to him."

I had to admit that would be the smart thing to do—if Tom still felt his life was in danger. But then both Eddie and Jessica at the bar were really convinced that Tom seemed to believe the worst was over. He had been reluctant to go out of his hotel at night all the time he was down there, but after he talked to Herson, he did not hesitate to walk out with Herson and then was seen standing under a streetlight, where he would have been an excellent target, talking with the tall man—or woman—wearing the Greek fisherman's hat.

Who was stalking Tom, as he put it? Was it Herson—or could Herson have hired someone?

"You don't really think that someone working in the White House would actually go out and hire a killer, do you?" Doreen simply could not believe that.

"Depends on what the stakes are," I replied. "Don't forget Mrs. Hunt. It's still possible that plane crash she was in was no accident. Remember, last month *The New York Times* said McCord had told the grand jury that Dorothy Hunt was the conduit for cash payments made to the Watergate burglars. Maybe she was getting ready to squeal to somehow protect her husband.

"And remember that with Herson, worries about Watergate were really secondary to his panic at the thought of his wife seeing that blackmail photograph. After all, Herson did tell Tom all he knew about Watergate in return for the photograph. If Carlotta Herson had seen that photograph, Herson's career would be over. He's just a jerk who really couldn't cut it in Washington without his wife's money opening the doors. I'm not sure he had the guts to kill anyone, and with his eyes he'd have a hard time shooting straight."

I had one more scotch. We ate Maryland crab cakes and continued the drive to the beach. We had turned onto Route 404, heading for Denton, and I was just dozing off when Dory said, "Of course, you should've gone to Beverly Turner immediately. You know Tom told you that if anything happened to him, she knew all about it. You probably should have told the police, too. And I'll bet she's just as attractive as Bernadette Harrigan."

"What makes you say that, dear?"

"If she was involved with Tom in any way, I know she must be attractive. Tom liked attractive women."

"Sounds like he must have made a pass at you. Did he?"

"No. Not even after he was separated from Elaine. He considered you a friend—and friends don't do that sort of thing. But . . ."

"But he might have if he wasn't a good friend."

"Yes, I think I can definitely say . . ."

And as she talked about the likelihood of Tom hitting on her, I faked a good snore and pretended that I was falling asleep.

CHAPTER NINE

Tuesday morning, May 8

As at home, mornings at the beach started with a thorough reading of the *Post* (from the little grocery store down at the corner) for Watergate revelations. This morning Attorney General Elliot Richardson, the Massachusetts public servant who had held more jobs than George Bush, would appoint a special Watergate prosecutor, and from Key Biscayne, the White House press office issued a statement denying any involvement by President Nixon in "the Watergate bugging case." *The Post* quoted: "'Any suggestion that the President was aware of the Watergate operation is untrue,' said Deputy Press Secretary Gerald L. Warren. 'Any suggestion that the President participated in any coverup activities is untrue. Any suggestion that the President ever authorized the offering of clemency to anyone in this case is also false.'"

And the *Post* announced that it had won a Pulitzer Prize for its reporting on Watergate. Much of the credit, of course, went to Bob Woodward and Carl Bernstein, who had been covering the break-in from the day it occurred—June 17, 1972. The two reporters were both in their late twenties. David Broder at the *Post* won the prize for commentary. But what really pleased me was the winner of the prize for editorial writing—Roger Linscott, Peter Potomac's op. ed. page editor at the *Berskhire Eagle.* I made a note to call Roger and congratulate him. Eudora Welty's novel *The Optimist's Wife* took the prize for literature. And W. A. Swanberg's *Luce and his Empire* took the prize for biography.

I was at the Turner house at 9:00 A.M. as agreed. It was only about two miles north of us in Dewey Beach. I was going to jog there, and was wearing a track suit. But then I decided I wanted this on tape and I also needed to take notes. Then there was the photo. Too damned much gear for jogging. I had told her that I would like to interview them separately, and she had agreed. Arthur Turner was driving down from Bethesda that morning and would be arriving around noon.

It was a beautiful morning made even more beautiful when Beverly Turner appeared at her door in a light-colored bathrobe that hung loosely open in the front. I was disappointed to see that she was wearing a bathing suit. But as soon as she closed the door, she took off her robe and threw it on a chair in the hall and said provocatively, "How 'bout joining me in my morning dip? I was just getting ready to go in." Then picking up a pair of bathing trunks that were sitting on the hall table and holding them to my stomach in such a way that her two hands touched the sides of my waist, she said: "I think these will fit."

"Oh, no, thanks," I said. "I just had breakfast. And the

water's still a little cold in May for my taste. You go ahead. I'll be setting up my tape recorder."

And I immediately felt like an old nerd for declining an opportunity that might have led to the beach scene in the movie version of *From Here to Eternity*.

"You'll be sorry," she said, patting my rear as she walked by me toward the door to a deck with stairs that went down to the beach. "This water will really start you stirring inside."

I was already stirred up enough, and she knew it. She could have been in and out of the ocean and fully dressed by the time I arrived this morning, so this little bathing suit fashion show was staged strictly for my benefit. Or maybe she was simply teasing a fifty-year-old writer, graying slightly around the temples.

Mrs. Turner went quickly into the water, swam out about ten feet, then caught a small wave back into shore. And she came into the house giving the impression of someone shivering with the cold. As she went by me heading for a door just off the living room, she started taking off the top of her bikini, revealing completely her well-formed left breast. "I've got to get on some dry clothes," she said as she disappeared into the room. "I'll be out in a minute—unless, of course, you want to give me a massage," she added as she slammed the door.

The last comment was made to sound like a joke, but I think she really meant it.

When she came into the living room she was wearing a brown track suit.

"That looks familiar," I said.

"I know. Arthur has one just like it, a husband-and-wife set that the kids, with a little help from Arthur, gave us one Christmas." Then, seeming a little embarrassed, she continued, "I am a little more relaxed now."

"Good." But she really wasn't.

"Let's sit over here," she said, "away from the window," which looked out on the beach. "There's not so much light." Beverly was still not only reluctant to be interviewed but even to be seen being interviewed.

"Well, I don't know how much of all this you can use in your article," she said nervously.

"Beverly," I replied, "you are in a great deal of trouble. The truth about Tom's death will come out sooner or later. I think you have much more to worry about than just being involved in a love triangle and blackmail. You are involved in a murder which might even be related to a historic national scandal. And I think you must know that you and your husband are suspects."

"Well, I know I didn't kill him," she said quickly. "What about the photograph? Have you shown it to the police?"

"Not yet. But I may have to. I assume you have talked to Herson."

"Yes. He called me. He's in sort of a panic. He thought all the photographs had been burned and he's terrified that you might show them to his wife. I think he's more concerned about that than your showing them to the police. I've never seen a man so afraid of his wife."

"That's easy. Carlotta Herson and her fortune are the key to his exciting and glamorous career in Republican politics. He's not the type to run for office, but with his wife's money and four years in the White House he could look forward to one good job after another like George Bush or Elliot Richardson. And then, after years of politics, he could sit back and enjoy those golden years of being the gray eminence, like a Jack Harrigan today."

"Not if I have anything to say about it," she said.

"What do you mean?"

"Dick Herson was terrified about what I might tell you."

"Why?"

Beverly seemed unsure how to respond. Finally I broke the silence. "Look, my main interest is in finding out what happened to Tom Cranston. I'm not interested in exposing a love affair between a White House aide and Tom's former lover. But if we can find out what happened quickly, we may be able to prevent the photograph and your affair with Herson—or Tom—from ever surfacing."

Beverly sighed and looked resigned to telling me what she knew.

I continued, "Let's start with the night Tom was killed. I guess you know Bernadette told me she kept your children."

"Yes, Bernadette told me and I'll explain all that. I guess she told you how I first met Tom at the beach and how the affair began—against her advice."

I nodded and Beverly went on, talking continually for the next hour. Trying to break off with Tom, she said, was extremely difficult. She began to drop hints that maybe they should stop seeing each other, but he was outraged. He said they had made a commitment to each other. He said he had ruined his career by not accepting the job with *The Los Angeles Tribune* and that the affair had ruined his marriage. And he told Beverly something else she had not known—that when Tom's wife, Elaine, had been mysteriously hospitalized, it was for an attempted suicide brought on by Tom's admitting to Elaine that he was having an affair with Beverly and that he did not intend to give her up.

This disturbed Beverly. In fact, it made the whole affair even more distasteful, and she knew it was over. She finally said, "Let's just think about it for a while. We both need a break from each other."

By now, Beverly and Arthur were virtually estranged and she knew if she was going to have male friends she must either ask for a divorce or spend the rest of her life in adulterous affairs. The idea did not appeal to her, but neither did she want to give up her husband and security. Like so many modern American women, affluent and well preserved, she wanted both worlds—a nice home, a secure family life, *and* romance.

He said he had been following her, off and on, for some time. He had quit his Senate job and was planning on going to work for the McGovern campaign, so he had plenty of time on his hands. Tom said that Beverly had gone too far. He knew the affair was over but that from now on, she would stay home and be a good little wife and not hurt anybody. This was his way, he said, of repaying Arthur for having cuckolded him. Tom was now going to guarantee Beverly's fidelity! He would tell Arthur everything if she did not behave!

Beverly was now developing an interest in politics, and Bernadette said that the best way to get into politics would be to work in the presidential election of 1972 for the reelection of Richard Nixon. Bernadette introduced her to a friend of her husband, Herson, who was just beginning to work for the Committee to Reelect the President. Soon Beverly was working for CREEP and involved in a casual affair with her boss, Herson. But she knew she had to be very careful not to make Tom suspicious. When she began as a volunteer in the campaign he was so furious at her for going to work for Richard Nixon that he did not even consider the possibility that she might become involved with another man.

Tom was working for the McGovern campaign and traveling most of the time, which gave him less time to annoy Beverly. After the election and Nixon's victory, Beverly continued to work at the committee and carry on her affair with Herson, although she was increasingly uncomfortable because Tom was back in town. He was out of a job and calling her a lot with annoying remarks about Nixon and "that bunch of crooks" she was involved with. She gathered from what she had heard and the way he acted that he was also drinking a lot. Arthur had run into him at Rehoboth on an all-male fishing weekend and he had a long talk with Tom. He had been drinking and seemed in terrible humor.

She did not know what to do. She did not want to break off her affair with Herson because he had talked seriously about finding her a job in the White House. And she could not tell him to be careful and make certain no one was following him because she did not want to let him know that she had had an earlier affair and was involved with a jealous ex-lover.

Then one day, she and Richard were meeting in a room at the Mayflower Hotel on Connecticut Avenue only a few blocks from the White House. They had ordered lunch, as they usually did. When the waiter arrived with the lunch, she went into the bathroom, while Richard paid the bill.

Suddenly she heard Herson yell, there was a loud crash and the bathroom door was abruptly flung open. It was Tom Cranston and he was holding a gun and motioning her to sit on the bed, where Herson was sitting in his underwear. When she sat down beside him, Tom suddenly put the gun in his pocket, produced a camera, took some pictures, and left, making a few obscene remarks about her abilities in bed.

Beverly was forced to tell Herson that she had once had an affair with Tom. It had been over for some time, but he was obviously still jealous. Two days later Tom called her. He was now very brusque and businesslike rather than emotional and sulky as he had been in the past. Beverly wanted to know just what he was doing, making a fool of himself and ruining her life. Furthermore, how did he know about Herson and that they were in the room together?

Tom said that when you are trying to apprehend someone in an assignation, if you know one person is being careful about being followed, follow the other one. When he had seen Arthur down at the beach a few weeks ago, he had a long talk with him about Beverly and learned that she seemed to have become very chummy with Dick Herson at the committee and that Herson had promised to find her a job in the White House. That's how he decided to follow Herson. He was sure Beverly could not tell Herson to be careful because that would make him think that either Arthur was suspicious or there was a problem with an ex-lover, either of which would make him uncomfortable.

He also said he knew that they probably met at least once a week so if he followed Herson at lunch every day for a week Herson would probably lead him to the rendezvous. Sure enough, the third time he followed Herson at noon, Herson led him right to the Mayflower Hotel. He had no trouble bribing the bellboy to let him be the one to knock on the door and tell Herson their lunch had arrived. He saw Herson meet Beverly in the hotel lobby and give her the room number, and it was easy to follow Herson to the room because Herson did not know Tom.

Two days later he called Beverly to say that he now had a good photo identifying her and Arthur, and all he wanted was for them to tell him everything they knew or could find out about Watergate! Tom said he knew enough about how politics and elections work to know that somebody in the upper echelon of the White House was aware of the break-in right from the start. He wanted to know who knew what and who authorized the break-in, and he knew Beverly was going to help him because he knew she wanted that photo.

A few days later, Tom contacted Herson and gave him the same message, hinting that he would send the photo to his wife. Herson was obviously upset and said he wanted to think about it. But he was stalling for time. Beverly and Herson had lunch one day in Annapolis to discuss the situation and Richard said he would not give in and that he knew how to take care of Tom. But she decided to tell Tom everything Herson had told her about Watergate, which was not much, but enough to cause the White House trouble. At the lunch, Beverly remembered telling Herson that she wished Tom were dead! Herson agreed and said he was going to keep stalling Tom until he figured out what to do.

Then, to let them know he was not bluffing, Tom sent a note to Arthur Turner hinting that Beverly was having an affair with someone in the White House. Arthur got the message and accused Beverly of having an affair with E. Richard Herson and threatened to have Jack Harrigan fire Herson.

So Beverly conceded to Arthur that several years ago, when Cranston was in the White House, she had had a brief affair with him. But the affair had been over for years. She said Tom was now blackmailing her to make her find out everything she could about Watergate and tell him, or else he would tell Arthur about the affair. Beverly knew Arthur was anxious to keep the Watergate affair quiet because Jack Harrigan had heard from Herson that there was a list of people who had contributed money to the fund that financed the Watergate cover-up, and Harrigan had informed Arthur that both of them were on that list.

Arthur was furious and asked how much she had told Tom about Watergate, and then roared out of the house, saying he did not know when he would be back.

A little while later, Tom called Beverly and repeated his demands. She was stunned at what he said next. She asked him where he was now, and he said, "I'm at the shore—playing volleyball."

"Playing volleyball!" Beverly exclaimed. "That doesn't sound like the kind of thing a blackmailer would be doing."

"You don't understand," Tom said. "I don't go out of my hotel unless I can be in a crowd. And you'd better stay away from that bunch in the White House because they're really bad. Someone is trying to kill me and the only person, other than you, who might want me dead is Herson."

Beverly could not believe it, but Cranston said that in Washington someone tried to shoot him with a silencer, so he'd came to the shore thinking it might be safer. But he thought someone had followed him because last night in Rehoboth someone tried to run over him.

Beverly asked if he was calling from Rehoboth and Cranston said, "Never you mind! But you better tell Dick Herson to call off his mafia friends. Not only is there the photo, but the tape recording I'm preparing tells everything I know about Watergate. And I'm arranging to have a friend send it to Bob Woodward at the *Post* if something happens to me."

Beverly was frightened. No matter how much she and Tom had been through, the thought of something happening to him was inconceivable, she said, "Despite all the ugliness and jealousy and spiteful things we had both done, I still had some deep-down feeling for him I could never overcome."

Beverly told Tom she could not believe Herson was trying to have him killed, but Cranston said, "You don't know how much trouble this bunch is in, and they'll do anything to stay in power." Tom finally convinced Beverly and she told him to be careful. He said he would and that he had bought a little .32-caliber revolver, just for comfort. Beverly promised to go to Herson, and if he was trying to have Tom killed, she would threaten to expose him herself. Tom said he thought that was the right thing to do, and hung up.

Beverly called Herson and made an appointment to meet him for lunch. She told him about Tom's note to Arthur, that it was written to let them know he was not bluffing, and that the next one would go to Herson's wife. But Tom had told her that he would rather know about Watergate then get Herson in trouble with his wife. She asked Herson, why not tell him, since it made no difference now, with John Dean getting ready to talk.

"Not necessarily," replied Herson. "The president will certainly stonewall it, and have a direct confrontation with Dean. And with his word against the president of the United States, who's ever going to believe John Dean?"

"Well, even if that happens, it doesn't change what'll happen to us. Your wife will leave you, and Arthur may throw me out. And your career in the White House may be hurt—if anyone is going to have a career in the White House under Richard Nixon. It's simply not worth it, just to keep things from leaking that'll come out anyway."

Richard was thinking. Finally, he said, "Beverly, there's more to it than just what might happen to me or you. You don't realize how important it is to keep Richard Nixon in office and to protect his credibility. We are developing a plan to literally take over this government! In our new appointments, we have Nixon loyalists in two or three key jobs in each agency—in the Public Affairs office, general counsel, congressional liaison, fiscal departments, administrative offices. And these men don't report to their secretary or agency head. They report *directly* to the White House—ultimately to the president. Now, this may not seem like much to someone who doesn't understand how this government works, but I tell you, it's a revolution!"

"You keep saying 'we are doing this' and 'we are doing that.' It sounds like you're very much involved in this plan."

"That's right, baby. I'm one of the three or four guys

charged with bringing about this little revolution. You can see why my reputation in the White House must be protected. And you can see why it's essential that Richard Nixon stay in office and that his credibility isn't hurt. We're hoping the resignations yesterday will put out this damned Watergate fire. Frankly, I was almost forced out with 'em. A lot of people thought I was responsible for some things that have leaked—and I probably was, because of what you told Tom. I think I weathered that all right, but I have to be more careful."

They ordered drinks and lunch, and when the waitress was gone, Beverly looked around to make certain that no one could hear them. Then she said, "Richard, something worries me. Do you remember that time we had lunch in Annapolis, after the incident with Tom at the Mayflower? We were both raging mad then at Tom's threat and I remember you saying something like, 'Don't worry about Tom, I know how to take care of him.' What did you mean by that?"

There was a long silence across the table. Then the waitress brought their drinks. When she left, Beverly said, "Well?"

Finally, Herson answered. "Do you remember, just before I mentioned my plan, you said, 'I wish Tom were dead'?"

"No, I don't remember saying that. I might have said something like 'I wish he would drop dead' but that was just an expression of anger. I didn't mean anything by it."

"Well, I thought you did. Frankly, I thought Tom Cranston had something else on you and that you had reasons of your own for wanting to get rid of him."

"Oh, Jesus, Richard! You can't really think I'd condone murder—even if Tom did have something else on me?"

"Why not? Tom's been cruel to you. He's treated you badly and blackmailed you. Women have been known to kill for less than that. I guess I didn't think you felt strong enough to kill him yourself, but I thought you were trying to tell me that you wouldn't mind if someone else did it."

"You *are* stupid! We can kill when we've been scorned or when we're insane with jealousy, or crazy at the thought of losing a lover. But we don't kill ex-lovers who never stopped loving us and even in blackmailing didn't do it for money. Tom's been ugly to me, but he's had good reason."

Richard swallowed the rest of his martini and looked around, trying to find the waitress in the dark. He loosened his tie, then took off his glasses and cleaned them with his napkin. He was obviously nervous, and Beverly could tell she was about to get bad news. "All right, Beverly. I'd hoped I'd never have to tell you about this. I never intended to involve you, but I felt I had to do what I did. I put out a contract on Tom!"

"Ohhh, God! Is that what I think it means?"

"Have you read *The Godfather*?"

"Yes."

"Well, then, you know what a contract means."

"I cannot believe you! I mean, Tom says you people are bad, but I can't believe you'd do that."

"Wait a goddamned minute, now. Don't get me wrong. This was not an official act, signed by the president. I did this on my own, I had to stop Tom from carrying out his threat, which would ruin me. After all, it was my fault he ever got the power and knowledge he has. I was the one who got involved with you at the worst possible time, and was dumb enough to let him follow me to our meeting place—and frankly, so *stupid* as to tell you what I knew about the president and Watergate."

"Was that really all you knew?"

"Yes."

"Tom says you know more."

"Not much more. But that's not all he wants. He wants me to start playing inside investigator and persuade people to talk, and then tell him. I can't do that. I told you how important it was to protect Richard Nixon's credibility. And not only for my personal gain. Sure, I'll be right at the center of power when we take over the government. But it's not just personal. We have to do it. As it stands now, the president simply cannot run this government. The bureaucracy's against him. He gives an order and it goes out to one of the Cabinet members and then nothing happens. Nothing! The bureaucracy smothers it. The bureaucracy's running this country. And we've go to put a stop to it. And if some people get hurt in the process, well, that's just tough shit. Getting rid of Tom was my idea—not Haldeman's or Ehrlichman's or Colson's."

"You are sick."

"No, just angry—and human. What Tom did to me at the Mayflower was humiliating. And the blackmailing was hard-ball, especially for what it might do to you. Imagine, trying to force me to spy on the White House by threatening to ruin your life, as well as mine! So I figured, if he wants to play hardball, I will too."

"So what did you do?"

"I told you."

"I want to know details."

Suddenly, the waitress appeared out of the dark and Herson ordered another drink. "All right," he said after the waitress was gone. "I used to practice law in New York before I came down here, so I know people with connections to the mafia. About three weeks ago I made arrangements through one of my Long Island contacts to have Tom, ah, well, eliminated, 'taken out' as they say. But not until I warned him that he was getting into dangerous waters and that it was risky business, blackmailing the White House. It didn't scare him. He said

he'd give me a couple of weeks, and then Arthur would begin
getting little messages in the mail. I thought he was bluffing."

"Now you know he wasn't."

"And now he knows *I* wasn't."

"Well. You've both had your little game. And it's time to
call them off or—"

"It may be too late."

"What do you mean, too late?"

"I mean, once you put something like this in motion, it's
hard to stop. You communicate through someone, who com-
municates with someone else, who then makes a contact with
the hit man. That sort of thing. And nobody really likes to talk
about it. You also put down quite a bundle of cash when you
make a contract."

"How much?"

"Never mind. It was quite a bundle."

"I'll bet it wasn't your money. I bet it came from the committee's political fund."

"I can assure you no one'll ever know where the money
came from—or for that matter that there was ever a contract."

"Not if you move fast, they won't." Beverly was raging mad.

"What do you mean?"

"I mean, unless you get on that phone right now and put a
stop to this stupid nonsense, I'll go to *The Washington Post*
myself. I know enough to blow you all out of the water—and
frankly I don't give a damn what happens to me. And if you
don't believe me, I suggest you get up out of here quietly and
just go back to the office without doing anything. I'll show you
what a woman can do when she's *really* mad!"

Beverly said she picked up her glass, but her hand was trem-
bling so much, she spilled her wine.

"Now, calm down, Beverly. I knew you wouldn't like this,
but I didn't think you'd ever get involved. This was strictly

between Tom and me. Look, Washington is a tough town. When there's so much power and money concentrated in any one place, you're going to find people playing rough."

"Look, you creep, let me tell you something! Tom Cranston has prepared a tape, which he is ready to send to a friend who will pass it on to Bob Woodward at the *Post*. He put everything on the tape that he knows about Watergate and the fact that you are trying to have him silenced. And when I add to the tape what *I* know, that *Post* reporter will have one helluva story. It'll finish you for good, and probably Richard Nixon. So I suggest you get to that phone right now and start trying to tear up that contract."

Beverly knew she had struck a chord. Herson gulped down his second martini and sat staring at his glass, which he was holding with both hands. Suddenly he stood up. "I'll be right back," he said, "I need to make a phone call."

When he returned Herson sat down and said, "Beverly, I called my contact to try to cancel the contract and he said he can't guarantee it. The man is obviously already on the job. It'll not only be difficult for my contact to reach his contacts, but the final contact will now have trouble reaching the man. I'm supposed to call my man back this afternoon, about four-thirty. He says he'll do the best he can. But bear in mind it'll not be easy. After all, if the hit man had not bungled the damned job, it would be done by now."

"You're really sick."

"Beverly, goddamn it, this is war. You don't know what the hell is going on. The liberals, like Tom, still control this country, *even after Richard Nixon has been in office four years!* The press, the Congress, the intelligence community, the bureaucracy, all controlled by the liberals. The president says, 'The bureaucracy still thinks Franklin Roosevelt is president.' And all the rest still think Kennedy's in the White House. Shit, a lot of us in the White House still are convinced Kennedy was responsible for the assassination of Ngo Din Diem and we know damn well he tried to have Castro knocked off. So what's one goddamn liberal jerk like Tom Cranston? He sure in hell's not going to stop us. I warned him he was getting into deep water, but he persisted in his little game of blackmail, and now he's going to find out we can be just as tough as the Kennedys. Serves him right. He used to work for those bastards. Now he knows what it's like to be on the outside, with the other guys holding the power."

Beverly shook her head while he was talking. The whole business was beginning to confuse her. She had wanted to work in the White House, but Herson made it sound so mean and ugly she wondered how anyone could stand it.

They were silent for some time. Dick, gulping his food, was obviously anxious to return to the White House. Beverly tried to draw him out on the latest Watergate developments, but he was hesitant to talk. He did tell her that John Dean had asked the president for immunity, and when he didn't get it, he went to the prosecutor's office secretly and had been talking to the grand jury. "That little bastard is singing and he is going to give us a real headache."

"Can he hurt the president?"

"Probably. But, as I said, in the long run it's going to be his word against that of the president of the United States."

"Is the president involved?"

Richard finished his coffee and stared at Beverly as if to say, Now, how in the hell could the president *not* be involved? But when he spoke, he said, "Beverly, my advice to you is to keep out of this and forget you ever had any interest in politics."

Herson said he would call Beverly back that afternoon, after he had heard from his contact. When he did, he told her, "I talked to my friend again and he simply cannot guarantee it can be stopped. He said he'll do everything possible. But when someone goes off on a mission like this, you just don't hear from them or know how to get in touch with them until the job is done. And even then, it may be weeks before they get back in touch, even to collect the money. They play it very cautious, as you can understand."

"Damn it, Richard, that's not good enough!" Beverly screamed. "You have to do something. Don't you know you have just as much interest now in stopping this as I do? I warned you—you'll be ruined."

"I know that, goddamn it. Hell, if I thought I could stop it, I'd go down to Rehoboth myself."

"Maybe that's not a bad idea."

"What would that accomplish?"

"Well, you could find Tom and confirm his suspicions that someone *is* after him, so he will be especially careful. Then you could try to intercept the killer and tell him the deal is off."

"Do you know where Tom is staying?"

"No, but it's a small town and there is practically nobody down there this time of year in the middle of the week. He's probably driving a white MG convertible with a black top and D.C. tags. It shouldn't be hard to find."

"Let me think about it. Maybe I can get down tonight. Trouble is, this guy wouldn't know me from Adam. The hit man never knows who places a contract. That's the way it works. Why in hell would be believe me? Maybe all I would accomplish would be to get shot."

"It would serve you right. But I'll tell you what you can do at Rehoboth. If you find the hit man, you could pay him the other half of the money and that would be that. He would believe you then, wouldn't he?"

"Yeah, and I wish it were that simple. Maybe I could find Tom. But you don't think the hit man is going to be sitting in a hotel window across the street with a rifle sticking out aimed at Tom's window. This isn't a movie. It's for real. Yeah, I could give him the rest of the money he'll get when the job is done. And how am I going to come up with that kind of cash this afternoon?"

"You had better think of something—and hope you get lucky when you go looking for that guy in Rehoboth."

Beverly was convinced something terrible was going to happen. By five-thirty she was so distraught she called Bernadette and asked her to come over. Arthur was not home. After talking with Bernadette, she decided to go down to the beach to try to find Tom, to tell him Herson had promised to try to cancel the contract, but that it was difficult, and he should be especially careful until she heard from Herson that it was off. She also told me that she was deeply concerned about Tom, maybe more than she cared to admit. Frankly, she said she decided that maybe she was still in love with Tom. Maybe she could find him at Rehoboth and move toward a reconciliation. At the very least, she could apologize for what she had done.

She, of course, let Bernadette know about Herson's contract, but she did not want her to know she was going to the beach, so she told Bernadette that she planned to take a sleeping pill and try to get a good night's sleep, and asked Bernadette to take her children for the night. Bernadette agreed, and after she was gone, Beverly drove to the beach.

She could not find Tom anywhere. She came back to the beach house, parked the Cadillac in the driveway and turned on some lights, all the while hoping Tom might come by, see the lights, and come in. Then Bernadette called. She figured Beverly had gone to the beach, and everything was fine at home, the kids were asleep. But she was worried about Beverly.

Maybe Herson would try to have her killed, too! Bernadette said the smart thing to do would be to turn out all the lights, take the car up by the Henlopen Hotel, park it, come back down the beach, and sneak into the dark house and spend the night there without turning on any lights. In this way, no one would know she was there and she would be safe.

Beverly agreed this was a good idea, but conceded to me that it also meant she would be unable to prove where she had spent that night.

The next morning, Beverly heard the news on the radio about Tom being killed and was horrified. She started home immediately but stopped in Annapolis and called Herson, accused him of killing Tom, and threatened to tell the police everything. Much to her surprise, Herson swore that he had canceled the contract personally! Through his contact, he had reached the hit man in Ocean City and he said he would cancel for $5,000 in cash, that night. Herson said he would raise the money and drive down immediately. He could only raise $4,000 so he called Beverly to tell her he had been able to cancel the contract and to see if she could raise another $1,000 from Arthur or someone. No one was home, so he called Bernadette to see if she knew where Beverly was, and Bernadette said she thought Beverly was home and had probably taken a sleeping pill and gone to bed. The children were with her and no one knew where Arthur was. Bernadette also told Herson she knew what was going on and that he was really getting in over his head. Herson said he told Bernadette the contract had been canceled and that all he needed was another $1,000 and then he was driving down to Ocean City to pay off the killer. Could she loan him the money?

Bernadette said she did not have that much cash around. Jack was out of town and she could not help him until morning.

Herson told Beverly that he then decided to go to Ocean City with only $4,000 and hope he could convince the hit man to take that and he would pay him the additional money later. When he got there, the killer said $4,000 was enough, and disappeared, after telling Herson that Cranston was hiding out at the Admiral Hotel in Ocean City.

Herson said he found Cranston in Ocean City and they had a drink in the Admiral bar, where Herson convinced Tom that the contract was off. He also said that if Tom would burn the photographs, the negatives, and the tape implicating Herson in an assignation, he would tell Cranston everything he knew about Watergate—provided Tom would keep his source confidential.

Tom agreed, so they went up to his room in the Admiral, where Herson witnessed Tom burning the photographs, negatives, and tape. Then Herson told Tom everything he knew about Watergate. When Herson left, Tom said he tried to call his contact on the Ervin committee but couldn't reach him. He planned to drive to Washington in the morning and tell the committee everything he had learned about Watergate, without revealing Herson as his main source.

Beverly said she did not believe Herson and accused him of killing Tom or telling the hit man to go ahead and do it anyway, after he had made a show of calling it off. Herson said Beverly was crazy, that he knew she would tell everybody what she knew if Cranston was killed and that he hoped she would keep her head now and not say anything until they found out more about what happened. Beverly promised to keep quiet—at least for now.

When she arrived home the next day a little after noon, Arthur was still not there. He came in a little later and Beverly asked where he had been. He would not say, and when Beverly hinted that maybe he had gone to Ocean City and seen Tom,

Arthur said he had spent the night with his old girlfriend, the one he had had an affair with in Baltimore at the time Beverly was pregnant with her second child. Arthur went out again, still mad, and Bernadette came over with the children. Beverly fell into her arms sobbing.

I had let her go on uninterrupted to get a sense of whether she was leveling with me or not. Near as I could guess, she was, and I knew I had to talk to Herson again in a hurry. I was also beginning to wonder if I should not get out of the detective business and tell Jenkins everything I knew. But I had some compelling instinct to keep going, like every writer when he knows he is onto a good story. When she had finished, I said, "Beverly, I can't understand why you didn't go to the police first thing Thursday morning when you heard on the radio that Tom was dead."

"I know that doesn't look good, but I wanted to talk to Dick first. I still had a hard time believing something like that could happen. And when I called him from Annapolis, he pleaded with me not to say anything for a while. I was confused. He knew how mad I was—and killing Tom wouldn't have kept *me* from going to the police. It would have made me even madder than I was. In fact, when I first called, Herson was terrified that I had already gone to the police. Then there was also the possibility that Tom had killed himself. He was drinking too much and not acting normal. In fact, he hadn't been acting right for almost a year."

"You were driving the blue Cadillac the night Tom was killed, right?"

"Yes."

"So your husband was driving the tan Oldsmobile station wagon?"

"Yes. He spent the night with his old girlfriend."

"Tell me about that."

"Well, back at the time I was pregnant with Broderick, our second child, I discovered Arthur was having an affair with his assistant. She was more than a secretary, you know, one of those very bright, articulate girls you find in most small businesses who seem to run the shop. Her name was Betty Sawyer. I don't know whether she ever married. It was really the turning point in our marriage. We almost broke up over it, though I decided to keep the family together. But we were never the same. I don't know what happened to Miss Sawyer. And he never mentioned her until the other night, the night of Tom's death, when he said he had spent the night with Betty and could prove it."

"Do you know where she lives now?"

"No. She used to live in one of the Baltimore suburbs, probably near the old Baltimore office. But I'm not sure where. Arthur can tell you."

"Well, he'll have to tell Jenkins about her. Do you by chance know if your husband was wearing his Greek fisherman's hat when he went out that afternoon?"

"I doubt it. He only wears it when we're in the sun sitting around the pool, or at the beach. In fact, he has another one he keeps here."

"Did you happen to notice if one of them was missing that night?"

"Oddly enough, I did notice the one he keeps at home sitting on the hall table when I left that night."

"And that was after your husband left?"

"Yes."

"I guess you know the bartender at the Admiral said he saw Tom talking with a tall man wearing what seemed to be a tan corduroy coat and a fishing hat after he left the bar, and that he drove off with him in a big, American-type station wagon?"

"Yes, Jenkins mentioned that, but he also said that the man was quite tall, maybe a little taller than Tom. And Arthur is short. If you saw him and Tom standing side-by-side, you'd immediately be aware that Arthur was much shorter."

I agreed and added: "And he's definitely not swishy, which was the way the bartender described that tall man."

"Definitely."

"Which made me think Tom met a woman that night— dressed as a man. What do you think?"

She paused for a moment looking puzzled. "I don't know. I never thought of that." Then, quickly shifting the subject, she said, "Herson says he didn't tell Tom anything that John Dean's not going to tell the Ervin committee, so killing Tom wouldn't keep the president out of trouble. He's still got a confrontation with Dean coming, although Tom's information might have succeeded in getting the story into the *Post* a lot sooner."

"Tom was also supposed to have something else," I said. "That list of people who had contributed to a special fund used in the Watergate cover-up. Your husband was on that list, right? And Jack Harrigan?"

"True," she said. "I guess that looks bad for Arthur, doesn't it? He really has a double motive. Do the police know about that list?"

"Not yet. And, of course, we don't know that Tom had a real list, just that he knew who was on it."

"Isn't it dangerous withholding evidence like we're doing?"

"Not if we can find out what happened soon. Then it would be forgotten. But that list also gives someone else a motive— Jack Harrigan."

"I suppose it does," she said. "But I just can't think of Jack Harrigan getting involved in something messy like this, and I certainly can't see him out on the beach at midnight shooting someone. That's really out of character."

"What about Bernadette?" I asked. "Herson says there are rumors about her, too. Could she be a lesbian? You'd certainly be the one to know, close as you are."

For the first time, Beverly seemed genuinely disconcerted. She obviously did not want to talk about it, but she said, "Mr. Hartley, I honestly don't know. I do know she is quite bitter about men. But I always attributed that to her very unhappy affair with the senator. She told you about that?"

"Not in detail."

"Well, I won't either. But it was a very passionate, intense thing for both of them. He was married, and when the showdown came, he chose to stay with his wife, as they usually do. Bernadette was crushed."

"Crushed at losing her lover or crushed at not becoming the wife of a senator?"

"Well, she was married, too, and I never heard her say anything about leaving Jack."

"But if she was in love she would have. Theirs is obviously a marriage of convenience."

"I suppose so, but I just don't know. I know we joked about becoming lovers, but we never did again."

"Did you tell her about Herson?"

"Yes. She knew I had an affair with him. I also told her Tom had surprised Dick and me, taken a photograph of us together, and was blackmailing Dick about Watergate."

The telephone rang and Beverly left the room to answer it in the kitchen. Here was a woman in pretty deep, I thought, up to her neck in adultery, blackmail, and murder. And promiscuous as hell, as I had just found out, involved with several men and on the edge of a relationship with a woman. Pretty heavy for a suburban housewife. Her marriage was obviously on the rocks, which might explain her promiscuity.

"That was Arlene Bradshaw," she said, reentering the room.

"We have a tennis date—and that will give you and Arthur a chance to talk alone. He should be along any time now."

"Good," I replied. "But I have one more question, if you don't mind. As pleasant as our little flirtation earlier this morning was, I have to admit I am a little baffled by it."

She thought for a moment, obviously quite embarrassed.

"I certainly was uptight physically as well as mentally. In fact, I was surprised at just how uptight I was. Seriously, a massage would have helped relax me. I wished that I had not committed to an interview this morning, but I did want to talk to you sometime. And if I shared a little intimacy with you now it it would make me feel I could trust you. That you are more interested in finding out what happened to your friend Tom Cranston than in publishing a sensational article. And that's what I want too. To find out what happened to Tom. After all, I was in love with him once."

"He did involve you as a pawn in his war with Richard Nixon."

"I guess I deserved that. I never should have been involved with that creep Dick. I never had any feelings for him. I was just playing the Washington game—using my body to advance my ambitions. I did want to work in the White House. And I must have been crazy."

"A lot of people wanted to work in the Nixon administration and a lot of them are going to jail."

"I hope Nixon goes with them."

"That would be nice."

We both heard the sound of a car pulling into the driveway, and Beverly walked to the window. I looked at my watch. It was quarter of twelve. "It's Arthur, and I suspect Arlene will be along any moment," she said.

I thanked her for her cooperation and said, "If I were you, I'd just tell Detective Jenkins the truth. Don't worry about an adultery scandal when you're facing a possible murder rap. I'd tell that to your husband, too."

"Tell me what?" Arthur Turner asked as he came up the stairs into the living room. He was wearing the mate to Mrs. Turner's brown track suit.

"I was just telling your wife," I said, as I shook his outstretched hand, "that when you see Jenkins this afternoon, you tell him all you know about Tom and what happened that night. You are both involved in a murder case."

Turner scowled, went to a little bar at the end of the counter that joined the kitchen and the living room, and started to fix himself a drink. "We both intend to tell the truth, naturally. You want something to drink, Hartley?"

Looking at my watch again, I said, "It's a little early for me, but I guess I could use a cold beer."

Beverly Turner left for her tennis match and I put a new tape in my recorder. Turner pulled up his chair closer to it before sitting down. I sat down and set up the tape recorder. "Mr. Turner, by now I know quite a bit of what happened Tuesday, May second, the night Tom Cranston was killed. Your wife said you were mad at the things you had learned lately and that you spent the night with an old girlfriend. Do you want to tell me about that?"

"Not especially, but I will. I've known Betty Sawyer for years. She used to work for me when I was in Baltimore. We had a brief affair. Beverly found out about it. Naturally she got mad and I broke it off. Betty left the company and we kept in touch after I moved to Kenwood, but I did not see her—until recently, when I learned that Bernadette was having an affair with someone who worked at the White House. There was a little confusion as to just who it was. She said it was Tom Cranston—when he *used* to work at the White House. But there was something going on lately and it was upsetting Beverly."

"Did you know it concerned E. Richard Herson, who works in the White House now?"

"I figured it was something to do with him. Beverly had worked for him during the campaign last year and he had promised her a job in the White House if they won, which they did. But she never got the job. Frankly, I thought Beverly was having the affair with him, but she insisted it was Tom."

"So what happened Tuesday afternoon?"

"I came home from work around seven. I was surprised to find Bernadette Harrigan's Mercedes in the driveway, but Beverly's Cadillac was gone. Bernadette said Beverly was on her way to the shore, looking for Tom Cranston. She told me some crazy story about Herson trying to have Cranston killed because Cranston was blackmailing him, but that Beverly had forced Herson to call it off. And she was going to tell Tom what had happened. Beverly, for some reason, felt partly responsible for the situation."

"Why do you think Bernadette told you what Herson had done?"

"I don't know why. For one thing, she seemed very upset and emotional, not like herself, really. She's usually very cool and collected. But she does confide in me some when it comes to what's going on at the White House and the Republican party. I make substantial contributions to the Republicans."

"Yes, I know. And did she, by chance, mention that she had learned that Cranston was probably in Ocean City, not Rehoboth?"

"Yes, Bernadette said she thought Herson was going down there too, to Ocean City, not Rehoboth. But Beverly left before Bernadette had a chance to tell her, so I think she thought Cranston was in Rehoboth."

"So, what did you do?"

"I was mad as hell. I was getting fed up. There was not only

Cranston but Herson having an affair with my wife. And I'm beginning to think there were others. I don't like her being so open about it. The children are getting older now. They're going to understand what's going on. I don't like it.

"Anyway, I called Betty Sawyer. She lives in Baltimore. I told her I was coming over and we could go to the Orioles game that night. She's a great Orioles fan, Colts, too. That's part of our friendship. She loves sports. I didn't tell her then that I planned to spend the night."

"You used your Oldsmobile station wagon, right?"

"That's right."

"And you went to the game?"

"Yes."

"I'm an Orioles fan and I remember they lost. How was it?"

"A lousy game. The Orioles couldn't hit Wood—that was the Chicago pitcher. But that's nothing unusual. Nobody can hit Wood this year. But the Birds looked dull in the field and they're not playing like they should. Palmer pitched a good game and Rettenmund and Baylor got some hits, but I don't know. They've lost nine out of their last twelve games and it looks like it may be a long season, although they're only a half game out of first place."

Turner seemed to have a good grasp of what went on. So I finally said, "Let me ask you something. A friend of mine who works for *The Baltimore Sun,* a big baseball fan, went to the game that night. I was talking about it with him a couple of days later and he mentioned that big blonde—I forget her name—the one who goes to ball games all over the league and likes to run out on the field and kiss one of the players."

"Yeah, I know about her," Turner said, "the one with the big tits."

"Yes. I'm sure you remember her. My friend said she came running out on the field that night, between the fifth or the sixth inning, and gave Brooks Robinson a big kiss. You remember that?"

Turner was silent for a moment. Then he said, "No, I don't really remember that. Must have happened when I went to the john and got some more beer. I did that once in the middle of the game. Maybe Betty'll remember. Why don't you call her?" He gave me Betty Sawyer's telephone number.

"Maybe I will," I said. "But not now, I'm running late. So what else happened that night?"

"Nothing much. After the game, we went back to her apartment and I spent the night. I went directly to work in the morning. I knew Bernadette had the children,"

"Did you drive your station wagon to the stadium?"

"No. We used Betty's car. I felt more comfortable. I don't like being open about seeing Betty."

"Because of the children?"

"Because of the children."

"It's pretty open at a ball game."

"That's different. Betty Sawyer used to work for me. We all used to go to the ball games together when our office was in Towson."

"Did you by chance wear your Greek fisherman's cap to Baltimore that night?"

"Of course not. That's my sun hat. I have two of them, one in Rehoboth and one in Kenwood. And I wasn't wearing either one."

I looked at my watch. It was nearly noon. I had to move fast because I wanted to call Herson before he left for lunch. We had to talk! Also I needed to see Jenkins. Hastily packing up my tape recorder, I told Turner I appreciated his answering my few questions and that I might have some more for him later.

I drove immediately into Rehoboth, found a phone booth,

and called Herson. When his secretary put me through, I said, "Herson, I know you don't like to talk on the phone, but we've gotta talk."

"You've talked to Beverly, haven't you," he said without that touch of hysteria in his voice I anticipated.

"Yes," I replied, "and I bet you have, too—maybe within the last half hour."

He was silent.

"I know your story now," I said, "but I want to hear it from you."

"When do you want to meet?" he said abruptly.

"I'm in Rehoboth now, but I'm driving up there immediately. I can meet you in Washington, at the same place we had lunch, around three. Can you make it?"

He said yes.

"See you then." I hung up and immediately called Doreen. "Dory, do me a favor. Make me a sandwich and have a beer and coffee ready to go in a few minutes. I have to go to Washington to see Herson. I can't tell you everything I learned from Beverly Turner, but we can talk in the car."

"No. I may stay here for a couple of days. There's so much to do before the renters come in. You go up to Washington and play detective. I can get a ride up with someone or take the bus."

"Or I'll be back in a day or so. But talking to Herson can't wait."

"How did your meeting with Beverly Turner go?"

"You wouldn't believe me if told you."

"Here we go again. What did she do, ask you to give her a massage?"

"Of course. Every woman I interview asks me to massage her first. They say it relaxes them."

"I'll bet it does, the way you give them."

"You never complained. And if you want, I'll give you one before we drive home."

"I'm not going home today."

"You mad?

"No, I just think I better stay. We have so much to do before the renters come in at the end of the month. But I'll have your lunch ready to take in the car. You can call me tonight when you get home. But please do it before you've had too many drinks."

"Now, damn it, Dory, you know I don't have that many drinks!"

"You do when I'm not there to fix dinner on time."

"Well, why don't you come with me, then?"

"No, I'll leave you free to see that Mrs. Harrigan. I bet you have to interview her again, too."

"No, but I have to interview her husband. He's in town now."

"Pity."

"Just fix lunch. I know the detectives you read about are always going around interviewing people, beating up or getting beat up by men and seducing or being seduced by women. But I'm just a middle-aged writer trying to make a couple of thousand bucks writing a profile—"

"And maybe get shot—and laid—in the process," she interrupted.

"Remember the insurance," I said. "I think it's double indemnity if I have a violent death. Look, you're right, I gotta see Jenkins. I'll see you in a little while."

Jenkins was sitting at his desk at state police headquarters, talking on the phone. He motioned me to sit down in a chair beside his desk, and when he hung up the phone he said, "That was the post office. They still haven't been able to trace that package. Just one guy remembers putting it in the bag that went to Salisbury and then to D.C. But the Baltimore people don't remember it coming in. It's been delivered now."

Shrugging my shoulders as if to say, What can we do about it, I asked Jenkins if he was making any progress.

"Not a helluva lot. I talked to Mrs. Turner yesterday and I'm talking to her husband today. She was at the beach that evening, but according to her neighbors she didn't spend the night there. She says she did, that they just didn't see her car come back. She said she had one phone call—from Bernadette Harrigan—and we're checking that out."

"Good."

"Here's another thing," said Jenkins. "My New York contact moved pretty fast on that Harrigan lead. He stayed at the Commodore Hotel all right, and they could keep track of him pretty much with his phone calls. But there was one big blank—from Wednesday afternoon from about four-thirty or five o'clock to the next morning. There were no phone calls during that period, even though he was on the phone all the time during the other periods he was there—from Monday afternoon to Sunday afternoon. And he was definitely not in his room Wednesday evening, or he wasn't answering his phone—because they remember he had several messages. And there was one curious thing: the hotel recorded one incoming call from Ocean City, Maryland, for Harrigan's room. But there was no message left and no record of whether it was a man or a woman calling. There were, however, several calls from his telephone number in Georgetown, presumably from his wife."

"That is interesting," I said. "I'll be talking with him soon. I'll see what I can find out."

Then I added, "Here's something else you might want to look into. Arthur Turner is going to tell you that he spent the night with an old girlfriend. Her name a few years ago was Betty Sawyer."

"He already told me, on the phone. She lives in Baltimore now. I'm talking to her this evening."

"Well, you better check out her phone calls for that night." Jenkins made a note of that.

"You know Beverly Turner had an affair with Tom Cranston?"

"Yeah. Mrs. Turner mentioned it and that's why right now her husband is a prime suspect, although it looks like Mrs. Turner was the one closest to Ocean City that night. But Baltimore isn't that far away."

"No, and neither is New York. You could drive it in five hours, you know."

"That's pressin' it," said Jenkins, "but it could be done. So you think Cranston could have been involved with Mrs. Harrigan too? Christ, he had good taste. This Alice Burton, who worked with him on that Senate committee, ain't bad either."

"And smarter than all of them, which would have appealed to Tom," I said. "So how'd you know about her?"

"She was the woman who phoned in telling us to look for a white MG after Tom's death was announced on the radio. We found it in Ocean City. And that's how we knew Tom was staying at the Admiral. The MG was parked near there and it was just a matter of asking around. I've already interviewed her."

"And what about Mrs. Cranston? Did you find out anything about her?"

"Not a thing. We checked most of the rental car agencies and only a couple of single women rented cars that night. We checked them out and none of them were Cranston's wife. But I have to say, she sure had the motives."

"But not the opportunity," I said as I stood up to leave. I felt much better, having given Jenkins some tips, making it look like I wasn't holding anything back—like evidence. "This detective business is just like writing a profile or a biography," I said. "You just try to find out everything you can—mostly by interviewing everyone who might know something about your subject."

"That's right, Mr. Hartley. Maybe you oughta have been a detective."

"And maybe you ought to have been a writer," I said as I headed for the door. Jenkins just laughed, turned around to a typewriter sitting on a table next to his desk and started typing furiously.

CHAPTER TEN

Tuesday afternoon, May 8

On the drive to Washington I speculated on why Herson had done such an evil, stupid thing, and finally decided that he must have assumed the contract would be executed quickly and efficiently. Then Tom would never have called Beverly, letting her know what was happening and getting her upset. Herson would simply have stonewalled Beverly, denying any part in Tom's death. And Tom would have been out of the way, eliminating a blackmailer who was threatening not only his marriage and career but the Nixon takeover of the government. There must have been a couple of days, at least, when Herson felt quite smug about things.

But then the hit man bungled the job, just as the Watergate burglars had bungled the break-in, and the White House had bungled the cover-up. I also began to visualize a scheme in which Herson might be quite useful.

After leaving the shore I turned on WTOP, the all-news station, as I usually do. It helps me to get back in that inside-the-Beltway frame of mind as I approach Washington on Route 50. In a few minutes there was a news report on the Cranston case:

"The Delaware and Maryland police are still investigating the death of Thomas W. Cranston, a former White House aide under Lyndon Johnson, and more recently staff director of the Senate Select Subcommittee on Oil Reserves. Although at first the police thought Cranston's death might have been a suicide, they have now ruled that out and are investigating the possibility of murder. They have no evidence that his death was related to government business, and a number of people known to be personally involved with Cranston are being questioned."

The traffic was light and I made good time, arriving at The Place Where Louis Dwells about quarter to three. I had a few minutes for some calls, first to Alice Burton, who said she would very much like to talk to me, alone and out of the office. I made a date to meet her at Billy Martin's in Georgetown at five-thirty.

Then I phoned Mrs. Harrigan and said I had to talk to her again. She said she would be delighted and that her husband was very anxious to meet me. "Why don't you come by for dinner tonight. Just the three of us—unless you'd like to bring your wife. Jack has to fly to Dallas tomorrow and he'll be gone for several days, so this will be our best chance to talk for a while. We have a dinner date tonight; the Kissingers will be there, but we can bow out gracefully. I know Jack is anxious to talk to you."

Passing up a dinner party featuring the Kissingers? He must really want to find out what I knew. "Yes, that would be nice. My wife is out of town, but I'll be there. What time?"

"How about sevenish? We'll make it an early night."

"Good. I'm having drinks with someone in Georgetown at five-thirty. I'll see you at seven." We hung up.

It might be an early night but it was going to be a long day, I mused, still impressed by the Harrigans passing up a dinner with the Kissingers to talk to me. I had five minutes before meeting Herson and I owed Sam Meyers a call.

Sam came on the phone saying, "How we doing, Marlowe? Cracked the case yet?"

"No, but I haven't been beat up and gone unconscious into the deep black pool that is always waiting for Marlowe. And I'm making progress."

"Can you tell me about it?"

"No. In two minutes I have a meeting with a White House creep—no pun intended—who I'd rather not name right now. We're going to be talking about Tom Cranston and the plot is getting thick. I don't know how much of all this we can use in the magazine, but it's going to be a good piece."

"Well, I knew that, Raymer. I can hardly wait to read it. Incidentally, we just heard that the Ervin committee will begin public hearings on May seventeenth and they're seeking immunity for John Dean. Things are beginning to break."

"They are. And maybe I can break them a little faster."

"Yeah? How?"

"Can't talk now, Sam. Just letting you know that I'm well, in Washington, and still on the case." I hung up.

When I told the head waitress in the restaurant my name and that I was meeting someone at three o'clock, she said my party had already arrived. After I was seated I said to Herson: "I talked to Beverly Turner this morning and I think you got some explaining to do."

"Goddamn it, Hartley. Beverly said she told you I canceled the contract, and, as I told you the first time we met, I personally went to Ocean City and gave Tom all the information he wanted. And he burned the photos, the negatives, and the tape, and that was the end of it—I thought. He also said that was the end of it with Beverly, that he never wanted to see her or talk to her again. He vowed that he never would."

"Well, you could have been lying to Beverly about canceling the contract. In fact, it seems odd to me that you were able to cancel a contract so easily. You made a pretty good case to Beverly on how hard it was to stop something like that once it's in motion."

"I know—and you're right. I just lucked out on that one. Just by chance, my contact was a personal friend of the hit man, his brother, I think, although he didn't say. And for personal reasons, he had been in touch with the hit man. He not only knew that the job had not been done, but how to reach his friend—or brother. He arranged for me to meet the hit man at an Ocean City parking lot and pay him off."

"Is that how you knew Cranston was at Ocean City and not Rehoboth?"

"Yeah. My contact told me that. Even Beverly thought he was at Rehoboth."

"So maybe you saw Tom, made your deal, but let the contract stand."

"Why would I do that?"

"To keep Tom quiet about Watergate."

"Look, this was a personal thing right from the beginning. I'd never have put out a contract just to stop Cranston from talking about Watergate. It was the photograph."

"Beverly Turner knew about the contract and threatened to talk. You had to convince her you canceled the contract."

"Goddamn it, I canceled the contract! But I had the photograph and Tom didn't have that much on Watergate, anyway."

"He did after what you told him that night. Maybe you told the hit man to wait until after you talked to Cranston, to see how much you had to tell Tom. Maybe it was a White House show from the beginning."

"Don't be crazy," Herson said, becoming increasingly agitated. "Cranston had more, yes. But all that's coming out anyway. You know John Dean's going to tell the Ervin committee everything he knows. I told you the first time, if we were going to kill anybody it would have been John Dean. Why kill some liberal jerk like Tom Cranston? He worked for a Democratic-controlled Senate committee; nobody would have believed him anyway. The Ervin committee is getting tips all the time from people around town. But they have to have more proof than Cranston had."

I was getting impatient. "Look, you bastard, you're in trouble whether you killed Cranston or not."

"So, what can I say? I've told you everything—I canceled the contract, and I didn't kill him. What about Jack Harrigan? He could've been the swishy guy that Cranston left the Admiral with. He's more than a little effeminate. He had a motive and so did Arthur Turner. They both had given a lot of money, some of which was used to finance the cover-up. If that ever came out it would ruin them. In fact, Arthur Turner had a double motive—he was a jealous husband *and* his wife's lover had his name on a list that could ruin his business. What about that?"

"They both have alibis," I said. "Turner spent the night with an old girlfriend in Baltimore, and Harrigan was in New York, staying at the Commodore Hotel. All that's been checked out by the Delaware police."

"Well, I still think they both have a lot of explaining to do."

I nodded that I agreed, but said, "Tell me something, Herson: by that night, who knew you had told Cranston about some of the people who had helped finance the Watergate cover-up?"

"Christ—just about everyone involved. I mean, I had told Beverly and I know she told Arthur. And when I talked to Bernadette Harrigan that afternoon before I went to Ocean City, she said that Beverly had told her. And I know she told her husband. So it was no secret."

"And to coin a phrase," I replied, "they all might have killed for it."

"Somebody sure did," Herson said, and he seemed to drift off into thought, shaking his head.

Suddenly I remembered my appointment with Alice Burton. As near as I could make out, my watch said four-fifteen. I knew the traffic would be slow going to Georgetown this time of evening and I had one more thing I wanted to talk to Herson about.

"So what about the photograph?" he asked, seeming to anticipate what I was about to say.

"I was thinking about that when I was driving up from Rehoboth."

Herson was silent.

When neither of us said anything, he finally responded, "Okay, let's hear it. I know it ain't going to be easy."

"It won't be hard. But I haven't got time to go into it now. All you need to know is that a friend has a note telling him where the photo is and what to do about it—in case anything happens to me. So you can tell your mafia buddy to stay home."

Despite the traffic I was able to get to Georgetown, park, and arrive at the restaurant around five-twenty. Billy Martin's is one of my favorite places, an unpretentious little restaurant, with booths for privacy if you are there early enough, draft beer, and good, reasonably priced food.

Alice Burton had not arrived, so I ordered a scotch and water. But the first sip told me it was too strong. This was going to be a long evening of interrogations, and I had to make sure I had everything right. It might be awkward to use my tape recorder at dinner with the Harrigans.

When Alice Burton sat down in the booth across from me she was absolutely gorgeous. I don't know what happened to her on the way from the Senate Office Building, but she had been transformed from an intelligent-looking, competent Senate committee lawyer into a very attractive, desirable woman. Maybe it was just the dimmed lighting or maybe it was her cocktail-time demeanor. She certainly did not have time to go home and slip into something casual and seductive before showing up at Billy Martin's. She was still wearing office clothes, but she had done something—brushed her hair? put on lipstick? opened her blouse a little more? Maybe it was just me. But her radiant appearance prompted an obvious question after we had ordered a martini and a glass of water to dilute my scotch: "Look, Ms. Burton, you're a very attractive woman. And frankly, considering how long you've known Tom and how closely you worked together, I just can't understand why you two were not, er, well, uh, living together or even married. I know you are Tom's kind of woman."

"Well, thank you, Mr. Hartley."

"Please, Ray, or even Raymer. That's what my friends call me."

"Ray, I agree. Tom and I were made for each other. When he separated from Elaine, I thought we were almost going to fall into each other's arms. But it didn't happen that way. He never said much about the affair he had going, but it quickly became obvious that although it was over, Tom was still somehow terribly involved. Whatever it was, he was not ready for me."

Tears were coming to her eyes, and I realized for the first

time that Alice Burton was the one person really hurt by Tom's death. She started talking to me, and for the next few minutes, she tried to tell me how much she had loved and admired Tom and about her hopes for the future. And as we both reminisced about Tom we gradually developed an unspoken bond, based on a mutual pledge to find out what had happened.

Finally Alice said, "Before I forget, I inquired around the Ervin committee the other day and I couldn't learn anything about the tape. They probably wouldn't tell me anyway, but my contacts say they don't know anything about it."

"Well, that figures," I replied. "By the way, Jenkins—the detective who's handling the case for Delaware—says you were the one who tipped them off about Tom's white MG."

"That's right. We had news of Tom's death in the office first thing Thursday morning, and when I thought about Tom being found alone on the beach, I thought the police might just be looking for his car—and I knew what it looked like. So I called the Maryland police and told them. I had given them my name, of course. But it was Jenkins who came to talk to me—yesterday."

"Oh?"

"Yeah. He asked all the usual questions, including where I was Wednesday night. I was at one of those after-hours staff parties that started in a bar on the Hill and ended up at my apartment, around midnight. I had plenty of witnesses—too many, as a matter of fact."

Then shifting the subject, she said, "Ray, I'm sorry about the tears a moment ago, but this is the first time I've really let go since Tom's death. I just knew he was going to say that his messy love affair was finally over and we were going to be . . . whatever you want to call it."

"Well, let's call it married," I said. "In my generation, that's the way falling in love ended. And then you lived happily ever after." As soon as I said it, I thought it was dumb, and a look at her face confirmed it. *And then it hit me!* That package the clerk at the Admiral said that Tom had mailed that night was a tape, all right—but not for me or for Bob Woodward or the Ervin committee. He had planned to deliver what he knew about Watergate in person. The package he mailed was to Beverly Turner! Tom was telling her what happened, and saying good-bye on a tape, *without having to see or talk to her again*. And he would have made his commitment to Alice Burton when he invited her to the beach that weekend.

Feeling that Alice Burton was composed enough that it would not be ungentlemanly for me to leave the booth for a few minutes, I said, "I just thought of something. I have to make a phone call. I'll explain when I come back."

I had to call Beverly Turner immediately; something Bernadette Harrigan had told me rang a bell. When Beverly answered the phone, I said, "Beverly, I want to speak to you privately. Are you alone?"

"Yes. Arthur's at the police station talking with Detective Jenkins."

"Good. I don't know whether anyone has told you, but the desk clerk at the Admiral Hotel in Ocean City says that Tom mailed a small package that evening before he went out. He bought the stamps from her and had the package in his hand. She's pretty sure Tom mailed it right there in the lobby. At first I thought it might be something he was mailing to me, but I never received anything. Jenkins knows about it and he had the post office try to trace it. But they never found it. I'm now almost certain that package was mailed to you. Have you received a package from Tom?"

"No, unless it came in the mail yesterday or today."

"You should have received it before that. Bernadette Harrigan says that you and Tom used to communicate through a post office box you kept somewhere. Do you still have it?"

There was a long silence. "Well, yes. But I don't get much mail there now. It was mostly from Tom."

"Where is it?"

Still another pause. "At the Palisades Post Office on MacArthur Boulevard."

"And if Tom sent you anything from Ocean City, he would naturally have sent it to the Palisades Post Office box. Right?"

"I guess so."

"Have you checked that box lately?"

"No. I haven't been there for a couple of weeks."

I thought for a moment and glanced nervously at my watch, confirming that all the post offices, except the main one near Union Station, were closed now. Finally I said, "Does anyone know where this box is?"

"No. Bernadette knows I have one, but not where it is."

"All right. I'll meet you at the Palisades Post Office tomorrow morning at nine A.M. sharp. You simply must come up to Washington tonight. It's very important. We'll open the box together, and I want to be with you when you play the tape I think is in it."

"Well, Mr. Hartley, this is a very private thing. I don't think that I can agree to that."

"I'm afraid you don't have much choice."

"Why?"

"Because with what I know I should call Detective Jenkins right now. He could detain both you and your husband in Delaware and impound that package, without you ever seeing it. That package is evidence in a murder case. I've been kind of hoping I could resolve it without having to tell the police everything I know. But it's frankly getting pretty sticky. So either you go along with me or I go to the police. What do you say?"

"Well, I guess I haven't any choice."

"Good. I'll see you at the Palisades Post Office tomorrow morning just before it opens."

"I'll be there," she said rather curtly, and hung up.

I returned to the booth and told Alice that with luck I would be hearing the tape tomorrow, and if there was anything on it about Watergate I would probably have to take it to the FBI or the police.

"I'd give it to the police," Alice said.

"Why?"

"Because the FBI may be more interested in suppressing it than publicizing it."

"You mean if Tom was about to expose something incriminating in the Watergate business—"

"Or the oil business," Alice interrupted.

"What do you mean? I thought you were more inclined to think if Tom was killed because of government business it was about Watergate."

"Well, maybe there's a connection. I've been thinking since we talked yesterday, and you know there're billions of dollars in profits for the big oil companies because of the mandatory oil import quotas, and lots of that money is floating around town here. It's gone to the House, the Senate, the White House, and I wouldn't be surprised if some of that White House oil money was used in the Watergate cover-up."

"Well, that's one thing Tom said when he called me from Ocean City," I replied. "He mentioned the money trail. I guess you know Jack Harrigan."

"I sure do. And I bet more money is funneled through Jack Harrigan from the oil companies to politicians than any single man in town. He's counsel for several oil companies. But that's just a front. I'll bet it's been years since Harrigan has worked on a case. He's really a bag man for oil money."

"Yeah, I figured that," I said. "And I know Tom had managed to get a list of names of the people who had contributed the money to pay the legal fees and help support the families of the bunch that broke into Watergate. Why the hell they keep such lists in the White House is beyond me."

"The reason they keep them," said Alice, "is that these are the people who deserve special favors when it's all over, the ones who came through when the going got tough."

"And the tough got going, unquote, John Mitchell," I said knowingly. "The list has disappeared. And do you know who's on that list?"

"Harrigan, no doubt."

"And Arthur Turner."

"Who's he?" asked Alice.

"The husband of Beverly Turner."

"And who's she?" asked Alice, still puzzled.

"You don't know?"

She shook her head.

"She's the woman Tom has been having an affair with—although recently it's been more like a feud." There was a long silence that I did not break, giving Alice time to absorb this information.

"Well, this does get complicated," she finally said. "So just how did Tom Cranston, a professional Democrat who hated Richard Nixon as much as any man in this town—and that's saying a lot—get involved with the wife of a Republican fat cat?"

"It's worse than that. Beverly Turner worked for CREEP and thought she was going to end up in the Nixon White House after the election, although that's been put on hold."

"Just how did all that come about?"

"It's a long story, and I know you don't want to hear details about the affair. But Beverly was really apolitical when they met. She had known Bernadette Harrigan since college days and after she broke off the affair with Tom—"

"She did the breaking?" Alice intervened. I nodded my head.

"I figured that, although I'd rather it had been the other way around."

"I understand. But I'm afraid that's the way it was. And Tom did not accept it. During the affair the Turners and the Harrigans became closer—especially after the Turners moved from Towson to Kenwood—although Jack Harrigan and Arthur Turner obviously don't have much in common."

"What do you mean?" Alice interrupted again.

"You know Jack Harrigan—smooth, urbane, sophisticated? Well, Turner is just the opposite. A typical Baltimore builder—unsophisticated, more interested in the Colts and Orioles than Republicans and Democrats. I'm sure it was Harrigan who talked him into giving money to Nixon. Turner didn't give a damn about Nixon or McGovern, but Harrigan convinced him it was good business to back the winner. And of course when Harrigan started raising money for the Watergate cover-up, Nixon was already a winner, but they had to keep him in office. I doubt if Harrigan even told Turner what the money was for."

"Well, it looks like we're getting close to the killer," Alice said. "And in my book the number-one suspect is Arthur Turner. He had a double motive."

"Trouble is, Turner's got an alibi. He and Beverly had a fight the evening Tom was killed, and Turner spent the night with an old flame, recently rekindled, in Baltimore."

"What about Harrigan?"

"He's got an alibi too, although he was in New York and could have driven to Ocean City. But it's hard to imagine Harrigan involved in anything like this, and I don't know that oil companies go in for paid killers."

"It's been known to happen. Or, at least, it's been suspected; I'll tell you in a minute. What about his wife? Could Tom have had an affair with her too?"

"There's no evidence of it."

"How about that list? Maybe she knew about it and went after it. If it surfaced and Jack Harrigan was ruined, her little world would certainly come tumbling down."

"True. But she had an alibi. She was in town that night, baby-sitting the Turner children."

"Where were the Turners? Or Beverly Turner? We know about Arthur."

"She was in Rehoboth Beach."

"Oho! That sure puts her on the list," Alice said quickly.

"I'm not so sure."

"Why?"

"I don't know. I interviewed her this morning in Rehoboth and for some reason I think she's telling the truth. She flatly denies killing Tom, although she doesn't have much of an alibi. She spent the night in her house with the lights out—at Bernadette Harrigan's suggestion."

Alice showed obvious disbelief at that, but because of my pledge to Herson, I did not want to go into the reason Beverly did not turn the lights on in her house that night or explain that Herson had put out a contract on Cranston. I had a plan, and for it to work, Herson's contract had to remain a secret.

But I could tell Alice about Tom blackmailing Herson. "There is one more suspect."

"Who?"

"E. Richard Herson."

"In the White House?"

"Right."

"How does he get in the act?" Alice asked, her interest clearly intensifying.

"After Tom, Beverly had an affair with Herson. Tom photographed them in the Mayflower Hotel and was using the photograph to blackmail Herson into talking about Watergate."

"So that explains it," Alice said.

"How's that?"

"Well," Alice replied, "a few days before he went to the shore, Tom acted kind of strange, implying, as I told you, that he was working on something big. In fact, I had the distinct impression he was going to tell me all about it that weekend, if he invited me to the beach. Although he had these recurring depressions, he really seemed to be moving toward resolving something. It could have either been the affair with Beverly Turner or the Watergate mystery."

"Or both," I said.

"Or both. Also, Tom may have found out about Harrigan's relationship to an oil company man who was killed under suspicious circumstances—which I'll tell you about in a minute. So what does Herson say?"

"Well, he denies having anything to do with it, of course, and makes a pretty good case that with his bad eyes, he couldn't shoot an elephant, especially in the dark. He also says he came home late from the office that evening to a cocktail party at his house, which I'm going to check out."

"So where does that leave us?" Alice said.

"Damned if I know! Maybe I'll have a better idea after dinner tonight. I'm dining with the Harrigans here in Georgetown."

Suddenly it dawned on me that I was probably overdue, and

as I looked at my watch I asked Alice, "Can you think of anything I should ask Harrigan?"

"Ask him if he ever heard of Enrico Mattei."

"Who's he?" I asked, motioning the waiter for the check, and adding, "I've got to run. I'm late now for the Harrigans."

"He was an Italian oil minister, head of the state-run Italian oil company, ENI, in the early 1960s. He's important in the oil business because he was instrumental in having Italy sign precedent-setting oil contracts with Iran and Iraq that eventually led to the formation of OPEC. He also negotiated for Italy the first oil contracts with the Soviet Union, which the oil companies denounced and the Senate, no doubt at the instigation of the oil companies, investigated on the grounds that any oil deal with Russia threatened NATO."

"Was he a communist?"

"I'm not sure. But most people thought he was acting not out of deference to Russia but because the Anglo-Iranian oil company, a British member of the international cartel, had double-crossed him in a deal. Whatever his motives, the cartel and the Western governments decided he was a dangerous man. He was killed when his private plane crashed near Milan. Nothing was ever proven, but the Italian government said there were some mysteries about the crash."

"So what's that got to do with Harrigan?"

"When he was with the Federal Power Commission, Harrigan was part of a task force that investigated Mattei's death. The rumors were that he located a cartel connection with the Mattei plane crash and used that information to negotiate his lucrative and powerful role with the oil companies after he left the government."

"Interesting, but what does it prove?"

"I'm not sure that it proves anything—except that if Mattei was killed by an oil cartel plot, it at least suggests that oil companies are not above having people who threaten them killed. And Harrigan, like Turner, had a double motive. In his Senate job, Tom was trying to blow the whistle on the Nixon–big oil partnership; and if in his freelance Watergate investigation he had obtained a list of contributors who were financing the Watergate cover-up, that would have implicated the oil companies."

I was getting fidgety. Alice had just dropped a little bomb-shell on the case and I wanted desperately to hear more. At the same time, I was already late for the Harrigans and I didn't want anything to go wrong at that meeting. Obviously, for some reason, the Harrigans wanted to talk to me as much as I wanted to talk to them.

"Alice, I really gotta run. Look, I want to talk more about this. Tomorrow is going to be another busy day, but I'll try to call you before noon to see if we can set up a meeting. What are you going to do now?"

She seemed a little stunned and disorganized. "I don't know. I guess I'll just stay here, have another martini, and then dinner. You've told me quite a bit. I just have to think about things."

I knew what she meant, and as I prepared to leave, I took a fifty-dollar bill out of my wallet and squeezed it in her hand. "Look, I'm on expense account and if I wasn't going to dinner with the Harrigans, I'd be insisting that you have dinner with me—which I can assure you I'd rather be doing."

Alice started to protest, but I squeezed her hand, saying, "It's on the magazine. Enjoy it."

As I left, she said, "Don't forget Mattei." And with my back to her as I hurried out the door, I waved my hand to show that I had heard.

CHAPTER ELEVEN

Bernadette Harrigan answered the door herself, and she was simply stunning in a subdued gold-colored blouse with a low-cut neckline and black velvet slacks. Her auburn hair was pulled back in a little bun, just as it was the first time I met her at the Turners'. Still wearing the tweed sport coat and gray flannel slacks I had put on that morning in Rehoboth, I immediately felt grubby.

"Mr. Hartley! So good to see you again." She held out her hand.

I gave it a squeeze, and said, "Me too, and I hope you'll excuse my clothes."

"Don't worry about your clothes. You look just like a writer's supposed to look."

And turning toward the hall and speaking louder, she said, "Mary, will you fix Mr. Hartley a drink?" And then, back to me, she asked, "What'll you have?"

"A tall scotch and water."

"Glenlivet all right? That's Jack's favorite."

"It'll probably spoil me, but I'd love it."

After we had moved into the living room and Mary had served a scotch and water—which was tall, all right, and mostly Glenlivet—Bernadette said, "Jack'll be here any minute. He had to work late, but Robert, our chauffeur, left some time ago to pick him up—"

And before she could finish, there was a noise at the front door. "Oh, that must be Jack now."

Jack Harrigan, a tall man with white hair, a tanned, wrinkled face that looked like a cross between Clark Clifford's and Eric Sevareid's, and dressed in a navy blue, double-breasted blazer, light gray flannel slacks, striped shirt with a button-down collar and a dark, solid knit tie, slowly entered the room, which he dominated immediately and would have even if there were a dozen additional people in it, all as dazzling as Bernadette. In other words, the moment you saw Harrigan you knew you were in the presence of a man who could walk and talk with kings and sit down at the conference table with the toughest, most hard-nosed men in the business world, which you had to do if you moved in the corridors of big oil. And as Bernadette introduced me, he extended his hand and shook mine vigorously. "Certainly pleased to meet you, Hartley." Then he disarmed me completely by moving quickly, with a smile on his face, to his library just off the living room, and returning with my book.

"I know you well from your fine biography of George Creel, and I hope you will do me the honor of autographing your book."

Immediately sensing my discomfort at not being exactly dressed for a dinner in Georgetown, he handed me the book, and said: "I'll be right back, I just want to get into something more comfortable. I had a board meeting at lunch today and feel dreadfully overdressed. Bernie, will you have Mary bring the usual to my room?" And he was gone.

But as I was trying to think of something clever to write in my book, he yelled down the stairs: "Bernie, do you know where my tan corduroy jacket is, you know, the one with the patches in the elbow?"

"Oh, I forgot to tell you. I gave it to Goodwill."

"Well, you should have checked with me first," he said, and I heard a door slam.

A conventional inscription was the best I could think of. In a moment, Harrigan returned wearing a light gray tweed jacket. When I handed him the book, he opened it quickly, glanced at the inscription page, and said, "Fascinating man, Creel. This is a town full of government information officers, yet I wonder how many of them ever heard of George Creel, the man who established all their ground rules in the summer of 1917. It was almost like Edgar Allan Poe setting forth the basic structure of the detective story, which has lasted for one hundred years, in the space of three or four short stories."

"You're absolutely right, Mr. Harrigan—"

"Why don't you call me Jack."

"Fine. When Creel set up the Committee on Public Information that summer to arouse the public support Wilson needed to wage the war, he showed, as you say, how government propaganda could work."

"I find the World War I period a fascinating time in American history," Harrington replied, "when the country began losing its freedom—all under the Democratic administrations, of course."

"Not exactly," I replied. "Don't forget Teddy Roosevelt took quite a bit of freedom away from the big trusts, including Standard Oil."

But Mrs. Harrigan interceded very abruptly. "Gentlemen, this is no time to talk politics. I promised Mr. Hartley it would be an early evening, and Jack, you know you have to fly to Dallas in the morning. I'm afraid it's poor Tom Cranston we should be talking about—a terrible thing. Mr. Hartley, do the police know anything more we haven't heard in the press?"

"I don't think so. I haven't talked to Jenkins—the Delaware detective—since this morning. But I think one thing is definite: they've ruled out suicide."

"Oh?" said Jack Harrigan. "I thought that was still the most likely consideration. What do you think?"

"Suicide doesn't make sense. Tom had just been relieved of what could only be described as a death threat and, at the same time, he'd just received some information about the Watergate affair. We think he was coming up to Washington the next morning to go to the Ervin committee with what he had. Hardly a time to be thinking about shooting himself."

"Nixon? Watergate? What's that all about?" Harrigan asked, doing a good job of expressing surprise through his cracked, wrinkled features.

"I know you travel a lot, Mr. Harri—Jack, and I don't know how much Mrs. Harrigan has told you about everything that has come to light about this tragedy. Beverly Turner, your friend," I said, nodding at Mrs. Harrigan, "has been most helpful. It's a complicated tale and not a very pretty one, and I think Detective Jenkins will be wanting to talk to you soon."

"He's already made an appointment for tomorrow evening," Bernadette said, interrupting me. "In fact, Jack's flying back from Dallas early especially to see him."

"Jack, the police have checked into your stay at the hotel in New York and discovered a couple of interesting things. First, that although you made and received a lot of telephone calls, there was a long, blank time from late Wednesday after-noon—before the night Tom was killed—and Thursday morn-ing. You made no calls and took no calls, although there were incoming calls, including several from your phone here. And late that night, you received a call from a pay phone in Ocean City—a pay phone not too far from the Admiral Hotel where Tom was staying, Jenkins and I both figure that there was enough unaccounted-for time in New York for you to rent a car and drive to Ocean City and back. Any comments on that?"

Jack looked a bit stunned.

"In the first place, if someone was calling me from Ocean City, it would seem to suggest that I was not there."

"Why?"

"Well, they'd expect to contact me there, wouldn't they?"

"Not if they didn't know you were coming. Then there's the possibility that you might have called yourself just to make it look, as you suggest, like it would be unlikely that you were in Ocean City if someone was trying to call you from there."

"Maybe. But I can assure you, I was not in Ocean City that night, although I'm not sure I can prove it."

"Who do you think might have been calling you from Ocean City that night? Dad you have any business dealings with any-one down there?"

"Not that I can think of, although if you have checked my phone records, you know that I get calls from all over the world all the time. And place them. I have a lot of things going on."

"So who do you think might have called you?"

"I don't know."

This was leading nowhere, so I shifted ground. "You said it might be hard to prove where you were that night."

He paused, looked at his empty glass, then moved quickly to the bar in the next room saying to his wife, "Darling, isn't dinner about ready?" and then to me, "How 'bout another drink, Hartley?"

"No, thanks," I replied, then settled back in my chair,

When he was finally seated and Bernadette had left the room to check on dinner, he said, "Hartley, I don't mind telling you—and Mrs. Harrigan knows this—I have a weakness for X-rated movies. She doesn't care for them and we never watch them at home. But they're my principal form of entertainment and relaxation on the road. Nothing unusual, I guess, many businessmen do the same thing. And in New York, near Times Square, as you know, they have the best concentration of X-rated theaters in the country. Usually, when I'm in New York for any time, I try to block out at least one free evening for an X-rated. I go down to Seventh Avenue, have a Chinese dinner, and go to one of those theaters. It just happened that on that trip, which lasted most of a week, I picked Wednesday evening for my night out, so to speak. Unfortunate timing, as it developed. But that's the truth."

"Well, the box office teller at the theater might remember you. You cut an impressive figure. I doubt if many people who dress like you buy tickets from them."

"More than you'd think. And anyway, I dress a little more casually on these evenings, as you might imagine.

"Hartley, I'm enough of a lawyer to know that for a district attorney to indict me for the murder of Thomas Cranston in Ocean City, it's going to take a lot more than the fact that my whereabouts in New York the night of May second are not known. I don't care what Cranston knew about the money oil companies contributed to the Republican party. Oil companies do not kill to achieve their ends. They buy them, which is very easy."

"Have you ever heard of Enrico Mattei?" I asked slowly.

He seemed startled at the juxtaposition, which was what I had in mind. "Yes, I know that name. Why?"

"The rumors are that Mattei was killed by an oil cartel plot because he was responsible not only for the oil contracts between Italy and Iran and Iraq that paved the way for OPEC but also for negotiating Italian oil deals with Russia. The fact, as I understand it, is that you, as a lawyer with the FPC then, were on the team that investigated Mattei's death. And another rumor says that you did establish a link with the oil cartel."

Harrigan went into his mode of official displeasure. "I did work on that investigation for FPC. The rumors are false. Mattei was a communist. He was killed in an airplane crash. It was that simple."

"It is generally assumed around town that the knowledge you gained from that investigation led to your profitable and successful relationship with the oil companies."

"Nonsense!" And he stood up quickly, as Mrs. Harrigan came back in the room announcing cheerfully that dinner was finally ready.

The dinner was as beautiful as it was delicious. Filet mignon with bordelaise sauce, salad, wine (which I never drink, so I cannot cite the vintage), coffee, all with candlelight and a beautiful hostess. Not exactly the proper setting to be asking questions suggesting that the host, and maybe even the hostess, were involved in a murder. But that's the way it is in Washington sometimes. "Mrs. Harrigan," I said while we were passing the bordelaise, "there were a number of phone calls from this house last Wednesday evening to the Commodore Hotel where your husband was staying in New York. Did you ever reach your husband on the telephone that night?"

"Well, no, I didn't."

"I tried to call her a couple of times," Harrigan said, "but her line was busy. Then it got late."

"Any particular reason you were calling her?"

"No, just checking in."

"Any particular reason you were calling your husband, Mrs. Harrigan?"

"Not that I can remember. I guess I was also just calling to check in. Maybe to tell him how upset Beverly was and that she was going to the beach and I was minding her children. That sort of thing."

"Weren't you a little surprised or disappointed that you couldn't reach him?"

"Heavens, no. Jack is often out of his hotel on business for long stretches. And, yes, I know he likes to take in an X-rated movie now and then. That doesn't bother me."

She had overheard our conversation, as I suspected. "And you spent the evening here with the children?"

"That's right."

"Can you prove it?"

"Certainly. That is, Mary was here." Mary was pouring the wine and Bernadette looked to her for confirmation.

Mary said, "That's right, Mr. Hartley, she was here all evening."

"And of course you called Beverly Turner that night at Rehoboth, didn't you?"

She paused as if trying to recollect, and then said, "That's right."

"Well, the police will check that out," I said. "And anyway, I suppose Herson could testify you were here." I said to Mrs. Harrigan after Mary had returned to the kitchen, "Beverly Turner told me that Herson called you that evening looking for Beverly, and that you told him you knew what was going on and that he was getting in over his head. He apparently agreed, said the contract was canceled and, in fact, asked if you had one thousand dollars in cash he could borrow that he needed to take to Ocean City."

Jack Harrigan was frowning at this, and I said, "Mrs. Harrigan, I take it from your husband's face that at least at that time, he did not know what was going on between Herson, Cranston, and Beverly Turner. Is that right?"

"Yes. I was hoping none of it would ever come out. I did not want to hurt Beverly and I was sworn to secrecy."

"You told Herson."

"That's different. He was involved. He knew all about it."

"Why didn't you tell me Sunday?"

"Same reason. I hoped it would never come out. And I still do. I hope we're going to find who killed Tom without having all that ugly business about Herson come out."

"I'm afraid you're wrong," I said.

Harrigan was looking at me in agreement but his wife was shaking her head as I added, "But of course, if the root of the evil is money—from the oil cartel to the White House—then maybe the affair can be kept quiet."

"What do you mean?" she asked.

"It's beginning to look more and more as though the key to this whole complicated business is that list of people who contributed money to the Republican National Committee to help finance the Watergate burglars. The burglars were now unemployed, had some big legal bills, and were virtually disowned by everybody in the party and the government. It appears that the names of Jack Harrigan and Arthur Turner were on that list and by the evening of Tom's death quite a few people knew about it—including E. Richard Herson, the Harrigans, and the Turners."

Before either of them could reply I went on, looking at Harrigan, "Am I right in assuming that Arthur Turner was not very happy when he learned that some of his money had gone to finance Watergate, and furthermore, there was a list of contributors floating around that had his name on it?"

"He was upset about that, yes."

"It hurt our friendship," Mrs. Harrigan added. "We used to take long walks together on the canal, the four of us. It was sort of fun then, before everything went wrong. I just love the canal. Whenever I have a problem and need to get away to think I go out on the canal. There's this one spot near the river. I remember a couple of times, the four of us sat on the edge just looking down into the rushing water and talked about how peaceful it was. Such a grand place to get away and think."

For a moment I thought I detected tears in her eyes, which was probably not so. Bernadette Harrigan was not the crying type. Having more or less neglected our food, we all lapsed into silence, concentrating on our plates and collecting our thoughts. Soon Mary came in with more coffee and dessert, a light, fluffy chocolate thing I could not resist, although the hostess declined.

The mood at the table was strained. There was noticeable tension between Bernadette Harrigan and her husband, and I was not sure whether one was trying to hide something from the other, with each afraid the other might inadvertently say something that might be damaging. Jack Harrigan, obviously annoyed, brought up George Creel again, then pushed back his chair and said, "Shall we take our coffee to the living room?"

As we moved out of the dining room, Bernadette excused

herself and went to the kitchen to talk to Mary. In the living room, Harrigan offered me a Royal Jamaican Churchill. I had long ago given up cigars, but was steeled enough in my resolve to be able to accept an occasional Churchill. He started to say something about Creel, but I said, "Before we get off the subject, I'd like to get your thoughts on the list of names we've heard so much about. Just how damaging would it be to you— and to Arthur Turner—if that list surfaced?"

"First of all," Harrigan responded in his best boardroom manner, "we have no specific evidence that such a list exists— except in my mind—and maybe Tom's."

"Well, Herson says—" I interrupted.

"I know, I know. But still no one has seen a real list, although I did tell Arthur that some of his money went to pay Watergate bills. I didn't want him to be surprised if it ever came out." He paused, long enough for a lengthy draw on his cigar. "Second, would the fact that our names were on this hypothetical list hurt us? That depends."

"On what?"

"On what the list—if there is a list—says. If it's just a list of contributors to the Republican National Committee or Richard Nixon's 1972 campaign, that naturally would not hurt anyone. It's no secret that I—and Turner, for that matter—gave money to the Republican party. We are Republicans, after all."

"I'm not so sure about Turner."

"He's a businessman," Harrigan responded. "It was just good business."

"It wouldn't be such good business now, if a list linking you both to money associated with Watergate surfaces."

"Again, that depends." All the while I was watching for Bernadette. When she came out of the kitchen I said, "Mrs.

Harrigan, I'd like to ask Mary a few questions before she goes home. Do you mind?"

My question caught her off guard, but she said, "Not at all, I'll go with you. And she doesn't go home. She lives here."

She moved toward the kitchen, but I said, "No, I'd like a few minutes alone, if you don't mind." And I walked by her, not giving her a chance to object. When I was alone in the kitchen with the maid, I said, "Mary, Mrs. Harrigan said it would be all right if I asked you a couple of questions."

"That's all right, Mary," a voice behind me said. Bernadette was standing in the kitchen door giving Mary the green light, obviously wanting to convey the impression that she was cooperating and had nothing to hide. For a moment I thought she was going to come into the kitchen and join us, but she suddenly disappeared.

When I heard Bernadette talking with her husband in the living room, I said, "Mary, you said that last Wednesday—the night Mr. Cranston was killed—Mrs. Harrigan stayed with the children. Did she have any phone calls?"

"She had one, I remember. Maybe more. But I only remember one."

"When was that?"

"Before dinner."

"How much before dinner?"

"Quite a bit. Probably late afternoon."

"Do you know who it was from?"

"No. She answered the phone."

"And you don't remember any more phone calls?"

"No."

"You say Mrs. Harrigan was here all evening. How do you know that? Did you see her or talk with her that night?"

"Well, not after dinner, I guess. When the dishes are done I usually take over the children and Mrs. Harrigan goes about her business—sometimes goes out."

"Did she go out that night, even for a short time?"

"Not that I know of. Whenever she goes out—especially when the children are here—she usually tells me where she's going, when she'll be back, and sometimes leaves me a phone number where she can be reached."

"But she didn't that night?"

"No. She went right to her room and stayed there all evening. Once, when I passed her bedroom on the way to the children's room, I could see the light on under her door. It's not unusual for her to spend the night in her room. It's more than a bedroom, you know. It has a large sitting room connected to it and a bathroom on the other side. She works in her room a lot and reads. Sometimes falls asleep reading."

"So you never actually saw her after dinner?"

"That's right."

"And you don't know whether she used the phone?"

"No."

"How about you? Mr. Harrigan said he tried to call home a couple of times that night and the line was busy. Could that have been you?"

"Not on his line. I have my own phone in my room, and I'm not allowed to use their line, especially when Mr. Harrigan's traveling."

"How about their relationship lately? Does there seem to be any special tension between them? Have they had any arguments?"

"No more than usual."

I looked at my watch and was startled to see how late it was. Tomorrow was going to be another busy day—for all of us— although I did not realize then just how busy.

"Thank you Mary, you've been very helpful. I suspect Detective Jenkins of the Delaware police will be wanting to ask you pretty much the same thing. You know he's coming up tomorrow to talk to Mr. and Mrs. Harrigan?"

"Yeah, I heard. Does that mean he thinks they did something wrong?"

"No. It's just routine police work. But they do think Mr. Cranston might have been murdered."

"Oh? Mrs. Harrigan said she thought Mr. Cranston must have killed himself. That's what she told me the next day. We were all so upset that morning."

"So Mrs. Harrigan seemed shocked by the news?"

"She sure did. Mr. Harrigan was in New York and she talked to him a couple of times and she seemed very upset— almost like Mr. Cranston was a close friend. But I didn't know they were very close. I know I never seen him around here."

"Well, he was once a close friend of Mrs. Turner's. I guess that explains it," I said.

"Maybe so," Mary said as I left the kitchen.

"You're very thorough," Jack Harrigan said as I returned to the living room.

"Yes."

"I assume you've been talking to Mary about my wife's whereabouts last Wednesday night. And I hope you are a good enough reporter to investigate where Arthur Turner was that night?"

"Then you think there was something to this list business? That maybe Turner would have killed to suppress it?"

"Or maybe killed the man who was having an affair with his wife," Harrigan suggested.

"I understand that Turner had gone back to his old girl-friend," I replied. "And, as I told you, Mrs. Harrigan, he spent the night with her in Baltimore. They went out to the ball game and I talked with him about that game. He knows quite a bit about what went on at Memorial Stadium that night, although he probably could have learned it reading the *Sun* and *Post* accounts. And Betty Sawyer, the girlfriend, confirms that they went to the game and that Turner spent the night with her."

"Just how much of all this," Harrigan asked, "is going to be in your profile? I hope you're not going to be writing about this mysterious list—at least, not until it actually materializes."

"I hope you don't have to get into Beverly's messy affairs with Tom or Herson," Bernadette added. "It would be hard on the children, you know."

It would be at that, I thought. People always think of the children—when it's too late. But all I said was, "I'll have to decide that later, when we all know more."

I did not tell them about meeting Beverly Turner the next morning at the Palisades Post Office, expecting to find a tape from Tom that could shed a whole new light on the case. I figured Bernadette, at least, already knew about it. "Have you talked to Beverly Turner this evening?" I asked her.

"Not yet. I told her I'd call her tonight, after you'd left. She naturally wants to hear all about our dinner."

"Naturally," I said. I knew damned well she already knew about my meeting Beverly in the morning, but I still preferred not to mention it. But as we were walking to the door, I said, "See you in the morning, Mrs. Harrigan, I'm sure."

I walked down the steps quickly, giving them no chance to respond. But they did have something to talk about after I was gone.

The first thing I did when I got home was to call Betty Sawyer. It was pretty late, but I was anxious to ask her about the blonde running out on the field that night at Memorial Stadium. I figured that Turner had talked with her about that by now. I let the phone ring several minutes, but there was no answer.

Then I called Doreen at the beach and told her about the evening's developments. When I said that Jack Harrigan was surprised and irritated when he learned that his wife had given his tan sport coat to Goodwill, Dory said, "That's it! Bernadette Harrigan did it, just as I've always thought."

"But you thought her husband was involved, too. And he wouldn't have brought up the coat in front of me if he thought it might be evidence."

"Maybe," Dory replied quickly, "they are working together to give each other alibis, with this maneuver designed to help establish Jack's innocence because, of the two Harrigans, he's probably the most likely suspect. At the same time, mentioning the coat then could have been a way of letting you know in a natural, unsuspicious manner that they had gotten rid of it."

"Yeah," I said just as quickly, "but the police could easily trace it through Goodwill—maybe establishing the fact that they never gave it to Goodwill at all; that they got rid of it some other way, which would arouse suspicion that it had something incriminating on it, like powder burns or blood. If we're going to talk about clothes the murderer was possibly wearing, let's not forget Arthur Turner's missing hat, which the person Tom left the Admiral with that night was also wearing."

Dory was quiet for a minute, then said, "I'll still take the Harrigans—one or both of them—over Arthur, although I do think he is capable of murder if he thought he could get away with it."

"Well, we can sleep on it. It's getting late and I'm meeting Beverly Turner at the Palisades Post Office at nine o'clock sharp in the morning."

CHAPTER TWELVE

Wednesday morning, May 9

The alarm startled me out of my deep sleep. Still dead tired from the long day yesterday, I had an unusually hard time getting started. There was no time for a workout. I was in the car and ready to leave when I remembered my tape recorder.

I got to the Palisades Post Office a few minutes before nine and was not too surprised to see Bernadette's yellow Mercedes parked in front of the little building. She was standing in the doorway of the post office, as sexy as ever in a black turtleneck sweater under a tan trench coat. It had rained during the night and was a little raw for May. After I parked my station wagon and joined her at the door, I asked: "Where's Beverly Turner?"

"She called this morning, told me where the key to the post office box was, and asked me to come by and pick up her mail.

I'll be taking it out to the house after an errand I have to do. She and Arthur were late getting away from Rehoboth this morning and she wanted me to be here to meet you."

"That makes some sense," I said. "But I'll take the package from Tom—if there is one."

"Why's that?" she responded with just an edge in her voice. "I'm perfectly capable of delivering it to Beverly. In fact she specifically asked me to. If it's a tape, I'm sure she wants to play it first, alone."

"I don't doubt that. But I'll tell you the same thing I told Beverly: I open the box, or I call the police now, from that phone in front of the post office. As soon as we establish the fact that there is a package, it doesn't go out of my sight until it is opened and—if it's a tape—until we play it."

Obviously angry, she pressed a key in my hand. "It's box five-thirty-one," she said, and started walking quickly to her car. The big yellow Mercedes gunned away from the curb almost before the door slammed. She was angry, but I was sure I would see her at the Turners' house in a few minutes.

I opened box 531 and there it was—jammed in with all the junk mail. A little package, about the size of a tape cartridge, covered with stamps and postmarked Ocean City, Maryland, May 2, 1973.

When I arrived at the Turner's the only car in the parking area was the maid's Pinto. As I drove up the driveway the two Turner children were standing near the side door. I could not remember their names but I called them over to my car and said I was a friend of their mother and father and that I had met them at their pool the other day. They wanted to know when their mommy and daddy would be home, and I said, "Any minute now. I have an appointment with them at a little past nine o'clock."

Then I decided this was an excellent opportunity to ask them something. "Do you remember last Tuesday, when you spent the night at Mrs. Harrigan's house in Georgetown?"

They both giggled and said that they remembered, and I continued, "Well, I was just wondering if you remember seeing Mrs. Harrigan after dinner that night. I mean, did you go to her room or did she come to your room, or did you only see Mary, the maid?"

They both seemed puzzled at why I might be asking them such a question and the boy—the youngest—showed no recollection one way or the other. But the little girl said, "I remember that night. I don't think we saw Mrs. Harrigan after dinner.

"So you don't remember seeing her after dinner at all?"

She shook her head and just then I could hear a car coming up the driveway. I turned to see the blue Cadillac approaching the house. Before it was even parked, Bernadette's yellow Mercedes came speeding up and parked next to the Turners'. As Beverly Turner stepped out of her car I approached her, holding out the little package.

"It's just the size of a cassette, and I have a tape recorder. Let's play it," I said.

She took the tape and walked quickly to the house with me on her heels. As we went into the Turner living room Beverly made arrangements for the maid to keep the children busy. While Beverly was busy with the children, I readied the tape recorder, always keeping the package in sight. When the children were gone, Beverly opened the package, and to no one's surprise, it contained the cassette. She stared at it and for one brief uncomfortable moment I thought she or Bernadette might make a move to destroy the tape.

Beverly's last message from her former lover would naturally be difficult for her to share with others, especially her husband. "Mr. Hartley," she all but pleaded, "I think you understand why I would prefer to hear this alone. It's my property, of course. The package was addressed to me. I promise to tell you anything that might lead us to Tom's killer—"

"Or," I intervened, "anything that pertains to the Watergate affair, which is what we assume Tom was working on."

But before I could grant or deny her request—and I really had no intention of letting her disappear with that tape—Arthur Turner entered the room. He said, "Hartley, play that tape now! I don't especially want to hear about my wife's love affair, but we're all involved in a murder and maybe there's something on that tape concerning a national scandal. If we don't play that tape now, I'll be the one who goes to Jenkins."

This was a curious twist. I wondered how Turner could be sure Tom would not say something that might incriminate him. And if there was damaging evidence on the tape, Turner's best chance of suppressing it would be to let his wife play it alone first, and then maybe decide herself to destroy it rather than permit the exposure of information that might ruin the father of her children and disgrace the family name. Turner was either innocent, as I speculated, or knew that Tom could not possibly implicate him. Beverly said, "All right, go ahead and play it, Mr. Hartley."

I put the cassette in the recorder and recognized Tom's voice immediately.

> "Greetings, Beverly. This is just a little surprise package to explain why I didn't call you this afternoon and also bring to an end to this charade we've been playing. I know I could call you on the telephone sometime to explain it all and no doubt your friend Herson will have talked to you by the time you receive this tape. But I've decided I don't want to talk to you again, so I'm ending our relationship this way."

Beverly sighed slightly, and Bernadette, who was sitting next to her on the couch, put her arm around her for comfort. Arthur, standing by the bar, took a long swallow from a drink he had prepared for the ordeal.

"First, about this afternoon, I didn't call at five o'clock as I said I would, because I was being followed by Herson's hit man—and I guess by now you know I wasn't kidding. To keep him away from me, I got involved in a game of volleyball on the beach with a bunch of young guys who work in construction down here. I figured this was a good way to keep the man at bay at least until dark. I could see him sitting up on the boardwalk watching me, but then, around quarter of six, he disappeared. I never saw him again. I knew it was too late to call you. I'm in Ocean City now, but will be leaving here soon, I guess.

"By the time you have this tape, Herson will no doubt have called and told you about our meeting down here and the contract being canceled. That was a strange deal, and believe me, you're in with some bad people. Herson said the president had nothing to do with going after me, that it was a personal matter—the photograph. And maybe I don't blame him. I was playing kinda rough. But we both figured we were playing for big stakes. He feels as strong about keeping Nixon in office as I feel about getting him out. But he also says maybe he went too far. I told him he was lucky not to have a murder rap on his neck—that his man probably would have been successful if I wasn't full of the bravado and dumb luck that goes with not really caring whether you live or die. A lot of heroes are made that way. Anyway,

we had a drink in the bar of the hotel where I'm staying
and he convinced me the contract was off. He said if we
went up to my room, he'd give me the list and tell me
all he knew about the president and Watergate—if I'd
burn the photo, the negative, and the tape.

"I agreed, so we went up to my room. I showed him
the negatives, the photo, and the tape, and we burned
them. And he told me the Watergate story. When Herson
left, I tried to call my contact on the Ervin committee,
but I couldn't reach him. I'll be driving up in the morning to tell them everything Herson told me. And I have
the list he gave me.

"I think you oughta know—briefly at least—just what
happened. Maybe it'll cure you of your infatuation with
that jerk in the White House and keep you from getting
involved anymore with guys like Herson.

"There has been, as most of us suspected, a cover-up
on Watergate going on in the White House—and for
good reason. Herson says that Howard Hunt's chief
contact in the White House was Chuck Colson and that
Colson was directing Hunt, no doubt acting with
Nixon's understanding, if not downright urging. It
seems Nixon was obsessed with trying to get something
on Larry O'Brien. No need to go into details, but
O'Brien has been on Howard Hughes's payroll, and the
president figured there had to be some kinda hanky-
panky between O'Brien and Hughes. He wanted to find
out what was going on and told Colson to do everything
possible to find out. At least that's what Herson says.
This led to putting taps on O'Brien's phone and another
guy at the DNC—Spencer Oliver.

"This was actually the second break-in. About three
weeks before the break-in when they were caught, they

had successfully broken in to the DNC offices, planted wiretaps on O'Brien's and Oliver's phones and photographed several documents. When they were caught, they were in the act of going back to check out Oliver's phone tap, which had not been working, and photograph some more documents.

"There was also some mysterious business about one hundred thousand dollars which Howard Hughes had apparently given Nixon's pal, Bebe Rebozo, to hold for Nixon. The White House, at least in Herson's opinion, also wanted to find out just how much, if anything, O'Brien knew about this deal.

"Since the break-in there has been a real cover-up. Some of the guys in the White House are no doubt guilty of destroying evidence and withholding information, which is a criminal offense. Plenty of people are involved, in the White House, the Justice Department, and the campaign staff—John Dean, John Ehrlichman, Bob Haldeman, Chuck Colson, John Mitchell, Jeb Magruder, Howard Hunt, G. Gordon Liddy, Egil Krogh, Robert Mardian. You wouldn't believe how many people are up to their neck in trouble. Herson says he managed to keep out of it, primarily because of what he's working on, the "Nixon Revolution," a plan to take over the bureaucracy.

"Well, that's what Herson told me—which is plenty. The whole business is over with Herson. I walked down to the corner with him and he left.

"Now—about us . . ."

I turned off the tape player for a moment to take some notes for my article. I was still worried that something might happen to this tape. I worked as fast as I could because I knew everyone in the room was tense. And I didn't trust any of them. When I finished my hastily scribbled notes I pushed the play button again.

> "After you broke off our affair, I admit I didn't act much like a man who was in love, and the truth is, I was a bum. I wasn't really sane. But now you're completely free and will never hear from me again. Everything is over. For some time, I have been very friendly with a woman in my office—her name is Alice—and lately I have managed to come to my senses and realize just how much I like her. In fact, I plan to ask her to marry me this weekend. And as soon as I make sure Nixon is on his way out of the White House, if Alice will go, I'll go back to Los Angeles and get a job on the *Tribune* writing editorials. It'll be a few steps down from that job they offered me after the election of '68, but that doesn't matter. If Alice does not want to leave Washington, I'll stay here with her—if she'll marry me.
>
> "Anyway, I just want you to know how much I loved you once and maybe still do, even knowing, as I do now, about your little affair with Bernadette."

With that remark, Beverly Turner abruptly drew away from Bernadette and awkwardly slid to the far side of the couch, obviously embarrassed. Arthur drained his glass and glowered at the two women.

> "Which brings me to the really funny thing that happened this evening. Right after Herson left and while I was standing on the corner outside, who should come along but your good friend, Bernadette! And I must say, she's really something. She was dressed up like a man

and looked great. If I was a girl, I'd have swooned right there on the street. I almost did anyway. My God, she is good-looking—even better-looking now than when I used to see her at the beach with you and Arthur.

"She said Jack was in New York and that she'd come to Ocean City to look over the new high-rise condominiums they're building north of here. She and Jack are thinking of buying one. She says she often dresses like a man when she's out alone at night, that she feels safer that way. Maybe she also tries to pick up girls, but I guess you'd know more about that than I do. I asked her to have a drink and she said she'd rather not go into the bar, but she'd go up to my room for one.

"We went up to my room for a drink and frankly I'm beginning to feel 'em—as maybe you can tell from the way I'm talking. She told me about your little affair— why, I'm not sure. But she insisted that she was the aggressor, that she was in love with you, but that you were really not responsive. In fact, she says she thinks you might still be in love with me, which naturally brought a big laugh from me.

"I didn't tell Bernadette about the Herson business, but I did tell her that I thought somebody was following me and I showed her the thirty-two revolver I bought for protection. And just to make her more uncomfortable, I handed her the gun, and said, 'Here, you keep it.' She took the gun, kissed me, and said I could use some sobering up, and what we needed was a long walk on the beach. That was a little while ago.

"So I'm about to go off for a walk on the beach with your lover, and that's some kind of an appointment, at least in Delaware if not exactly in Samara. Or is it? Anyway, Bernadette must have taken the gun with her, so there's no chance of my shooting anyone accidentally or otherwise. She's gone now and I'm supposed to meet her downstairs on the corner in about half an hour. She said she had to make some telephone calls.

"I'll mail this in the lobby downstairs on the way out and I guess this'll be the last time I'll be talking to you. Have fun with Herson and Bernadette. I'm gone."

I reached down and pressed the stop button on the little tape player. I looked at Arthur Turner, who was pouring another drink. He did not look happy. Beverly stood up abruptly and left the room in tears. When she returned, the silence in the room was still deafening until she broke the tension. Staring at the tape, avoiding meeting anyone's eyes, Beverly tried to explain, to Arthur, with obvious embarrassment, what had happened between her and Bernadette:

"That night when Tom was killed," she said, not looking at Bernadette, "Bernadette came over to the house when I was getting ready to go to the shore and you wanted to go with me. I did submit to her advances; in fact, they were almost welcome. I was distraught—worried about Tom, concerned about what you would do, and furious at Richard. I probably responded a little too much—enough, perhaps, to let you think we might become lovers, Bernadette. I didn't really have that in mind. But I can assure you, I was emotionally muddled that night."

Then, after a pause, Beverly looked at Bernadette, and said, "But I think you're the one who has some explaining to do. It would seem you were the last one to see Tom alive; you went out on the beach with him—and *you had the gun!*"

Bernadette had a cigarette in her hand and was fumbling in her pocketbook, apparently looking for a match. But as I reached for the tape recorder, she said, "I'll take that," and drew a small black automatic pistol from her pocketbook and pointed it at me.

Everyone in the room froze in disbelief. Keeping the pistol pointed as us, she looked at Beverly, and said, "Beverly, I have been in love with you for years, as I told you that evening. And, yes, I did go to Ocean City that night for a couple of reasons. But most important was that list of Republican contributors who gave money to the party that was used to support the families of the Watergate burglars. Jack was convinced that Tom had the list and that his and Arthur Turner's names were on it. But I assure you I did not kill Tom, although I had that in the back of my mind when I went to Ocean City. But I left him on the beach, with the gun, after I managed to get that list from him without a struggle. He didn't seem to care that much about it. And don't worry, Arthur," she said, looking at Beverly's husband, "I have destroyed it, which is my only crime—destroying evidence. Although I am about to commit another one—with this tape."

Suddenly Bernadette dropped the unlit cigarette, pressed the eject button, took the tape out of the cassette player, and put it in her pocket. As she moved toward the door, she kept the gun pointed at us. "All right, friends. Now I have this, shall we say, historic, tape. And what would you suggest I do with it? If this tape is ever used to help break open the Watergate affair, Tom, Beverly and Arthur, and Bernadette will go down in history associated with murder and the political crisis of 1973."

She hesitated for a moment, seeming uncertain what to do next. Then she said, "Frankly, I can't honestly say what happened to Tom, although I have an idea. There was someone else on the beach that night standing not too far from us. And I think I know now who it was, although I couldn't be sure at the time. It was very dark. I just wanted to get off that beach, and home as soon as possible. I tried to get Tom to come with me, but he just said, 'No, I want to stay here and think awhile. It's not that long a walk back to the hotel.' And he turned away and started walking toward the ocean. So I just threw the gun down, yelling, 'Here's your gun, Tom. Be careful with it.' And then I ran toward the car. I'm pretty sure Tom did not shoot himself—unless it was an accident. He was drunk all right. But *not* suicidal. He was too excited about going to the Ervin committee the next day."

Suddenly, Bernadette walked quickly toward the door, still holding the gun on us. She had the tape in her pocket. When I heard the side door slam as she left the house, I made a move to go after her but Arthur Turner virtually tackled me, temporarily knocking the wind out of me. "Let her go, you fool," he shouted. "She's still got that little gun! Someone could get hurt. I don't want a scene with the children. The worst she can do is destroy that tape. But we have three witnesses who heard Bernadette Harrigan confirm that she left the Admiral with Tom. All we have to do is call Jenkins and he'll swear out a warrant for her arrest."

"You don't believe her?" I said.

"Hell, no. Do you? That story was quick thinking on her part, after she heard Cranston implicate her."

Bernadette had lied to me all along to keep everyone from knowing that she was the one who left the hotel with Tom. But she could have gotten that list away from Tom without having to shoot him. That was her main objective. And I knew she was a bright woman—bright enough to realize that that phone call from Ocean City to Beverly could trip her up. But now she was saying someone else was on the beach with them. I really had to tell Jenkins about that, and that the tape Tom sent Beverly revealed that it was Bernadette who had left the hotel with Tom.

Arthur went to the phone and called Jenkins in Rehoboth.

His assistant said he was en route to Washington for his meeting with the Harrigans and to follow up some other leads.

Almost immediately after Arthur hung up, the phone rang. Mrs. Turner, being the closest, picked it up. Then after listening to the caller, she handed the phone to her husband. "It's for you, Arthur, a woman from the Hertz Rent-A-Car Company."

Turner took the phone, and said "This is Arthur Turner. What can I do for you?" There was a long silence while the woman from Hertz explained what she was calling about. Then Turner said, "I'll call you when I get to the office and can find my file. Is that okay?"

It seemed to take care of the problem, and he hung up.

"When did you rent a car, Arthur?" Beverly asked.

"It was office business. The office must have told them I was still home."

Beverly Turner started to say something, but the phone rang again and Arthur Turner picked it up. Holding his hand over the mouthpiece of the phone, he said, "It's the office, excuse me." He listened a few minutes, scowled, and said, "All right, I'll be right over."

He hung up the phone, and after glaring angrily at his wife for a moment, he said, "I have a minor crisis at the office. I've got to go. I assume when Jenkins calls you'll tell him about Bernadette."

As he started out the door with Beverly following him, presumably to have a few words in private with her husband, I said loud enough so he could hear me going down the hall, "I certainly plan to tell Jenkins about Tom's tape. Bernadette is going to have a tough time convincing the district attorney that she went out on the beach with Tom but did not kill him." By now they had gone out onto the driveway. I was standing at the window watching the Turners in a heated discussion as they walked toward their Cadillac, when I suddenly thought of something. But first, I had to call Alice Burton.

I dialed her office, hoping I could catch her before she went to lunch. She answered the phone. "Alice, I promised to call you this morning. Have you got a minute?"

She said yes.

"I haven't got much time, but I just wanted you to know I hadn't forgotten you. We played the tape; there was dynamite stuff on there about Watergate. Tom did sign off with Beverly, and incidentally, he said he planned to ask you to marry him this weekend."

I gave her a moment, and then continued. "But the most fascinating item on the tape was that the tall, slightly effeminate man wearing the Greek fisherman's hat that Tom left the Admiral with was Bernadette Harrigan—in drag, you might say. They ended up on the beach, where Bernadette managed to get Tom to give her a list of names incriminating, or at least embarrassing, Jack Harrigan and Arthur Turner, but insists that she did not kill him."

"So what did happen?"

"I'm not sure yet, but Mrs. Harrigan has a lot of explaining to do. For now, don't say anything about this to anyone. I've got to move fast, but I'll call you later. Jenkins is on his way to Washington and this whole thing may be over by tonight."

I hung up and dialed Betty Sawyer's number in Baltimore. A recorded message said she was at work and gave her office number, which I dialed next, hoping she'd not gone to lunch. She had not.

"Miss Sawyer," I said when I finally reached her and introduced myself, "Arthur Turner may have mentioned me. I am writing a magazine profile about my friend Thomas Cranston, who was killed last week."

"I thought it was suicide," Miss Sawyer responded. "That's what Arthur says."

"Well, the police aren't sure yet. But there is evidence to suggest murder. That's why it's routine, but important, that we know where everyone was that night. Arthur Turner says you and he went to the Orioles game that night. We got to talking about that the other day, and he couldn't remember an incident that occurred that evening. He said it might have happened between innings when he went to the men's room and got some more beer. So he suggested I call you to see if you might have remembered it."

"What was that?" she said.

"It was a woman running on the field. Do you remember?"

"Oh, yes, Arthur told me you wanted to know if I remembered seeing her while he was gone. No, I don't remember seeing anyone like that running onto the field at all. And I don't know how we missed her, because we were never out of our seats at the same time."

"Well, thank you, Miss Sawyer. My friend must have been mistaken." When she hung up, I began looking through the yellow pages. The phone rang. The Turners were still talking heatedly at their car, so I picked up the phone. It was Jenkins.

"Am I glad to hear your voice," I said. "Look, we haven't got much time. You know that package we've been trying to trace in the mail? Well, it was sent to Beverly Turner. It's a tape, and we played it this morning. It was, in effect, a good-bye note to Beverly Turner. Tom also said he was going to meet Bernadette Harrigan on the beach that night."

"Well, that figures," Jenkins interrupted.

"What do you mean?"

"We checked out that phone call from Mrs. Harrigan to Mrs. Turner at Rehoboth that night, and no call was placed from her house in Washington. But Mrs. Turner did get one call—the only call—from a pay phone in Ocean City. The same pay phone that placed a call to the hotel where Mrs. Harrigan's husband was staying that night. She must have been in Ocean City."

"She was. She managed to get a list of names from Cranston."

"So why did she go to all that trouble to get a list?"

I lied when I replied, "I'm not sure. It was some sort of list of names of people who had contributed to the 1972 Nixon presidential campaign. But those names are not secret. Mrs. Harrigan seemed terribly confused trying to explain. And she says she saw someone else near them on the beach. She thinks she knows who it was. She left Tom there alive with his gun on the beach."

"You're kidding!" Jenkins said.

"After we played the tape, she pulled out a gun, grabbed the tape, and left!"

"I guess my appointment with the Harrigans is canceled," Jenkins said. "She seems to be admitting her guilt."

I agreed and added: "There was also some personal stuff on the tape, which I imagine she would just as soon not have appear in the press. Look, there's something else. I need some police help. Could you have a Maryland detective meet me in a little while at the Hertz Rental Car agency in Bethesda? I need to check really fast on who rented a car, and when, and what kind. But I can't do it without police credentials. Can you go over there?"

"Not soon. I'm at a gas station off the Beltway near I-Ninety-five. I'll send over a man."

"Good. I'll explain it all to you this afternoon. We'll meet at the Harrigans' in Georgetown. I'm betting Jack Harrigan—and maybe both—will keep your appointment this afternoon."

"I'll swear out that warrant as soon as we hang up."

"Good," I said. "I'm going directly to the Hertz place. If there's any problem with getting a detective over there to help me, leave a message at Hertz." I gave him the number and he hung up.

I hung up the phone and stood there looking at Beverly Turner walking slowly toward the house. Arthur was gone. The phone rang again, and I looked at my watch; it was exactly noon. It was Bernadette Harrigan calling.

CHAPTER THIRTEEN

Wednesday afternoon, May 9

I was hoping you'd still be there," Bernadette said. "Do you believe what I said?"

"Bernadette, even if you are telling the truth—which you are going to have a hard time proving—you are still in a jam. That tape is evidence in a murder case; it implicates you, and you stole it from its rightful owner—at gunpoint. I've already told Detective Jenkins about it. My advice to you is to keep your appointment with Jenkins this afternoon. There are three other witnesses who heard what Tom said about meeting you that night, so there's nothing you can do about that."

There was more silence before she said, "All right. I'll keep the appointment with Jenkins. But Ray, I want to talk to you first to explain what happened that night on the beach. I did a foolish thing grabbing the tape and leaving. I know it makes me look guilty. But I did not kill Tom. Can you meet me now?"

"Where are you?"

"At the entrance to Great Falls on the Maryland side— where the C and O Canal runs close to the Potomac River. Do you know where that is?"

"Yes. I'll come on one condition."

"What's that?"

"Remember, you are now the prime suspect in this murder case, and you have a gun but I don't. I'm bringing Beverly with me—"

"Good," she interrupted.

"You be standing at the rear of the parking lot and as we approach you, I want you to put the gun down somewhere I can see it and make sure you don't have it. Got that?"

"I understand."

"Okay. We'll see you there in ten or fifteen minutes."

When I hung up, Beverly, who had returned to the house, said, "I'll be with you in a moment," and left the room. Which gave me a chance to call Hertz. I had decided not to tell her what I was looking for unless I found it. When I got the Hertz agency on the phone, I told them, "A Maryland State detective should be coming to your office soon looking for me. Tell him I called and will be a few minutes late, and ask him to wait, that it's urgent. Got that? I'll explain later."

When I hung up, Beverly was back and I started moving her toward the door. "Come on, we're going to talk to Bernadette."

"Where is she?"

"Great Falls. She wants to talk to me about that night on the beach. When I said I was bringing you she said 'Good.'"

The phone rang just as we were leaving and Beverly answered it. She was silent for a moment as she listened to whoever called and then I heard her say: "We're going out to

Great Falls to meet her now." She was silent and then she said to me: "It's Arthur. He wants to know what's happening; have you talked to Jenkins yet about Bernadette?"

"Tell him 'Yes'" I replied. "And he is going to swear out a warrant for her arrest."

She repeated that to her husband, then hung up.

We took my car and as we drove toward Great Falls, Beverly became more and more distressed. When we arrived at the entrance to Great Falls we could see Bernadette seated at a picnic table back in the trees. As we slowly approached her, I could see the little automatic sitting on the table, out of her reach. Her purse was sitting next to it. When we arrived at the table, I put the gun in my pocket using a hankerchief, and then quickly looked in the purse, hoping to find the tape. It was not there.

"I told you I hid the cassette," she said.

I did not have time to pursue its whereabouts, and as Beverly and I sat down on the bench, I said, "Bernadette, I'm very anxious to hear what you have to say, but it has to be quick."

"All right," she said. "The first thing I want to say—again—is that I did not kill Tom! In fact, as I drove back, I began feeling very bad about leaving him alone on the beach with that gun. He was definitely not suicidal then—in fact, he was very excited about going to the Ervin committee the next morning. But he was being very careless with that gun. And then, as I was driving back, I remembered seeing in the Fenwick Towers parking lot that another car had joined the two there when we arrived—a nondescript white car—maybe a two-door coupe, something like that. The police can check to see if anyone in that building owns a white two-door."

"Good idea," I said. "I'll tell Detective Jenkins."

"Anyway, when I reached home I was in a panic and had to take two sleeping pills to go to sleep. But I lay in bed and recalled my last moments with Tom after deciding I could not kill him. I still had the gun and I had pointed it at him demanding that he give me the list that would otherwise ruin us.

" 'Hell, I don't care if you have it,' he said. 'It's no big deal, anyway. If the list went public it would damage the reputation of the people on it, maybe even ruin their careers, but I don't think they'd go to jail because I don't think they knew what their contributions were being used for. I only scanned the list, but Arthur Turner and your husband's names were definitely on it.'

"Then, as he handed me the list, he said, 'I got what I need and I'm going to the Ervin committee tomorrow with the whole business I got from Herson—the story of the cover-up, Dean, Ehrlichman, Haldeman, Mitchell. Even the president. They're all going to jail!'

"I tossed the gun on the sand and walked away. But I turned around for a moment and saw Tom silhouetted there against the distant lights of Rehoboth. He was waving his hands at the ocean and shouting, 'They're all going to jail! Hyyyaaa!'

"The next morning, when I heard Tom was dead, I was sick. I felt it was my fault for leaving him alone with that gun. I also knew that damned phone call from Ocean City to Beverly would come back to haunt me. Or rather, the phone call I did *not* make from Washington. I figure you were onto that, Mr. Hartley."

"Not me, the police. But what about that other person you said you saw on the beach?"

Bernadette paused for a moment, then looked directly at Beverly and said, "I can't be sure but I think it was Arthur. He came along right after I had gotten the list from Tom. I'm sure he didn't know Tom had given it to me."

Beverly seemed stunned. "So what made you think it was Arthur Turner?" I asked.

"I couldn't see his face clearly and he definitely wasn't wearing a hat. But his general size and shape looked like Arthur's. And he was wearing a track suit, although it was too dark to really be sure of the color. I know Arthur's is brown, but it could have been blue. I know I could never positively identify him—or anyone else—if I had to testify in court."

"You're right about that," I said. "The track suit is not enough. I have one myself—a blue one."

"And," Beverly added, "mine is a mate to Arthur's."

"Well, be sure to tell that to Jenkins," I said. "Look, I have to go to Bethesda now. Can you two wait here for me? I'll be back in less than an hour."

But before I left, I paused and held out my hand to Bernadette. "I think maybe you had better give me that tape."

She shook her head. "No. I've hidden it."

Bernadette stood up to leave and Beverly said, "Mr. Hartley, when you come back, you'll find us about a hundred yards down the canal's towpath toward Washington. There's a clearly worn path to the right over to the river. It's our favorite spot out here; we'll wait for you there."

"Good," I said. And as I went to my car, they started walking along the towpath toward Washington.

When I reached the Hertz rental agency, a Maryland State Police car was parked in front of it. I went in and a man who could have been a Maryland detective was talking on the phone. When he saw me, he asked, "Are you Hartley?"

I said 'Yes.'

"Jenkins wants to talk to you."

I grabbed the phone and, covering the mouthpiece with my hand, said, "Tell these people we want to see the records of their rentals for the night of May second."

"Goddamn it, Hartley, you got to tell me what's going on."

"Arthur Turner may have rented a car the night Tom was

killed, which he could have used to drive to Ocean City. Hang on a minute while I try to confirm this."

"I'll hold."

I went into a back office to join the detective and one of the yellow-jacketed Hertz employees. She was pulling out a bunch of forms, which she handed to the detective, who turned around and handed them to me. The Hertz girl showed me a little table in the corner where I could begin my search. The forms appeared to be in alphabetical order, so I was in luck. There it was, it almost leaped right out at me: Arthur Turner had rented a white, two-door Chevrolet Malibu the night of May 2. He had paid cash, so there was no credit card involved. But there was no way he could have rented a car under a phony name, because you can't get a rental car without a valid license, period. The mileage was 356—more than it took to travel the 35 miles to Baltimore and back. It was about 165 miles to Ocean City and 356 miles would have taken him there and back—by way of Baltimore.

I asked the Hertz agent why she'd called Turner at home this morning, and she said Turner had put his company name, address, and phone number on the form, but the company man she talked to didn't know anything about the rental. So she called Turner at home.

I grabbed the receipts for the Turner rental and said to the Maryland detective, "Do me a favor and tell the young lady that this receipt is evidence in a police investigation and she'll get a photocopy of it back for her files."

"Okay," he said. "Don't forget Jenkins. He's hanging on the phone."

I grabbed the phone. Jenkins was still there. "Okay, read this fast. I think we got it. Arthur Turner rented a car, a white Chevrolet Malibu, the night of May second. It had three hundred and fifty-six miles on it when he brought it back.

Bernadette Harrigan says that after she left Cranston on the beach that night she noticed another car parked in the Fenwick Towers parking lot. A nondescript white car, she says, which is the way you would describe a white Malibu rental. Right?"

"Right!"

"Could you have your people check out the Fenwick Towers again to see if anyone living or working there might drive a white Malibu?"

"Got it."

"Also, Mrs. Harrigan says she thinks the other man she saw on the beach that night was Mrs. Turner's husband, Arthur."

"Well, I'll be damned!" was all Jenkins could say.

"And," I added, "I think if you really put the pressure on Betty Sawyer, telling her about Turner's three hundred and fifty-mile trip in a rental car that night and threatening her with prison as an accomplice in a murder, she'd blast Turner's alibi right out of the stadium, like a Boog Powell home run."

Then I had one of those intuitive flashes. "Christ," I said to Jenkins, "I think Bernadette Harrigan is in real danger—and Turner knows where she might be. She's out on the river at a picnic place the Harrigans and Turners used to go to, and Bernadette's car is visible in the parking lot. If Turner went there and saw it, he would know right where to go."

"Is she out there alone?"

"No. Beverly Turner's with her. Look," I almost yelled at Jenkins, "this Maryland detective and I are heading to Great Falls. Meet us at the parking lot there. Ask someone for directions and look for a Maryland police car, number eight-fifty-six," I said, looking out the window at the number on the police car. "If you can't make it out there, I'll see you at the Harrigans'."

I hung up without giving him a chance to reply. Out front, the detective was standing by his car. I said, "Look, we're going as fast as we can to Great Falls. Jenkins knows what we're doing. You know where that is?"

He nodded.

"Good, I'll follow you. Use your light and your siren if you have to. But don't go too fast, I want to arrive in one piece."

Then as we were racing through Bethesda with his light flashing, I began to worry about Bernadette Harrigan out on the edge of the river with one—and maybe two—Turners, by the time I got there.

We went through a red light in Potomac and sped down Falls Road toward the river. As we roared into the Great Falls parking area I noticed that Bernadette's yellow Mercedes was still parked back in the corner, under some trees. But not far from it, I noticed another car, a tan Oldsmobile station wagon.

"We gotta hurry," I said to the detective as we got out of our cars. "I think our man might be here."

"Our man?" the detective replied, obviously puzzled.

I had forgotten to tell him what I had found at Hertz, so I quickly brought him up to date. I also explained that the suspect's wife was with them, and for all I knew, she might be involved, too. "They're out on the river about one hundred yards down the towpath that way," I said, pointing toward Washington. "You take a right, where you see a path leading to the river. You run on ahead; I'll catch up with you."

"Gotcha," he said, and took off at a sprint that I could not keep up with. He was a much younger man, and as he ran ahead I noticed that he pulled out the revolver that was buckled to his belt.

Fortunately, I jog almost every morning so I was not too far behind the detective when he reached the path and headed toward the river. As I approached the turnoff, I noticed a sign on the towpath that read:

Danger
Deadly Current
Slippery Rocks
Even Wading Can Kill

I reached the turnoff and went toward the river, but suddenly I ran into the detective talking to Arthur Turner, who appeared to be heading back from the river. He was wearing a T-shirt, slacks and loafers.

"Where are Bernadette and your wife?" I asked him.

"I don't know," Turner replied, quite disconcerted. "I thought they would be out here, but they weren't. They must have gone farther down the towpath. I was just going to look for them."

"We'll come with you," I said. "They were supposed to meet me here about now and they wouldn't go anywhere else, because they knew I wouldn't be able to find them. And Bernadette very much wanted to talk to me."

"Officer," I said, running to the Maryland detective, "We're going to look out here on the river, where I was supposed to meet them."

We reached the little clearing by the river—a beautiful spot, a mixture of jagged rocks and the brown churning Potomac River below—but there was no sign of the two women. Then over near the edge, I spotted something—Bernadette's handbag! "Looks like they were here," I said to Turner. "I saw Mrs. Harrigan with that bag about forty-five minutes ago. What do you think?"

"I think she left it here when they decided to go farther down the river."

"I don't, Turner. I think something happened out here. And by the way, we have some new information."

"What information?" Turner said contemptuously.

"The Chevy Malibu you rented the night of Cranston's death."

"Hartley, I was nowhere near the shore that night! So my company rented a car! We do that all the time."

At the same time, Turner was edging toward the river and I didn't know what he was up to. So I said to the Maryland trooper, "Officer, I know I don't have the authority to ask you to do this, but I think it would be a good idea to handcuff this man."

The trooper said, "I'll do it," but as he put his gun back in its holster and started to ready his handcuffs, Turner turned and leaped into the river and immediately disappeared underwater. The detective was taking off his jacket, ready but not eager to go in after Turner. "I wouldn't do that," I said. "This river is really treacherous. People drown all the time in this water. Let's go downstream and watch for him to come up below the falls."

The detective agreed and picked up his gun. But when we looked to the edge of the river it was obvious that with the rocks and the underbrush we could not make it downstream very fast. I yelled at the detective, "The best thing is to go back to the towpath and run downstream and then go back onto the river when we see a path. Come on!"

We both ran back to the canal and as we reached it I could see Detective Jenkins walking rapidly down the path in our direction. I waved at him to hurry up and he broke into a jog.

"I'll wait for Jenkins," I said to the detective. "Why don't you go on downstream and find a place to go back to the river and look for Turner."

He sprinted on down the path and as Jenkins approached, I said, "You arrived just in time. I'm sure Arthur Turner is our man. I was supposed to meet Mrs. Harrigan and Mrs. Turner out there on the river, but when we got here, only Turner was there and he said he hadn't seen them. I told him we knew about the rental car and I asked the detective to put handcuffs on him—and Turner jumped in the river, went under, and never came up. The detective has gone downstream looking for him."

"That wasn't very smart," Jenkins said. "What about the women?"

"We haven't seen them and I'm worried—at least about Mrs. Harrigan. I think Turner is trying to get rid of her, figuring that she was the only person that might identify him as the other man on the beach. After all, what was Turner doing out here anyway? He left his house saying he had a minor crisis at the office."

"All right, Hartley. I'm going to help the detective. You go back up there," he said, pointing toward the entrance to Great Falls, "and find a park ranger. Tell them to get a rescue squad out here fast. If you can't find a policeman, the trooper in my car—his name is Scottie—can call someone on the car phone. Then tell him to join us. You wait for the rescue squad and tell them where to go."

"I think I should go back to Georgetown and wait for Jack Harrigan, tell him what happened, and bring him out here. His wife may be in serious trouble. And you're supposed to be meeting with the Harrigans about now at their house. Isn't he coming back from Dallas especially to see you?"

"You're right. Tell Scottie to wait for the rescue squad, then you and Harrigan come back here. I'm going to need you and that evidence you got. You know where the tape is now?"

I shook my head. "Bernadette Harrigan has it. She said she hid it."

"All right, get moving," Jenkins said as he started down the towpath.

CHAPTER FOURTEEN

Late Wednesday afternoon, May 9

I drove back into Georgetown through heavy traffic—the beginning of rush hour. I found a parking place virtually in front of the Harrigans' house and knocked on their door. Mary answered.

"Mr. Harrigan here?" I asked.

"No. But he's coming back from Dallas, and he should be here any minute now."

"Could I wait for him? He has an appointment here with me and a policeman."

"I know," she said, as she ushered me into the hallway.

I did not want to tell her about Mrs. Harrigan. No use alarming her and possibly the children until we knew for sure what had happened to her. I said I would wait in the library and killed time browsing through Harrigan's books, although I was really too edgy to concentrate. So I moved over to the window looking down on O street, figuring that as soon as Harrigan's cab arrived I would go down to the street and meet him.

Pretty soon an airport limousine pulled up in front of the house and I met Harrigan on the front steps.

"Oh, hello, Hartley," he said brusquely. "Is Officer Jenkins here?"

"Mr. Harrigan, you should come with me. Your wife is out at Great Falls with Beverly Turner and she may be in some danger. Jenkins is there. I'll explain on the way." We took my car.

For the first time in my brief acquaintance with Jack Harrigan, he appeared ruffled and disturbed. And he seemed to pale a little when I told him about his wife. "Damn," was his first reaction. "I've had a premonition something was about to break—ever since she told me she was meeting you at the post office this morning. She said Beverly told her you were expecting a package from Tom that might have been mailed there—to that post office. Maybe a taped message for Beverly."

"Then you know about that?"

"Yes. Where is she now?"

"I found Arthur Turner in a little clearing by the river where I was supposed to meet your wife and Mrs. Turner. But they were not there, although your wife's handbag was. Turner said he hadn't seen them, that they must have gone down the river to some other place."

"Uh-oh," Harrigan mumbled.

"There's enough evidence on Turner that Jenkins is going to arrest him for the murder of Tom Cranston."

"What evidence?"

"Turner rented a Chevy Malibu that night and put more than enough miles on it to have driven to the beach and back."

"That wouldn't convict Arthur of murder."

"Right. But when I told Turner of knowing about his rental car, he leaped into the river and disappeared."

Harrigan said, "The river is really treacherous there. I guess Turner's gone, although he's a pretty good swimmer. At Rehoboth, I've seen him swim out of sight in the ocean. He said he had heard that Bobby Kennedy used to do it. Damn-fool thing to do. He must have known he was taking a chance on the river."

Harrigan stared out the window, muttering impatiently about the traffic. We were in the middle of rush hour now, going along MacArthur boulevard at a snail's pace. *The Sound of Music* was playing at the MacArthur. Dory and I had planned to see it this week.

"What did your wife tell you about Tom Cranston?" I asked.

"She told me she saw him on the beach that night, but didn't kill him."

"And you believed her?"

"If she had killed him, she would tell me. I've been sort of acting as her lawyer. Because of the phone call to Beverly that night, we both knew how much trouble she was in, just being over there. We also knew you were onto something about that sport coat."

"Did she explain all that?"

"Yes, in great detail, and it made sense."

"Do you want to tell me?"

"Might as well. When Bernadette left Beverly's house late that afternoon she was very confused. She told me she thought she was in love with Beverly— and, yes, we talk about that sort of thing, too. She realized Beverly was not in love with her and did not want that kind of relationship. But that night all she could think of was being with Beverly—"

"And the list."

Harrigan was silent.

"Harrigan, there's no use being coy about that list any-more," I said. "Your wife told us about it."

"And she probably destroyed it. That needed to be done for everyone's sake." He fell silent again.

Then he said, "Beverly was very upset, worried about Tom. Bernadette figured Arthur would be getting home late, if at all. She knew he was furious at Beverly. Then Richard Herson called Bernadette and said he had tried to reach Beverly but she did not answer the phone. Bernadette told him she thought Beverly was probably asleep, after taking sleeping pills. She really didn't believe that. Then she went out to Beverly's house to see what had happened to her. Beverly was gone, but while Bernadette was stlll there, Arthur Turner came home, before he went to see his girlfriend in Baltimore. He wanted to know where Beverly was and Bernadette said she had gone to Rehoboth. Bernadette also told Turner she doubted Beverly would find Tom in Rehoboth, that he was probably in Ocean City."

"That wasn't too good," I said.

"Bernadette said she regretted it later, although she didn't suspect Arthur of anything then."

Harrigan paused, looked at his watch, and continued.

"Bernadette said that while she was talking with Arthur a crazy idea was forming in her mind. She would go to Ocean City herself to see if she could find Tom or Beverly or both. If she found Beverly with Tom, she didn't know what she would do. Beverly had told her Tom had a gun. So she started think-ing about the gun and how she might get hold of it. And she confessed she was thinking about shooting Tom and making it look like suicide if she could find him alone and get the gun away from him."

"She must have been in some emotional state."

"You're right. Bernadette's usually so cool and collected. But she admitted that her motivation was quite muddled—a mixture of jealousy of Tom and a desire to shut him up. I had convinced Bernadette that our life would probably be significantly changed if oil company money was linked to Watergate. Anyway, she thought the way she had it set up at home she could get away with it. She didn't think the children would find out, and if Mary discovered she was gone, Bernadette knew Mary would tell the police whatever she told her to tell them. She thought I might call a couple of times, as I did, and get a busy signal but would think nothing of it, just that she was gossiping, as usual. As it turned out, Mary never did discover she had gone out."

"But your wife didn't get the alibi she wanted," I said. "I talked to the Turner children and the little girl said they didn't see Mrs. Harrigan that night."

"But they didn't say anything to anyone but you, did they?"

"I don't know."

Harrigan continued. "Bernadette decided to dress as a man, which she had done before, rolling up her hair in a bun. She even had a hat, Arthur Turner's Greek fisherman's cap, which she had found sitting on the hall table at the Turners'. She drove her station wagon to Ocean City and the first thing she did was make a search for the cars. She found Richard's red Porsche at Fifth Street, parked just down from the old Admiral Hotel, right near the corner. She figured Richard had found Tom, so she parked the station wagon where she could watch Richard's car."

Harrigan was getting more and more fidgety, continually looking at his watch as if the time made any difference.

"Pretty soon, they came out of the Admiral and walked to the corner. They stood talking for a moment, then shook hands and Richard got in his car and drove away. Tom stood there for a moment and then began walking back to the hotel. She caught up with him and pretended that she just happened to run into him as he was entering the hotel. It was all very smooth. Tom didn't recognize her at first. But he seemed to accept her explanation for the way she was dressed. Tom asked her to come in for a drink. She said she'd rather not, but would come up to his room, if he didn't mind being seen with a 'strange man' in a hotel. He said it might be interesting."

Harrigan paused for a moment while I ran a red light, then continued. "By this time, Bernadette said, she figured Tom and Richard had reached some kind of agreement and the contract was off. But it also occurred to her that if Tom were killed that night and they decided it was not suicide, Beverly would always be convinced that Herson was responsible, no matter what he said. And Herson would certainly be implicated when it became known he'd put out a contract on Tom. She began to think that if she could just get hold of that gun, she might pull off the perfect crime.

"And, to her surprise, getting hold of the gun was no problem. Tom just handed it to her in the hotel room. And his apparent willingness to be the victim gave her the courage to carry out a plan that had been forming in her mind. But she decided she needed a little time, so she left Tom for about half an hour."

"That must have been when Tom made the tape which we played this morning," I interrupted.

"Leaving Tom was a big mistake," said Harrigan.

"Why did she do it?"

"She said there were some things she had to do to make it the perfect crime. First she had to call Beverly in Rehoboth to make her think she was still in Washington and make sure Beverly was not on the way to Ocean City to find Tom. For all she knew Herson might have reached Beverly in Rehoboth and told her about canceling the contract and where Tom was staying. So she called Beverly from Ocean City and confirmed that Beverly was in Rehoboth, and convinced her that she was still in Washington. Beverly obviously had not heard from Herson. Bernadette, of course, did not tell Beverly that the contract had probably been canceled. Later, she decided that the call was a big mistake. She also tried to reach me in New York, although that was not a serious error."

"No, but that first call was. The police have already traced it."

"That's right. Another reason Bernadette left Tom," Harrigan continued, "was that she wanted to know just how much noise a thirty-two caliber revolver made when fired outdoors, but muffled by something like a coat. So after calling Beverly, she drove north to a turnoff that led to Asawoman Bay, got out of her car, and wrapped the gun in the coat she was wearing— which was my tan corduroy sport jacket. And she knew you were onto something about that."

"Actually," I said, "it eliminated you as the person who left the Admiral with Tom. If you were wearing the coat that night, you wouldn't have made such a fuss about it last night. But it made your wife even more suspect."

"Very astute, Mr. Hartley. I wouldn't have mentioned it if I had known Bernadette had worn it that night. She didn't decide to tell me everything until after you had left."

"Why?"

"Because in her muddled state, she hoped she wouldn't have to tell me or anyone she was there. But the more she thought about the phone call, the more she realized she couldn't hide it. The coat just made it worse. Anyway, although the gunshot made more noise than Bernadette thought it would and she was wavering a little, she was still thinking about the perfect crime. But she needed to find just the right spot—a lonely stretch of beach, but with a place to park the wagon where it would not be investigated by a passing police car. She had to drive farther north than she had planned, but she found it. The Fenwick Towers, just north of Fenwick Island, across the Maryland border in Delaware. It's a single high-rise condominium with lots of lonely uninhabited beach north and south of it. But a station wagon parked in its parking lot wouldn't be noticed by the police, or anyone else.

"So she had her plan. But if anything went wrong at any stage—until the trigger was pulled—she could call it off and shift to the role of the good Samaritan, trying to console a drunken, despondent friend of a friend.

"She raced back to Ocean City, parked the station wagon on the corner of Fifth Street at Baltimore and walked back to the corner to wait for Tom. In a few minutes, he came along and they drove north to the Fenwick Towers. They parked and Bernadette said she was delighted how inconspicuous the wagon looked parked in the Towers lot.

"But by the time they walked north on the beach and into the dunes, Bernadette said she was confused. She was getting hold of her emotions and losing her nerve. The loudness of the gun had shocked her, and walking up the beach she remembered the phone call to Beverly and thought it might be traceable. She even thought about the mileage she had put on the station wagon. But she still wanted that list.

"She had thought that once they were alone on the beach, Tom would try to make love to her. But it didn't happen. The more they talked, the more emotional Tom became—first about Beverly and then about Richard Nixon. He also said he had met a wonderful woman and that he wanted to marry her. At that moment Bernadette said she knew she could not kill Tom. But she still had the gun and decided to make an effort to get the list—"

"And then Tom just gave the list to her without a struggle,"

I interjected. "She told Beverly and me what happened on the beach, and that Tom was going to the Ervin committee this morning."

"But somebody stopped him."

"And we know who did it, although we may never see him again."

"Or my wife," Harrigan said grimly.

Suddenly I noticed a flashing light and a gathering of people ahead on the left. "Look," I said, pointing toward the light. "That must be the search party."

We were nowhere near Great Falls: in fact, we had just passed the Little Falls dam. But the river was rushing so fast beneath the falls where Turner had gone in that anyone would have been carried down here by now. "You're right," Harrigan said. "Pull over there and park."

The flashing light I had seen was an ambulance that had driven down to the towpath. As we approached it, we could see a young man in a white uniform standing by the ambulance, but most of the excitement was over near the river's edge. Harrigan started toward the river, obviously concerned about his wife, when I grabbed his arm. "Look," I said, pointing up the canal toward Great Falls. Two women were making their way down the path toward us. They looked like Bernadette Harrigan and Beverly Turner.

I motioned to Harrigan and said, "Come on." And as we ran toward them, I looked over at Jenkins, but he was preoccupied with what was going on in the river— presumably the search for Arthur Turner.

When we reached the women, Harrigan hugged his wife and then Beverly. "We were very worried about you both. Hartley thought there was a chance Arthur might have attacked you and thrown you in the river. Have they found him yet?"

"No," Bernadette said. "And he might have tried to get rid of us, but he never had a chance."

"What do you mean?" Harrigan replied. But before Bernadette answered, I started to pull the two women into the brush, so Jenkins could not see us if he came back to the ambulance. "There's something I want to say to you both before we see Jenkins."

But as we were moving off the towpath into the underbrush and trees, Bernadette continued without giving me a chance to finish. "When we were waiting out there on the river's edge for Mr. Hartley, I told Beverly that I thought it must have been Arthur's car that was at the parking lot when I left. He was, after all, the only person other than Richard Herson, Beverly, and me who knew Tom was in Ocean City—"

"Except me," I interrupted. "He called me the day before."

She nodded and went on. "Beverly said that she had had a talk with Arthur that morning before he went to the office and practically accused him of going to Ocean City that night. He denied it."

"So what happened? You two should have waited there for me."

"As we were talking out there," Bernadette replied, "we both got worried about Arthur, that he might come after me. Beverly had told him we were coming here. Remember?"

"Yes. Just before we left their house."

"Then we remembered that my car was parked up front in the Great Falls parking lot, and if Arthur came out here looking for us he would know we were still here. So we started to rush back to the falls entrance—"

"And you left your handbag there," I said.

"Yes. In my excitement I forgot it. But then as we reached the towpath we could see Arthur's station wagon pull into the parking lot. So we hid in the woods near where we were, hoping Arthur would not find us."

Beverly nodded, adding, "We were both terrified. I knew Bernadette was in danger and by now I was also afraid of what Arthur might do to me. We heard him approach the path to the river and go out to the ledge and then we heard someone running down that path. That was about the time you arrived."

"We heard everything that went on between you and Arthur," Bernadette said, "and we also heard you tell Detective Jenkins that you were going back to get Jack."

"So what did you do then?"

"Not much. We knew we couldn't do anything for Arthur. So we just waited up here for the rescue squad to arrive. Also I didn't want to talk with anyone until you came back with Jack. After a while, the rescue squad arrived and went down the towpath. Then, after giving you enough time to get into town and back with Jack, we began walking toward the ambulance, which had gone out of sight down the towpath."

Looking back down the path to make sure Jenkins was not coming, I said, "There's something I want to say before we see Jenkins again. I think we should keep Herson, what he did and the list, out of this. I know both of you will agree to that," I said, looking at the Harrigans. "And I don't think Mrs. Turner wants it known that the father of her children contributed money—even inadvertently—to help the Watergate burglars."

"I agree one hundred percent," Jack said, looking out toward the towpath to see if Jenkins had spotted them yet. "I don't care what happens to that fool Herson, but I am concerned about knowledge of that list surfacing. Of course, it would ruin me with the oil companies and in Washington. Neither I nor Arthur had any idea what our money was being used for. When I found out, I was furious. So was Arthur, and I don't blame him."

"Yes, he was," said Beverly, "and I would be happy if we never hear about it again. Although, frankly, I don't give a damn what happens to Richard now."

"Well, I do," I said. "I have plans for him which you do not want to hear about."

"Agreed, then," said Jack Harrigan. "But what about the tape?"

"That's right," I said, turning to Bernadette. "You said you hid it."

"Yes."

"Where?"

"In the river! That's a pretty good hiding place, isn't it?"

"Damn good," said her husband. "But what will Jenkins think? About the list, too. You did tell him, didn't you, Hartley?"

There was a long silence before I spoke. "Yes, I told him about them both. As for the list, he seemed to lose interest in it when I lied and told him that it was of people and organizations that had contributed to Nixon's campaign in 1972 and that the names were a matter of public record."

"And in a way, that's quite true," said Harrigan. "Our names *are* on some master list of GOP contributors. So what about the tape?"

"I told him that it was mostly a good-bye message from Cranston to Beverly Turner, but that there was also some personal stuff on there about Mrs. Harrigan that she was afraid might someday go public. You know how Washington is. So she wanted the tape."

"You think Jenkins bought that?" Bernadette Harrigan asked.

"No," I replied. "In fact, he has sworn out a warrant for your arrest. He thinks the tape shows you were the last one to see Tom alive, that you had the gun and a motive, and that you would not have stolen the tape at gunpoint if it did not somehow incriminate you."

"Not good," said her husband.

"But, of course," I said, "that was before Arthur Turner became a fugitive. I'm sure Jenkins will think that is proof enough of guilt. And with the Hertz rental car evidence, and when Betty Sawyer changes her story about what Turner really did that night—as I'm sure she will now—that will be all the Delaware district attorney's office will need to close the case."

"I hope you're right," said Jack Harrigan, looking toward the towpath. "Here's Jenkins now. Let's see what's happening."

When we returned to the search area, Jenkins said that Turner had still not been found. Beverly stayed with the search team; the Harrigans decided to go home after they had a talk with Jenkins. I decided to go home, too. I gave Jenkins my phone number and asked him to call me if they found Turner. In my opinion, the case was closed, and I was exhausted.

I was home in about fifteen minutes and the phone was ringing when I walked in the door. It was Beverly Turner. "They found Arthur, Ray," she said flatly, as if she was in a trance. "He was dead. He had apparently hit his head on a rock and was knocked unconscious. So he couldn't have pulled himself out of the undertow, even if it had been possible."

"I'm terribly sorry, Beverly. But maybe it's for the best. It would be an ugly, difficult trial for you—and the children."

"I know. But I can't believe it. I just didn't think Arthur would go that far."

"You never know. Jealousy, pride, and, of course, the understandable but panicky desire to keep his name out of the Watergate scandal all played a part. You all right?"

"I guess so. I'm going home to tell the children. Jenkins is coming out soon. He needs to get some information."

"All right. I may be out in a bit. But I want to call Dory at the beach now."

I fixed myself a scotch and water, then called Dory and told her about Arthur.

"So why did he do that?" was her first question.

"By that time we had evidence that Turner had rented a Hertz car that night and put three hundred and fifty-six miles on it—enough to drive to Ocean City and back."

"But are you sure he killed Tom?"

"No. And we may never be certain now. But the case against him is strong. When a detective was about to handcuff him, he leaped into the river at that place below Great Falls where so many people have drowned. Arthur must have known he was taking a risk doing that. He either panicked or thought he was a strong enough swimmer to keep from drowning. But he hit his head on a rock."

"So everybody's just assuming Turner was the killer?"

"There's also the motive. And Turner had two, at least in the eyes of the police. One, he was the jealous husband; and two, he wanted to silence Tom because he knew about the list of campaign contributors whose money had gone to the Republicans and possibly the Watergate burglars. And he knew he was on it. Then there is the fact that he had the opportunity—assuming that he drove to Ocean City, and he arrived late at Betty Sawyer's apartment, where he spent the night. Finally, he also had a gun, thanks to Bernadette—"

"*Cherchez la femme!*" Dory interrupted.

"In the tape Tom sent Beverly—"

"So that was the tape Tom sent—not one to you. Was it at the post office?"

"Yes. We played the tape at the Turners' house and on it Tom told about the contract, that Herson had successfully called it off and that he would tell Tom all he knew about Watergate if Tom would tear up the photograph and burn the tape. And it was Bernadette, dressed as a man, who Tom went off with that night."

"And you believe that!" Dory said.

"Jenkins didn't. When I told him that after we played the tape Bernadette pulled a gun and went off with it, Jenkins swore out a warrant for her arrest."

"Sound like he's a lot smarter than you are."

"Well, that was before Turner went into the river and before I had confirmed that Turner had put three hundred and fifty miles on a rental car that night."

"So how did Mrs. Harrigan explain what she was doing with Tom that night?"

"You are not going to believe her story, but she says her intent was to get that list of names from Tom. She went out on the beach with him hoping she could use her feminine charms to get the list from him. She even had in the back of her mind using the gun if she had to. They had Tom's gun, he was a little drunk and had been making jokes about committing suicide."

"So how the hell do you know she didn't use it?"

"I don't. But she says Tom was quite emotional and that he had met a woman he wanted to marry. He was not responsive to her advances, but she had no trouble getting the list of names. Tom had it memorized. Anyway, she said she knew she could not kill him, and when she told Tom she was going back to the hotel, he said he would rather walk to the hotel on the beach. So she left the gun with Tom and went back to the Fenwick Towers parking lot, where she saw that another car had been added. It was a white sedan—and she told me this *before* I learned at Hertz that Turner had rented a white two-door Chevy Malibu that night. So we're assuming that it was Turner's rental car at the parking lot and that he was the last one on the beach with Tom. And he bolted after the police tried to handcuff him."

This seemed to silence Dory for a moment. Then she said, "So nobody wants to be seen handcuffed. Think how that would look to his children when he showed up on television."

"So how 'bout the headline, 'Jealous Maryland Builder Shoots Wife's Boyfriend?' That look any better?"

"You could make a good case that Arthur Turner and the Harrigans were in this together. Did you ever think of that?"

"Yes, but not for long. I eliminated Jack Harrigan after he made such a fuss about his missing sport coat. If he had known that Bernadette got rid of it because it had gunpowder on it, he never would have mentioned it. But I was suspicious of Mrs. Harrigan, especially after I decided that it was a woman dressed as a man that Tom went off with. Then when she pulled a gun and took the tape I was sure she was the one. But I'm afraid I have to believe her now. And so does Peter Potomac."

"You were always a sucker for a well-built woman."

"You mean like you? And I'd believe you if you said you didn't kill someone who tried to ruin my reputation—even if you were alone on a beach with him late at night, had a gun and, incidentally, were smart enough to figure out that you had made a phone call that put you at the shore that night."

"Well, that's why I love you—and, incidentally, I wouldn't have made that phone call."

"And that's why I love *you*."

"That's nice. And I'm not married to Peter Potomac, even if he does write better than you."

"You're not married to him, I am. And he doesn't write better than I do. But don't forget I'm just a registered Democrat. He's a registered trademark. You can look it up."

"I like Democrats better than trademarks. It's been my experience that they're better in bed."

"How much experience?"

"Well, I've only slept with one trademark."

"Peter Potomac, I presume."

"God, no! My diaphragm. I forget its name."

"We gotta stop this. You're getting me distracted. I think you can figure out why I don't want Jenkins and the Delaware police trying to find out if Bernadette Harrigan, or her husband, is involved in this murder."

"Because you want to have lunch with her again sometime when her husband is out of town?"

"No. Because if they continue snooping around it will inevitably lead to Herson. And I don't want him brought into this if I can avoid it."

"Why?"

"Because I want him to remain in place—in the White House."

"Why?"

"Because I plan to continue where Tom left off. First, I am going to tell Herson that I want him to leak information about Watergate to the press—preferably Bob Woodward. I still have the photo, and Herson is more concerned about that than anything else, even his desire to carry out Nixon's takeover of the government."

"That's not smart!" Dory replied. "Look what happened to Tom when he tried that. If Herson's mafia friend had been more efficient Tom would have been killed before he called you and before he sent his tape to Beverly. Herson would not have had to tell Beverly and he probably would have gotten away with it."

"Don't worry. I've thought of that. And I'm going to fix it so that Herson will be more worried about something happening to me than if it didn't. And I'm not going to tell you about it, for your own good. Here's the thing. Tom said he might or might not be sending me a little package to give to Bob Woodward. I'm sure the package was a tape containing information he had already learned from Richard Herson. He didn't send me that package because he no longer felt his life was in danger. And he planned to take everything he had to the Ervin committee. But he did send Beverly a tape—mostly personal stuff, although he did talk some about Watergate. The point is that Tom never sent a package to Woodward. Or, I don't think he did."

"So what are you going to do? Send Woodward a tape?"

"No. What I will do is drop Woodward a note telling him that a second-level staffer in the White House named E. Richard Herson knows a lot about what's going on and might be persuaded to talk—for reasons I won't go into."

"Aren't you the mover and shaker."

"It's the least I can do for Tom."

While I was talking to Dory, I had been looking around the living room and something did not seem quite right. Lamps out of place; couch cushions askew; magazines and books on the coffee table not the way I left them. Then I realized: someone had been searching the house.

"Guess what?" I said to Dory, "Somebody's been searching the house."

"Of course, the photographs. Herson's still trying to get the ones you kept. Did they break anything?"

"Not that I can see. And you must be right about the photographs."

"So where *did* you hide them?"

"You'd be the last person I'd tell."

"So what if something happens to you? Shouldn't I know where they are?"

"Then they might try to torture you, trying to force you to tell them. They might disfigure your beautiful body. You know how much that would upset me."

"You know I'd never tell them. And anyway, you'd be dead."

"I forgot."

"So what if they tortured you?" Dory replied.

"I'd say you were the only one who knew; that I let you hide them because you're so good at hiding Easter eggs. Look, darling, I've got to run. We can talk about this tomorrow when we're not on phones that might be tapped. I'll drive to the beach in the morning."

"I'll be waiting at the door. But if you happen to go into our grocery store before you come here, don't be alarmed if some of the clerks look at you a little strangely."

"Why's that?"

"It's because of the Saran Wrap."

"The Saran Wrap?"

"Yeah, the guy at the checkout counter wondered what I needed twenty boxes of Saran Wrap for."

"I'll just tell him I like to stick you in the microwave before dinner. It always warms you up."

We both slammed the phones down at the same time and I didn't even have to check to see if the photographs were still there. I had hidden them in the backyard, like Whittaker Chambers, but not in a pumpkin—in a waterproof box. I went immediately to the Virginia phone book to look up E. Richard Herson, but before I could dial the number, I noticed that there was a flashing light in front of my house. It was a Delaware State Police car.

CHAPTER SIXTEEN

Wednesday night, May 9

There was a loud knock on the door. I opened it and Detective Jenkins said, "Evening, Ray, you got a moment? It won't take long, but I got a couple of questions."

"Sure, but would you turn out that light? I don't want to alarm the neighborhood."

"So, what'll they think?" Jenkins said, turning to the street, motioning with his arms and yelling.

As the car went around the corner, I said, "They'll think you got a James Bond car that will do anything you yell at it to do."

"No such luck. I got my trusted deputy, Scottie, with me, and he'll do anything I tell him to do. Right now, he's standing guard out there watching for anyone that might come after you."

"What the hell does that mean?"

"Just kidding. But when the FBI came in, I thought this case would turn out to be government related. We knew Cranston was working for a Senate committee that dealt with oil quotas. And there were rumors that he was working for the Senate Watergate Committee, although we were never able to confirm that. Then the FBI went out as fast as it came in—almost as if they knew something we didn't know."

"That's odd," I said. "Did you have your talk with Jack Harrigan?"

"Yeah. We had a chat down at the river, just before I came up here. It wasn't much of a talk, now that the case appears to be over. But he was one reason I thought there were government connections. He works for the oil companies."

I nodded yes, and said, "You want a beer?"

"Don't mind if I do. I guess I'm off duty now."

"So you're satisfied the case is closed now?"

"I guess so, but there are a couple of questions. Maybe you can help me."

"I hope so," I said, "although I think you know more about the case than I do."

"Are you kidding? I'm waiting to read your story. That was a brilliant stroke, thinking of the rental car."

"I was lucky on that one. I just happened to be at Turner's house when Hertz called with a question about the car."

"Maybe. But you know, there's still one thing that bothers me about this case."

"Oh? What's that?"

"That beautiful dame, Harrigan's wife. I just can't understand why she would pull a gun on everybody, grab the tape, and disappear. That was evidence in a murder case and if Turner's actions at the river hadn't more or less confirmed his guilt, Mrs. Harrigan would be facing serious charges of destroying evidence and obstructing justice—if not murder."

"You're absolutely right. And I told her to give that tape to you. In fact, I tried to take it away from her. But apparently she had already thrown it in the river."

"So why did she do that if there was nothing on that tape to implicate her?"

"Did you ask her?"

"Of course. She said there were personal things on the tape that she would rather not talk about and hoped would never go public. So I didn't press her. But . . ." Jenkins said, fixing me with a stare that made me sure what was coming next. "That tape is still evidence, and you heard it—in fact, I can't quite figure what you were doing in the act anyway. It was a personal tape from Tom Cranston to Mrs. Turner. How come you were there when it was played?"

"Well," and I paused for a moment, not too long, I hoped, "Mrs. Turner knew I was a good friend of Tom's and was just trying to help me find out what happened to him—and not just for my article."

"And Mrs. Harrigan was there because?"

"Same thing, I guess. She's Beverly's best friend, since college. Mrs. Turner knew she was upset about Tom—as we all were—except Arthur Turner, of course."

"So why didn't someone there—especially you, considering how cooperative I had been with you—say that we got to get his tape right to the police?"

"Good question. To me, it depended on what was on the tape. It turned out to be a farewell letter to Mrs. Turner. Even so, I was prepared to insist that Mrs. Turner give it to you, and I planned to talk to you about it. And I did. But Bernadette surprised us all by taking it herself."

"And I'm asking you—officially, as one who has heard this evidence—what was on the tape that might have prompted Mrs. Harrigan to do such a criminal thing, assuming she was innocent of any crime?"

I arose from the chair I was sitting in, walked slowly to my little bar, and fixed another scotch and water. Jenkins still had half a beer. When I sat down again, I said, "I hope you treat this as confidential—unless, of course, you are going to continue your investigation of this case—but I think I know what was on the tape that worried Mrs. Harrigan. Frankly, there were references to a brief love affair between Mrs. Harrigan and Mrs. Turner, in which Mrs. Harrigan was the aggressor and Mrs. Turner not really responsive. If this tape ever got to the media, Mrs. Harrigan—and her husband—would be ruined socially in Washington. And what lobbyists mostly do, other than give money to candidates for political office, is give and attend parties. That life would be over for them if a scandal like that came out."

Jenkins just sat there staring at his beer, seeming temporarily at least at a loss for words. "I guess you're right," he finally said.

"Of course," I continued, "the tape also indicated that she had gone out on the beach with Tom, and appeared to be the last one to see him alive."

"That didn't make a lot of sense either," Jenkins said. "She says she was out there trying to get a list from Cranston. But you said the list was a matter of public record anyway."

"The whole business of the list was overblown. It was just the names of people who had contributed to the Nixon campaign in 1972. Harrigan and Turner were both on it. But there's a campaign oversight committee that keeps track of that stuff and anyone can get the list when the records are available."

"Well, if Turner hadn't come along and implicated himself by fleeing the law, Mrs. Harrigan would be in some kind of trouble," Jenkins said. "She would still be the number one suspect."

"And what would I be?"

"I don't know," said Jenkins. "But if Betty Sawyer changes her story, as I think she will when we convince her of the trouble she's in, I'm sure the district attorney will label the Cranston affair as another case of a jealous husband's rage at the man who cuckolded him and will close it. But I have to say that you seem to know much more about this Cranston business than just a reporter writing a story."

"And there's Mrs. Cranston. You know, until you found that Turner had rented a car that night, I was almost convinced she was the one. There was the insurance; and she wanted a divorce, and she just happened to be in Washington from California that night. Still looks bad, doesn't it?"

"I guess it does."

"You seemed to be one step ahead of me all the time. But I want you to know how much I appreciate all the help you gave me. I told you once, you ought to be a detective."

"There's not much difference between a good detective and a good reporter—except that a detective can open more doors."

"Well, you seem to have opened a few more than I did. I'll be reading your article to see how much you didn't share with me. Don't make me look bad with the Delaware district attorney's office or I might have to start looking into what the hell Cranston was really doing in Ocean City in the first place.

"You got another beer for the road? I have a designated driver tonight, so I might as well relax on that two-and-a-half-hour drive back to the beach. If you ever need the police in Rehoboth, just give me a call and I'll try to give you the same efficient treatment we gave Cranston."

I watched Jenkins swagger out to his car with a can of beer in his hand, and as he walked away I had to admit I was much relieved. There wasn't any doubt in his mind who the killer was, and that was enough for him.

It was time to deal with Herson, to take up where Tom left off. I called him at his home and when he answered, I said, "Look, you bastard, I know you're looking for that photograph and I want to tell you right now, you're wasting your time."

"Who am I speaking to?" Herson said coldly.

"This is Hartley, and you know it!"

"I think I've asked you not to call me at home on such matters," he continued in his all-business White House mode.

"I know you're scared your wife might hear you talking about Beverly Turner," I said.

"May I call you back in a moment? I have the number."

"I'll give you five minutes and then I leave for your house with the photograph." I slammed down the phone.

It took him about four minutes to find another, more private, phone, and when mine rang, Herson said, "All right, Hartley, what's this about someone looking for a photograph?"

"You know what I mean, and you're taking a mighty big risk!"

"Look, I gave quite a bit to get that item back from your friend and he said he destroyed it."

"He didn't. He hid it and I found it. And here's what's going to happen next. Do you want to go to a secure phone?"

"I'm talking from one."

"O.K. First, you may have heard that Arthur Turner—Beverly Turner's husband— drowned this evening trying to elude the police who were going to place him under arrest for the murder of Tom Cranston."

There was a long silence before Herson said: "Jesus! No, I've not heard that. We're having guests for dinner and have not been listening to the news. It doesn't surprise me too much."

Then another pause before he said, "If the Cranston case is closed then you're going to give me back the negative and all copies of that photo."

"Not exactly. Here's the deal. The negative of the photo and the copies I made are all hidden with someone who has very specific instructions what to do with them if anything unusual happens to me. You couldn't possibly guess who it is, but I'll give you one hint. He—or she—knows Bob Woodward personally. They won't have any trouble getting the photo into the right hands." (I was lying here. But the photos would be in Roger Clayton's hands tomorrow morning when I stopped by his farm on my way to the beach.)

"God damn it, Hartley! I can't have that photo floating around for every Tom, Dick and Harry to see! That breaks the understanding I had with Cranston."

"Now you're going to have a new understanding with me."

A deafening silence. Then Herson said: "Okay. What's the deal?"

"Assuming I can keep the police from finding out about your involvement in this affair—and I think I can. The only people who know about your involvement are people who do not want that information to surface."

"I know who they are and I don't trust them."

"You have no choice. You're going to stay at the White House and learn everything you can about Watergate, and you're going to start leaking what you learn to me or Bob Woodward."

"Christ, Hartley, I can't do that."

"I'm going to make it easy for you."

"I'll bet."

"Very soon, Woodward will be given your name as someone at the White House who is willing to talk."

"Now, that's going too far."

"Not at all. You say you have not been involved in the
Watergate cover-up—and I believe you—which makes you a
perfect candidate to be whistle-blower. You won't be blowing
it on yourself. In fact, you'll be saving your own neck. I know
damn well that photo is the most important thing in your life.
I'm betting that if it hits the media, humiliating your wife,
she'll leave you in a minute, taking her money with her. Your
political career will be over."

"So what do you get out of this, Hartley? Why don't you
take what you've learned and run with it? You're a journalist."

"Good point. But frankly, I don't want to gain personally
out of what is obviously a blackmail attempt. But maybe I
could rationalize it if the stakes were high enough. Right now it
looks as though the Watergate caper stops at Haldeman and
Ehrlichman. But I got a hunch that it goes higher—right to the
top. But I don't know for sure; and I don't think I could ever
get close enough to find out. But somebody in the White house
might. I doubt if you know for sure now, but I think you are in
a position to find out. In fact, you're going to be a lot better off
if you do, because if Richard Nixon resigns his office before
the election of 1976, that's when the last copies of the photograph get torn up—and that's a deal!"

Herson said nothing for some time. Then, finally, "Okay,
Hartley. You got me by the short hairs."

"And one more thing. Remember, you'll be in real trouble if
something unusual or suspicious happens to me. My friend

knows exactly what to do. So cross your fingers and pray that I die of old age and natural causes."

"Can't you hear me praying?" were Herson's last words before we hung up.

Epilogue

The Delaware police closed the Cranston case. On the advice of a lawyer, Betty Sawyer admitted that she and Turner did not go to the Orioles game and that he arrived at her house early in the morning driving a white rental car.

Turner had told Sawyer that he went to the beach that night, hoping to catch his wife with Cranston so that he could start divorce proceedings. He'd said he did follow Cranston and another woman out on the beach, but the woman was not his wife. He insisted that he did *not* kill Tom Cranston, that he left Cranston alive and alone with the other woman, that he knew who she was and would lead the police to her, if they did not find and arrest her. Hence it was all right for Sawyer not to say anything to the police about Turner going to the shore that night. He had also promised to marry Ms. Sawyer after his divorce, which gave her a vested interest in keeping him free.

Doreen, however, continued to believe that Bernadette, and maybe her husband, too, were involved. She would not change her argument that Arthur, whom she'd always liked even though she knew him only slightly, dived into the river to avoid being photographed handcuffed. He didn't care that it made him look guilty because he was convinced Bernadette had done it and would eventually be found guilty, with the tape revealing that she was the last one on the beach with Tom and the gun.

Dory, as usual, had a good argument. But I still believe it was Turner, not Bernadette, who killed Tom. First, there were the two motives: the jealous husband (which impressed the police the most) and the desire to obtain a list that linked him to contributions to the Republican party, which, in turn (he thought), would also link him to money being used to support the Watergate burglars.

And I don't think he would have risked his life and leaped into the Potomac River at that notoriously dangerous point below Great Falls if he were convinced that Bernadette was the killer and he could prove it. Diving in there was simply too big a risk just to avoid being handcuffed for a crime he knew someone else had committed.

But if the Harrigans were involved, it never came to light—and Dory devoured the newspapers for months looking for any clues that they might have been. Like many people on the fringe of Watergate, soon after Nixon left office, the Harrigans moved to New York, where Jack continued to work for the oil companies, but he was not involved with their government relations. Then they moved to Europe in the 1980s and disappeared from the industry and the social radar. We never heard of them after they left New York.

The incredible thing is how long President Nixon managed

to remain in office after John Dean's testimony before the Ervin committee, which the White House never cracked, despite every effort to discredit Dean. For a while, I thought Dean had taken Herson off the hook. On June 25, 1973, approximately five weeks after Arthur Turner had dived into the Potomac and drowned, Dean appeared before the Senate Watergate Committee and read a six-hour, 245-page statement and was then interrogated for a week. But although Dean said that President Nixon had taken part in the Watergate cover-up for eight months, had even tried to pressure the CIA into taking responsibility for the Watergate break-in and had sanctioned a host of illegal espionage and sabotage operations by his reelection committee, by the end of the first month of the hearings it began to appear that Richard Nixon might escape. Ron Ziegler, the White House press secretary, reportedly told a White House speech writer that Dean had not "laid a glove on" the president, and the Nixon establishment began quietly and effectively to put the blame on John Mitchell, who, in his testimony at the hearings, accepted it and defended the president.

Nixon did not resign until August of 1974. In the interim, Vice President Spiro Agnew was forced to resign because of a corruption scandal in Maryland and Nixon picked Gerald Ford to replace Agnew. And it was Ford who pardoned Nixon after the president resigned.

But Nixon may not ever have had to resign, except for the now-famous Watergate tapes, which first came into the Watergate drama when Alexander Butterfield, who headed the Federal Aviation Administration, testified before the Ervin committee less than a month after John Dean's testimony. Butterfield said that when he worked in the White House he was aware of a taping system that was rigged to enable the president to preserve his Oval Office conversations on tape for posterity. Almost immediately the tapes, not the Ervin committee and John Dean, became the focus of the Watergate investigation. And this led to Nixon's most serious mistake during the whole sordid story: The Saturday Night Massacre.

When Watergate Special Prosecutor Archibald Cox, who had been appointed by Attorney General Elliott Richardson, requested that Nixon release the tapes, Nixon refused, offering instead to furnish Cox with transcripts of relevant portions of the tapes. When Cox refused to accept the transcripts, Nixon ordered Attorney General Richardson to fire Cox. Richardson refused and resigned. Nixon then ordered Deputy Attorney General William Ruckelshaus to fire Cox, and he refused. Then Nixon made Solicitor General Robert Bork the acting attorney general, and Bork fired Cox.

This unleashed a torrent of mail to Congress eventually totaling, according to one estimate, three million letters and telegrams. The President lost what few supporters he had left on the Hill and the House began an impeachment inquiry. But still the President held on to his office for ten more months until the new special prosecutor, Leon Jaworksi, requested the White House relinquish the tapes. The President refused, and the Supreme Court decided 8–0 on July 24, 1974, that the White House must comply. Facing the court order and impeachment, Richard Nixon resigned the next month.

The Watergate tragedy was the most sordid period in American history since the Harding administration, but it was a great time for column writing. For almost two years the media was given one new story after another. The *Post* reporters, Carl Bernstein and Bob Woodward, said that Nixon and his aides literally launched wars that began in 1969 against whatever groups or individuals were perceived to be a threat to their remaining in power in 1972. "First it was the radicals," one source told the reporters, "then it was reporters and leaking White House aides, then the Democrats. They all got the same treatment: bugging, infiltration, burglary, spying, etc." The collapse of the Muskie campaign—assuring that the Democratic nomination went to George McGovern, who began as the choice of only five percent of the Democrats—was attributed in large part to the Nixon saboteurs.

In addition, possibly as much as a million dollars of the money raised for the campaign was contributed illegally. Then came the cover-up, the frantic attempt to make it appear that a handful of lower echelon employees got out of hand in their misplaced zeal. Again, laws were violated in an attempted obstruction of justice. And the power of what is the most respected office in the land, the White House, was used to try to keep the truth from surfacing. Add to that disgusting performance the greatest crime against the American people: the use of agencies of the Federal government not only to gather information used in some of the sabotage efforts, but to cover up the activities of this frightened little group of power-hungry men.

Bad as it was, fortunately we will never know just how bad the Nixon administration might have been. The plan Richard Herson was working on to take over the government of the United States more effectively than any president had ever done was not a figment of Herson's imagination. It was later outlined in *The Plot That Failed* by Richard P. Nathan. "While riding on an airplane in the spring of 1973," Nathan said in the preface to his book, "I overheard a conversation about Watergate. One comment was, "Nixon, Haldeman and Ehrlichman are on the verge of taking over the government." And in his book, which he developed as a Brookings Institution fellow, he showed the extent to which Nixon had succeeded. By the spring of 1973, the Nixon loyalists were all in place in the major government agencies. As John Ehrlichman is reported to have said, "When we say jump, they will only ask how high." Only Watergate prevented the plan from being fully executed.

And instead of taking over the government, Nixon's men did a good job of filling the nation's jails: Attorney General John Mitchell was sentenced to two and a half to eight years, H.R. Haldeman and John Ehrlichman got the same, plus Ehrlichman received an additional twenty months to five years for plotting to burglarize the office of Daniel Ellsberg's psychiatrist; John Dean was sentenced to one to four years. Twenty-two other Nixon operatives received similar sentences for a variety of crimes, including the Watergate break-in. And the articles of impeachment that the House of Representatives voted against Richard Nixon contained the harshest indictment any president has ever received, ranging from crimes against the Constitution to crimes against American citizens, contempt of Congress, and crimes against the government.

When Nixon, Haldeman, and Ehrlichman left the White House, the plan to take over the government collapsed. And I like to think that Tom Cranston and the photograph he took of Richard Herson and Beverly Turner played some role—perhaps more than Tom could ever imagine—in the departure of Richard Nixon. Herson was a Nixon loyalist and a true believer in the revolution they were plotting in the White House.

Unfortunately, we'll never know what role Herson might have played in the dismantling of the Nixon administration because at about the time of the president's resignation, Herson also abruptly resigned his White House job, and he and Carlotta disappeared, turning up in Switzerland a few months later. He and Carlotta were killed in an automobile accident in 1975 while driving through the French Alps.

Was Herson one of the secret voices that enabled Woodward and Bernstein to help expose the mysteries of Watergate? If he was, we would know for certain that there was more than one Deep Throat, because Woodward and Bernstein had begun getting information from "him" way back in late 1972, when

Herson was still very much a Nixon loyalist. But there are many today who think Deep Throat was more than one person, including Alexander Haig, who was then in the White House and has always been a prime suspect for the role of the anonymous informer. In 1989, Christopher Buckley, who was writing a piece for *The Washington Post Book World,* said that Haig told him, "I don't think there was a Deep Throat, I think there were several."

Leonard Garment, who succeeded John Dean as White House counsel, thought Deep Throat was John P. Sears, deputy White House counsel, and Garment published a book, *In Search of Deep Throat*, in 2000 to support his case. Sears, of course, denied it, saying he thought it was Chuck Colson, who followed Sears as deputy counsel. Colson also denied being Deep Throat, saying that although Deep Throat was a composite cover, it was mainly John Sears.

Woodward and Bernstein were still getting information from some Deep Throat after I put Herson in action. In Woodward's and Bernstein's book, *All the President's Men*, the authors say that Deep Throat had mentioned Alexander Butterfield to them, and in fact sometime in May 1973, Woodward asked a Watergate committee staffer if anyone had interviewed Butterfield. They had not until then, but they did, and when they did so, Butterfield mentioned the existence of Nixon's White House taping system, which virtually no one knew about then.

Not too long after the existence of the tapes was revealed, I could see that Nixon was on his way out, so I destroyed Tom's photo, taking me out of the blackmail business for good. I never did tell Herson, and he never called to ask. I guess he trusted me to go through with my end of the bargain.

We all want to be part of history, if only in a footnote, so it is my conceit, which I will keep at least until Woodward and

Bernstein tell us who "Deep Throat" really was, that somehow my continuation of Tom Cranston's pressuring E. Richard Herson could have caused Herson to leak the fact that the tapes existed, which directly led to Butterfield's testimony, and eventually to the resignation of Richard Nixon.

I stayed in touch with Beverly Turner, who has a new married name, which was also taken by her children. She gave me the green light to go ahead and tell this story. For many years she taught in the local middle school.

The Orioles won the Eastern Division but lost in the playoffs to Oakland. Junior graduated from Boston University Law School, went into a law firm in Massachusetts, married a Wellesley girl, had two children, and eventually became involved in Democratic politics on the fringes of the Dukakis campaign in 1988. The Sophie Kerr Award at Washington College was won by Mary Ruth Yoe. Karen is happily married and unhappily still trying to sell her first short story to *The New Yorker*, which may be a career in itself.

I wrote the profile of Tom Cranston for *Washington* magazine, but did not tell all I knew. Sam was not entirely happy with my limiting the article to Tom's public career.

The murder of Tom Cranston disappeared immediately from the media, and Watergate continued to escalate to its inevitable conclusion—Nixon's resignation on August 9, 1974.

I still remember that great day when Richard Nixon climbed aboard his helicopter and left the White House, never to return. Dory and I were watching it on television, and as the helicopter rose dramatically over the Mall behind the White House, we lifted our champagne glasses in a toast: "To Tom Cranston," I said, "who wanted to make a difference—and probably did."